Hurdles in Hobart

Hurdles in Hobart

C.R. Page

Turn the Page Creations

Also by C.R. Page

Bedside in Berlin

Paradox in Paris

The Ride to Work

This book is published by Turn the Page Creations.

Fullarton SA 5063 Australia

Cover designed and created by Alison Page Photography

ISBN 978-0-6454757-3-9

A catalogue copy of this novel is held by the National Library of Australia

First published 2023

To Dad, the true master of the Mechanical Monkeys.

15 May 2023

HELEN

Considering the publicity surrounding a couple of his near-fatal accidents, it surprised me that there was no mention in the media when he passed. He had attained celebrity status during his career, yet not sufficiently to maintain this once he had retired. He liked it that way. Given his claim to fame was failure, it was a relief for that fame to disappear.

Failure is an interesting concept. Everybody has dreams as they grow up and it's a very small proportion of people who achieve these. I wanted to be a movie star, while other kids I knew dreamed of winning Wimbledon, being ballerinas, singers or the first person in space.

The dreams of most people fade into obscurity. These people aren't ridiculed for that, yet the person who shows sufficient courage, determination and hard work to make it furthest gets noticed. From that point, any margin by which they fall short of their dream gets seen as a failure. The more they continue to dust themselves off and continue to strive, the more they are noticed and the more that the term failure is applied to them. On that score, nobody was a greater failure than my beloved husband, the centre of my world for seventy years.

Lucky O'Shaughnessy and I celebrated our 62nd anniversary shortly before he passed away. I couldn't imagine how I would live without him, and in the time since he's gone, my life has regressed to mere existence.

There is little meaning in anything. The pain doesn't reduce each day, it remains constant. It isn't feeling like a constant this morning, for I feel much worse now than I have at any time since the funeral.

Lucky was something of a legendary figure in this city half a century ago. Year by year the legend has diminished, and eventually, he was largely forgotten. To the world outside of our island state of Tasmania, there was nothing to forget, for his reputation never seemed to extend beyond Bass Strait. I don't think that's a bad thing, as the way he was thought of was an oversimplified and largely false creation. Lucky the man was someone so much deeper than the public figure. That may be the case with most people in the public eye, but in those cases, the spectacle lies in the success, and the human failings are hidden away. With Lucky, the profile worked in reverse, with his story only reported when a failure occurred.

We constantly see the media claim to be reporting on stories. The truth is that they less frequently report on stories than they create them. They make their money by selling papers or getting eyes on the screen. They don't report based on the importance of a story, but on what story will sell. While an important enough story may be guaranteed exposure, a created story that appeals to the masses seems to be just as significant to some media outlets. That is how it was at the height of Lucky's career, and it seems nothing has changed.

I knew the article was going to be published in today's paper and I had thought it would be a tribute to the man I loved. How foolish I was. It was not a tribute but a tasteless parody. It may not be meant as a callous piece, but every action has a consequence and there appears to have been no thought given to the consequences of this. Perhaps an old woman like me doesn't warrant thought or consideration. How difficult would it have been to prepare me? More to the point, how difficult would have been for the reporter to ask a couple of questions and write something that rounded the story more accurately? Lucky's claim to fame was failure and I wouldn't expect that to be ignored, but that is just one part of the picture. There is always balance within every life story. His failures couldn't have happened without successes that put him in that position. It was bad enough that these were ignored all through the years, but at the time of his passing, a tribute to the man should surely give reference to the joys amongst the pain. He was a man, not a caricature.

Barely a day passed in the first half of his life that he didn't have feelings of failure that were reinforced by the words of others. Eventually, his perspective changed once he realised who he should be listening to. Now I was the one who felt destroyed by the words of those who shouldn't be listened to, but unfortunately, their voices were being heard across the state. While Lucky always had my voice to drown out all others, there was nobody now to play that role for me.

It may seem petty or pointless, but I feel like I owe him this. History may be written by the winners, but history needs to be written with accuracy and balance. He may have been *Hobart's Biggest Loser* to a lazy journalist, but he was Hobart's Biggest Hero to me. I will make it my mission to ensure that people hear why.

15 May 2023

ZANIYA

There was some part of every trip where I'd be made to feel guilty for making the rest of the family wait while I had my sleep-in after a big night out. Usually, on our first full day in the city, it was the opposite. My excitement at the new place had me ready early and everyone else moved slowly after the journey of the previous day.

We flew into Hobart late yesterday afternoon. Our taxi brought us into the city to our hotel on Davey Street, the Grand Chancellor. Whether by chance or design, Dad had booked the best hotel in the city. It is one of the biggest and most impressive buildings in Hobart and is ideally located, right on the waterfront. The interior is every bit as welcoming.

I am sharing a room with my brother Oliver. There was a time when that was the great downside of our travels, but since he moved to Coventry for university, we have spent little time together. Now we both appreciate the rare opportunities we get much more. Oliver is not just my brother but my closest friend. I think most people in our respective social circles find our closeness strange but to me it is natural. We have been brought up together and lived through a very similar set of experiences. Everyone is shaped by their experiences and for us this has meant that nobody understands me better than Oliver, nor does anyone understand him as well as I do.

Mum and Dad's room was on the next floor up. The check-in staff were apologetic about our rooms being on different floors, but I couldn't be happier to have the space between us. There was no reason for this; Oli and I never got up to anything that we'd need to hide from our parents, but sometimes it's nice to have that extra feeling of freedom and independence that a minor buffer provides. The only downside from my perspective, was that while Mum and Dad had a spectacular harbour view, our room faced the opposite direction with an interesting, but less enticing view of the city and Mount Wellington. I couldn't complain. The room, like every other aspect of the hotel, couldn't be faulted.

Mum and Dad are both incredibly relaxed and our relationships are as good as you would find in any family. They must be. You don't continue to choose holidays with your parents at 18 and 20 respectively if your relationships with them aren't so good.

Over the past decade, we have seen so much of the world together. None of us had travelled much before 2012 when we were convinced to ignore travel advice and go to Pakistan for a family reunion on my mother's side. Listening to her speak, my mother could not be more English, but her heritage was Pakistani. She was born in Lahore in 1965 but moved to the north of England with her parents the following year. She had been back on a couple of occasions but not since we were born.

She had faced persecution for her race all through life. Possibly this is what encouraged her to demonstrate such a traditional English manner. It certainly helped her build a level of resilience that she has instilled in Oliver and me. We have both had to endure similar attitudes, albeit less common in our theoretically more enlightened age.

On appearances, our father was the stereotypical Englishman. He has pale skin and light-coloured hair that had evolved from blond to grey at an early age. He has a wonderful sense of humour, leaning typically towards the type of comedy Britain was famous for. He was a regular at Chester-Le-Street whenever the English cricket team played there, something he considered to be the quintessential English experience.

He was an equally enthusiastic football supporter and made sure he caught a couple of matches each season at St James Park watching Newcastle United in the Premier League. He drank copious amounts of tea, almost as an opportunity to further connect to the stereotype.

Nobody is ever as simple as they seem on the surface, and my father was a testament to that fact. The sports fan who himself was fit enough in his late fifties to be running a great time in a half marathon last year was also an incredibly widely read man with a vast array of intellectual and artistic interests. He loved history and encouraged the same in us. He, rather than our mother, had encouraged that first trip to Pakistan and had been the driving force in the regular travels in subsequent years. He had a hunger for knowledge that we'd all followed suit with. Our travels always had plenty of stops for good food, drinks and entertainment, but everywhere we went we came back enriched and wiser from our experiences.

In the years after our visit to Mum's homeland we have travelled to such diverse places as the United States, Sri Lanka, Malaysia, Canada and Turkey. It was a shared passion and one that wasn't likely to see our family trips stop anytime soon. Oliver is seeing someone back home and we had wondered whether he would be willing to leave her for this trip, but he did. Maybe she will join us on our next trip this Christmas time.

Between work and study, it is hard to get more than two weeks at a time to travel. A place as far as Australia needed far longer but necessity forced us to break it into stages. Family connections had led us down here for a wedding in northern Tasmania and while we'd have loved to have visited more of the country while down here, we were restricted. Our total stay was just over two weeks and was originally going to be a few days each in Melbourne, Sydney and Brisbane before flying south for the wedding, but Mum intervened.

I had given Mum a travel book about the ultimate 500 travel destinations for her birthday last year. When Mum read that Hobart's Museum of Old and New Art was listed before the Louvre or the Hermitage Museum, she was adamant that it was an essential part of our itinerary.

When she pointed out that Tasmania had two other destinations on the list, making it the most heavily represented Australian state, we were all intrigued. The natural wonder of Cradle Mountain and the history of Port Arthur ensured we were all keen on seeing as much of Tasmania as we could. We were all willing to leave Sydney and the rest of the country until our next trip down under.

After we had checked in, we had agreed to keep the evening reasonably quiet. We did a quick wander of the area adjacent to the hotel in the quest for a tempting dinner, deciding to walk until we found a place we could agree on. All of us were hungry enough that it didn't take long before we reached agreement and settled in for seafood on the waterfront. The restaurant didn't look anything fancy, but the meals were sensational. No doubt, we will be having a lot of seafood while we are here.

The harbour is very pretty, and we found a bar to have a few drinks at which gave us a great view of it. From the edge, as you look back to the main part of the city the buildings are dwarfed by the mountain behind it. Hopefully, we will head up to the summit at some stage while we are here as the views from there would be amazing.

We hadn't made any significant plans for this morning but had decided we'd organise the day over breakfast, which is why I had waited so long despite my hunger. As was so often the way by the time arrived to meet the rest of the family downstairs, I'd become distracted by my phone and ended up being the last one to arrive.

Barely receiving a nod of acknowledgment as I sat down having grabbed my urgently needed coffee on the way through to their table, Dad continued to be preoccupied with the newspaper.

'Listen to this. It's an article on a former jockey who recently passed away. *Tasmania's biggest loser, Lucky didn't just fail to ever win a race, he failed to even finish one. Forty-five career rides resulted in forty-six falls, as in one race he fell off his horse only to remount it as it hadn't galloped away. All this was to no avail as he fell off a second time at the next hurdle.*'

Mum and Oliver laughed in unison with him, more at the joyful expression of Dad's reading than the story itself. I noticed the old lady at the adjacent table looking across with tears in her eyes and I asked her if she was alright.

'That story is not funny. It is highly offensive,' she said. 'Lucky was no loser. His life was a triumph, and nobody knows it more than me. I was married to him for 62 years.'

'I'm so sorry,' Dad said, feeling genuine remorse for the poor woman.

'Don't be. I'm upset at the person who has written that and the newspaper that has published it. And some of the sources quoted within it should have known better.

'Articles like that fill space in the newspaper and entertain the readers but shouldn't there be some level of respect and understanding for the deceased and their surviving loved ones? If anyone wants to know the story of Lucky, I am only too willing to tell it, but coming and doing that research must be a little too much for journalists.'

'I would love to hear his story,' I told her. 'I can't promise you the paper here will give the article I write the same exposure as this one, but I can promise that you'll see the story that you want reaching some people.'

'You're a journalist?'

'I'm studying journalism.'

'So, this will be for a university newspaper in England, will it?'

'I shouldn't think so,' I said. 'I've had works published in various spots as a freelancer. Maybe there will be a story that is published somewhere, but maybe not. Maybe there'll be something that is merely an account that has been written that you can cherish. At this stage, I am more interested in his story, one person to another, rather than as a journalist to a subject.'

'I would also be intrigued,' Dad added. 'I grew up just near a racecourse in the north of England. I never followed the sport as a punter, but I had a fascination with horses as a child and have retained a general interest ever since. I know that jockeys are participating in the most dangerous sport imaginable, particularly those who ride over jumps. It requires courage, possibly too much so. Surviving that career is a triumph in itself.'

The lady told us she was staying at the hotel as she had several appointments in Hobart over the next couple of days. She'd asked about the length of our stay and said that if we could make some time, we should come to her home on Bruny Island.

'It's an essential part of a trip down here anyway. It is such a beautiful part of our state. You will have missed Tasmania's most sparkling jewel if you don't visit.'

We introduced ourselves formally, having neglected to do so before we began making plans. Her name was Helen O'Shaughnessy. Having been married for sixty-two years she must have been over eighty.

We discussed plans over the coming days, and we agreed to spend some time together in the lounge area of the hotel after breakfast followed by another session tomorrow morning before we headed to Port Arthur. We also committed to heading to Bruny Island on Monday.

'What else do you recommend we see and do in Hobart?' Mum asked.

'We are all different,' Helen said. 'I have travelled to the mainland just a couple of times in my life, and never have I been overseas. I can't imagine a place being sufficiently special to have an impact as great as what a special person can. For me, joy was always about who I was with, not where I was or what I did. I'm probably not the best person to ask.'

'I share your view,' Oliver said, building rapport with Helen. 'We now are separated as both Zaniya and I are at universities in different cities. The opportunity to spend time together when we travel makes these experiences special. I enjoy the new places we see, but it wouldn't have the same impact without those I love.'

I could immediately see the sense of pride on my mother's face as she heard this comment. I must admit it felt nice hearing it from him as I did feel the same way, at least to some extent. I love to travel and I feel certain that I would be happy travelling alone, albeit in a different way.

Being alone in a strange land would challenge my comfort zone and I think be the ultimate experience. I can't wait to do that. This is something different. Not better, not worse, just different. When I get back to England I will reflect on the sights of Australia, and they will always go hand in hand with the family I love.

'I do wish to go back to my room to freshen up,' Helen said. 'I will return to the lounge area in say 15 minutes if that's long enough for you to finish.

'Yes, that's perfect' I said.

Helen stood up and walked out of the breakfast room looking strong and mobile for someone of her age. I returned my focus to getting through what was on my plate before returning to the buffet for a croissant and some jam.

'Oli, can you please grab the pen and notebook that are next to my bed and bring them back down,' I asked when he was finished. I still had half a cup of coffee and was running out of time. This wasn't a formal interview, but I wanted to take down all I could. I really couldn't envisage that there was much to it, but if a city's main newspaper could run a significant story about the man, there had to be enough substance to create something from it.

'We're going to have a bit of a walk and pick a few things up from the supermarket,' Mum said.

We wandered across from the restaurant area to the lounge and saw both Helen and my brother come out of the lift.

'We will leave you two to talk,' Mum said. 'We'll see you when you're finished.

As my family headed to the hotel's front entrance, Helen and I took a seat.

'They weren't interested?' she asked.

'They were, but they felt it was best to allow us to start one on one. They know how I operate and thought it was best to give me the space to speak to you in private and prepare the story that they'll be excited to read. Of course, when we come down to see you on Monday, they'll get to hear more from you. Don't worry, they are very interested. They're both people who admire stories of human triumph.'

She nodded her head, impressed at my reasoning. 'So where should I start?

'As far back as you can.'

3

28 October 1947

HELEN

The legend of Lucky O'Shaughnessy came to the fore as a ten-year-old at the Royal Hobart Show. When he recounted the day in later years, he added a whole lot of falls off various rides, but he was prone to exaggeration. The way that Lucky would tell the story, he would have you believe that his first ever fall came moments after birth when the midwife was handing him over to his mother. As much as it wasn't true, he was never short of finding a different example to give of him falling.

Patrick and Iris O'Shaughnessy welcomed Luke Patrick into the world on January 3, 1937, a brother for Kathleen who was two and a half. By the time he turned eight, the nickname Lucky was all that he was ever known by.

Lucky's childhood was not too uncommon for the era. Born just before World War II and in the aftermath of the Great Depression, life wasn't easy. Patrick had been a labourer from the time he had left school, even managing to stay in work most of the way through the Great Depression. He'd been employed on the Mount Wellington Summit Road project and then the Hobart Bridge construction but when war broke out few opportunities were remaining. With Iris, Kathleen, Luke and now a third child Jenny as dependents, he reluctantly decided to enlist in the Army. He served with the Australian 8th Division and left for Malaya in late 1941. He was wounded soon after New Year and was evacuated back to Australia, eventually returning home to his family almost 12 months after he had last seen them.

Patrick returned a changed man. While the physical scars were significant, having lost his right eye, it was the mental scars that marked the biggest change. Iris had spent the past year being the sole parent, and in many ways, her husband's return didn't change this. Patrick was able to re-join the workforce in late 1943 and with manufacturing increasing partly in response to the war effort, there was plenty of work for him. By this time, he was willing to work long hours, preferring to be an absent provider. He struggled to rekindle the close bond he'd had with his children and felt uncomfortable that this was the case. He got no satisfaction from work but found it easier to cope with than playing the role of father at home.

Young Luke was first referred to as Lucky by a couple of kids at school because his father had come back from the war. Most kids in the class had fathers who'd gone to war, but they were either still fighting, prisoners of war, or had been fatally wounded. To have his father sufficiently wounded to be home made him considered very lucky, but these children had no concept of the price Luke's father had paid. Luke himself couldn't understand this, but he did feel relieved to have him home. While his father's return had been the origin of the name, it became more universal as a result of a day out with his father.

In 1947 Patrick took Lucky to the Royal Hobart Show with him and headed straight to the games of skill in sideshow alley. He'd once previously played the Mechanical Monkeys game and after watching and playing for an extended period he'd become quite adept at it. Now with his son at his side, he set to work on teaching what he had learned and hopefully winning a few games to help fund their day out.

The Mechanical Monkeys game saw up to twelve people competing, each trying to get their monkey up the pole first. This was done by pressing down on a handle to make a ball jump through a hoop. Winning required an understanding of the game's technicalities. It was essential to learn what force you needed when pushing down on the handle.

The second, and rarer understanding, was related to timing. The ball would not register while the monkey was already moving. While most players impulsively kept pushing as fast as they could, those who understood the game waited for the exact moment when their next play would register. Patrick had been obsessive enough in his monitoring of this game to understand it, unlike most of the people he competed against.

It cost a shilling to play and if you won, you won a box of either chocolates or cigarettes. The value of these would probably only be a couple of shillings, to make sure that the sideshow was making money, especially as you didn't always get a full house of players. Due to the rationing that had commenced during World War II, the value of these prizes had become far greater.

Lucky wasn't used to getting too much attention from his father, so when Patrick was so focussed on teaching him the skills needed for this game, he listened. He decided the time was right to play after they'd watched three games and he'd explained the intricacies.

'Watch me closely Luke,' he said as he handed over his shilling. He'd taken a place right at the end of the line, not because the position was relevant, but because it gave more room for Lucky to be at his side.

Patrick missed with his first push, and it took until nearly halfway through the 30-second race before he caught up to the leader.

'C'mon Dad,' Lucky said, starting to get excited as he closed in on the leader. With the patient timing he'd stressed, he got three balls through in a row and the bell rang as his monkey reached the top of the pole.

He played another game and won this won even easier.

'Can I play now, Dad?' Lucky said.

'Not yet.' He didn't want his son to get caught up in having fun with the game. To Patrick, this was serious, and until his son was ready to win, he didn't want to waste an extra shilling. Patrick won a third game and then got up from his seat. He walked behind the game and spoke to the owner, asking how he got their cigarettes due to all the rationing.

'We can't get enough so we do buy some back of players that don't want them. If you're interested, we'll buy them back off you – four shillings a packet.'

'No don't worry, I can get far more than that for them at work. I'd get a pound for three packs.'

'Ok – five shillings a pack. That's the limit, as in some games we barely take in more than that.'

Patrick agreed and handed over the packets he'd won. As a non-smoker, they were of no value but currency. Taking five shillings now for convenience was better than hanging on to them in the hope of an extra shilling or two. Rationing wouldn't continue forever, and the quicker he traded cigarettes now, the better off he was.

He now took his son to get something to eat and to go for a ride on the Ferris Wheel. Their first stint at the Mechanical Monkeys had resulted in a twelve-shilling profit. Spending half of that on his son now was reasonable.

When they went back to the Mechanical Monkeys, the game was full, and they had to wait for two more games before Patrick got back on.

'I want to win one more, then when we can get two seats together, you can play too.'

Patrick wasn't successful in his first game back. A player right next to him seemed to be equally expert and once he'd fallen behind this new-comer, he panicked and wasted a couple of balls by pressing too fast. He knew the margin of defeat was too great to be the result of just a simple error or two and was worried about his plans for the day. Luckily, as he turned to his victor, he saw him get up from the seat with his prize and walk away. He motioned to his son to quickly sit there.

'Lucky,' Patrick said.

'That's what they call me at school. First time you've called me that.'

'I meant it's lucky that man left. He was very good. Maybe your presence was the good luck that made it happen. If we keep going well, I might keep calling you Lucky.'

In the next game, Patrick dominated. Spending two shillings a game now to pay for Lucky as well, Patrick won the three that followed. In each of the four games they played at this time, Lucky was doing better. In the last of these, he came second and felt sure that his time for victory was not far off.

The stallholders were happy to see Patrick stand up. To some people who'd been watching, he seemed an unbeatable foe. His presence was likely to stop a few other people from playing. He gave Lucky three shillings to play the next few games and told him that he'd be watching from further back.

Lucky again finished second in the next game before having a bad game in the following one. With his last shilling left, he managed to piece all his father's advice perfectly. After being behind for most of the game, he perfectly timed his last three balls to take his first victory. He fell from his seat, excitement overcoming him, and nearly forgot to collect his prize as he sought out his father. Patrick was making his way back showing little emotion but feeling overwhelmingly proud.

Father and son spent several more hours at the Show. While they managed to spend time wandering the Showgrounds and seeing most of what was on display, they kept returning for more stints at the Mechanical Monkeys, Patrick winning about a dozen more games and Lucky having three more successes himself. In the most exciting of these, he was successful in a game that Patrick had also entered. While Patrick had made a mistake early in that game, he had tried as hard as he could to win. It was a deserved win by his son.

As they left to embark on the long walk home, Patrick reflected on the financial result of the day. Lucky was keeping two boxes of chocolates that he had won, but the other two, plus seventeen packets of cigarettes had netted them nearly six pounds. Even with all of the money they had spent, he was still returning home two pounds better off than he'd left home with, even after giving five shillings to his son as a reward.

'You wouldn't believe how well Lucky and I did today,' Patrick said to the family when they arrived home.

'Lucky?' Iris said.

'That's what they call him,' Patrick said. 'And now, it is what I call him too.'

From that point onwards, everyone did.

4

15 May 2023

ZANIYA

'I'm sorry dear,' Helen said as she wiped the moisture from her eye. 'It is all still very new to me. I get teary so often.' I don't know how much opportunity she's had to talk in-depth about her late husband, and it was impossible for her not to get emotional at times. There's a degree to which this should be therapeutic, but any form of rehabilitation doesn't succeed without difficulties along the way.

'You do want all of this, right? I mean, it isn't relevant to what made him famous.'

'It is probably more relevant than what made him famous. What I want to capture is less about the jockey everyone knew and more about the man they didn't know. The greater my understanding of him, the truer the picture I can paint. So often, a glimpse into the childhood of someone allows us to make sense of the scrambled elements of their adulthood.'

'That is very true with Lucky.' Sure, I thought. He fell as a child, and he never stopped. I knew this was the furthest thing from her mind, but occasionally my dark sense of humour strikes at inopportune moments.

Her voice was shaky, and I told her I would get her a glass of water. As I walked across the room, I noticed heavy rain falling outside. Hopefully, conditions clear quickly as these conditions would compromise our plans for the rest of the day.

'It is bucketing down out there. I hope you don't have to go too far for any of your appointments,' I said returning to Helen.

'I'll have a taxi taking me from door to door, so it won't impact me. It may be having much more of an effect on your family, out there walking in it now.'

'In the north of England, we are pretty used to days like this. It doesn't quite fit the image of Australia we're so used to seeing.'

'You may be half a world away from home, but climate-wise, Southern Tasmania is probably not more similar to Northern England than the north of Australia. It suits me. Our part of the country is far more beautiful for it. Very green. I love it.'

Getting away from the topic of Lucky had helped her mood lift. As much as this wasn't helping me get the information I sought, clearing her mind was likely to be the most beneficial way forward for me.

'Does Hobart still feel like home even though you live on Bruny Island now?'

'When I lived in the city, and ever since moving to the island, the whole of Southern Tasmania has seemed like home. I've always been happiest in a more rural setting, but that doesn't mean Hobart isn't home. Still, home is where the heart is, and with Lucky gone, I feel a little homeless.'

Keeping Lucky away from the conversation was never going to be easy, but I decided to try a little more.

'We are going to Port Arthur tomorrow and stopping at some of the spots on the Tasman Peninsula. Is there anything in particular we must not miss?'

'Take your time. There is beauty everywhere, and the slower you go, the more you will get to appreciate it. And stop at Dunalley. It's just a small town, but it is where I had wanted to move to many years ago.'

As we continued to chat about the family's plans throughout our stay, my drenched family came back through the door.

'That wasn't a good decision,' Mum said.

'We couldn't have timed it worse. It's just starting to clear up now,' Oliver added.

'You better get out of those wet clothes,' Helen said. 'Your daughter has been telling me about your plans for the coming days. You can't afford to be getting sick with so much to do in such a short space of time.'

They didn't need to be told and were happy to leave us be. We were leaving in about an hour for a day that was centred on a trip to MONA. We were all keen, but for Mum, it was the major reason that she wanted to come to Hobart. I wasn't going to need the time to get ready and could devote that now to Helen, but I had to remain conscious of the time. Mum was not going to be understanding if we missed our ferry.

The break in the conversation had been sufficient for me to turn things back to the main topic at hand. Lucky's youth.

5

29 October 1947

HELEN

The previous day's success on the Mechanical Monkeys had been the greatest day of Lucky's life. The show had last been held before the war, and it had been a miserable event for him as he'd fallen off a horse on the merry-go-round. The fall was nothing serious, with his pride wounded more than his body, but it still ruined his day. He couldn't have remembered the experience, having been just three at the time. Memories impact us in strange ways, and many of our fears and dislikes stem from moments we can't remember. The angst they cause remains every bit as real.

Seven years later the new Royal Show experience had been transforming. He had learned that for the lack of ability he had shown in any field so far, he could concentrate, work hard and improve. Once he found his true direction, he could use these attributes to get somewhere. More importantly, he had seen his father proud of him and happy, two things he'd wondered if he would ever see again.

'Dad, if I can make a pound a day, couldn't I just play the Mechanical Monkeys forever and be rich?'

'Nothing in life is impossible son, but that might be close. The Royal Show is not on here long enough. If you have to pay to follow the shows around the country it will cost you considerably more than a pound a day. Plus, they won't ration chocolate and cigarettes forever.

Once that's over they won't pay so much to buy back the prizes as they'll access them cheaper elsewhere. Fewer people will be playing as they won't be inclined to spend a shilling to win three shillings worth of prizes when they can just buy the products. That means less frequent games and fewer chances to win.'

Patrick knew this was beyond a ten-year-olds understanding, but he wasn't going to sugarcoat truths for the boy. Seeing the disappointment in Lucky's eyes he chose to minimise the impact. 'Still, there is next year, and we can see how we go then'.

Despite the disappointment that his hour-long career dream had been crushed, he took it as a victory that his father was showing joy in making plans, which hadn't happened in a long time.

'Don't they have shows in Launceston and Devonport? Can't we go there?'

'Maybe. They're some way off now anyways, but we'll think about it when the time comes. In the meantime, how about you put the same focus you gave the Mechanical Monkeys into riding your bike.'

Most boys at the age of ten spent plenty of time riding their bikes around the streets, but despite owning a bike he wouldn't be seen out the front of his house on it. He'd had the same bike for three years and had just about outgrown it. The major issue wasn't so much the size of his bike, but his inability to stay upright on it. His parents weren't inclined to get him something bigger, reasoning that he'd merely be falling further in those regular accidents he seemed to find.

'Once you're comfortable riding it in the street, then we can look at replacing it with something bigger and better,' Iris said. She wasn't too sure if this would ever happen, wondering if he'd be driving a car before riding a bike successfully.

Lucky practiced out of view in the backyard but time and again he'd end up on the ground. Patrick had started teaching him before the war, and progress was slow while the bruise count was high. In the subsequent years he'd tried teaching himself with little more than encouragement from Iris but all to no avail. Even with training wheels Lucky just couldn't stay balanced. He'd been determined to get permission from his parents to ride to school next year, but after saying this for three years he still couldn't be trusted on the bike. He wasn't so uncoordinated that he couldn't ride it at all, but just the slightest distraction or sudden need to brake would inevitably see him lose balance and hit the deck.

With Patrick's words in his ear and the memory of the Show Day, there was finally progress. His parents rewarded this with a new bike for his eleventh birthday and he practiced constantly before being willing to be seen riding up and down the streets around their tiny home. Before too long he finally had their permission to ride to school. Lucky was the proudest child at Goodwood Primary School when he arrived on his bike, but the feeling disappeared fast as he fell off trying to dismount at the bike sheds. While the nearby children laughed heartily at him, one of the teachers came rushing to check that he was alright.

'It's alright miss. I tend to fall off a lot, so I'm used to it,' he told her.

'I think you should do a vertigo test Lucky,' she said.

'No, I'm no good at tests, Miss,' he said before quickly finding an opportunity to get away from the site that had caused his embarrassment.

Out of the sight of others he persisted, and before too long he was riding to school every day. He managed to find his share of trouble, falling off more than one time on his way to school, but it was usually not a case of his balance, but being in the wrong place at the wrong time.

Already the name Lucky was considered ironic to most people, but by now it had been universally adopted for him. Family, kids, and teachers all called him Lucky. His mother had been the slowest to transition, but even she couldn't escape it.

In late 1948 the O'Shaughnessys moved into a new home in a public housing development in Goodwood. A couple of weeks later, the adjacent house was occupied by its new owners.

Two families at the same stage of life in the post-war era were always likely to have enough symmetry to see friendships build and that quickly became the case with the O'Shaughnessy and Sorenson families.

The Sorensons had two daughters who were the same age as Lucky's sisters Kathleen and Jenny. The two families became close immediately. Like most times in life, Lucky remained somewhat of an outsider as the only boy in the two families. Kathleen quickly became best friends with Ann Sorenson. They were both at Montrose Bay High School and were spending most of their time together. Jenny was building a similar friendship with the younger Sorenson girl, though she ended up ensuring Lucky didn't remain the odd one out for too long. After all, the younger Sorenson girl was me, Helen.

6

15 May 2023

ZANIYA

When we allocated six nights for Hobart, I thought it was excessive. Over the years we'd spent less time in great cities like Berlin, so there seemed little need for so long in such a small city. Helen had immediately changed that view. I now had a purpose and could have happily spent far longer digging my way through remnants of Lucky's life.

The same wasn't true for the rest of the family, yet we now had enough of a plan in place for our time that suited everyone. With tomorrow set aside for a full-day trip to Port Arthur and the same for Bruny Island on Monday, it left us with today, Saturday and Sunday to cover inner Hobart. Mum knew how the best-laid plans didn't always come to fruition and had locked in MONA first, so that was our plan for this afternoon. We were all keen to visit the Salamanca Markets on Saturday morning, which many people had recommended as one of the city's greatest highlights. We decided to leave that afternoon free for whatever else we found along the way. After a bit of research, I found that there were races on Sunday and everyone agreed that we'd spend part of the afternoon there, both to experience something new to us and also as an opportunity for me to hunt down some independent opinions on Lucky.

When I got upstairs, Oliver gave me a rundown of their walk. I hadn't missed anything other than the rain.

'So, you just wasted your time?'

'Pretty much. I had wanted to see some more of that street art we'd spotted yesterday. Once the rain started, we were stuck without cover, so we didn't make it to the spots I'd intended to see. We did get more of our bearings of the city though.'

'Anything worth going back to.'

'Plenty of options. We went past the Art Gallery, the Tasmanian Museum, the Maritime Museum and the Elizabeth Street Mall. I don't think there's anything essential amongst them, but if we don't have anything else on at times over the weekend, they'd all be worth a look. We also stopped at the Visitors Information Centre. They recommended a tour of the brewery, so Dad and I might do that after the markets on Saturday. You and Mum mightn't be as keen.'

'I'm sure we'll find something that would be of equal disinterest to you,' I said.

'Dad was most interested when he saw the sign for *The Mercury*. He wanted to go in and find out about getting your article published.'

'What?'

'Don't worry. The sign was still there but the building was abandoned. Their headquarters have moved, so he didn't get the chance. We did pass a community newspaper headquarters, and I kept him from going in. We did get some contact details though, so if you want to follow up with them, you can.'

Oliver knew me well. It wasn't that I didn't appreciate help at times, but once I had committed to a project, I wanted to do everything my way. Having Dad, or anyone for that matter, pushing my cause wasn't something I responded well to.

While Oliver continued getting ready, I took the opportunity to make a start on the tribute. I didn't have much to work on as yet, but I already knew the essence would be to focus on Lucky's successes rather than the failures that were synonymous with his public image. To an extent both things were the same, it was merely how the events were framed that indicated whether it was a success or a failure.

Life often works that way. At university, we pass or fail in a subject, yet success is not defined based purely on a grade, but on numerous other factors. A distinction may be a failure for some, while a minimum pass can be the ultimate success for others. An athlete may achieve their life's dream by qualifying for an Olympic team while another may feel they have failed when winning a silver medal. There are people with seemingly everything they could wish for, yet are dissatisfied for the few things they lack while others with almost nothing can have greater contentment for the little they possess. Who defines each success and each failure? We all can do that for ourselves and others, but we all shine our light with our perspective. I want Helen's perspective shone on this story because I think that is what makes it special. If constant losing is what makes Lucky so significant then surely anyone could emulate it. What can't be so easily matched is the character that got through all of that. To endure, to survive and to have the courage to continue a journey when every bit of evidence showed that he would never reach the destination of his dreams. That was the defining story of his life. Falling from horses was merely the backdrop and any other field of endeavour could have provided a similar story.

Mum and Dad knocked on the door, not wanting to take chances on us being ready in time. Dad got straight into mentioning the former newspaper headquarters and said he subsequently found that they are now based in Salamanca Square, so we could go in there a little later.

'Why? 'I don't think they would want foreign journalism students knocking on the door and telling their editors that they can investigate and write more newsworthy copy than their current staff. I will send them the finished product and let the work stand for itself.'

Salamanca Place was where we headed, not for the newspaper, but to see the Hobart of yesteryear. On Saturday the area would be flooded with half of Hobart as the famous markets would be on, and as much as we were keen to experience that, we also wanted a taste of the area in its quieter more regular state.

The perception of Australia that I, and possibly most people have, is youth. A young country. Sport and its young athletes are revered above anyone. Modern architecture, arts and ideas are dominant. In Europe, we focus on the traditions that have led us to a point in time. The future isn't ignored, but today is seen as the point of natural progress from the past. In Australia, the ideals of the future seem to dictate today far more than the memories of the past which seems to result in a very different psyche. While Britain and Australia share a commonality, the perspective from which the two nations approach that point shows a real cultural difference. My father made a big point of this to us years ago when he took us all to an international cricket match against Australia.

'It is such an English sport and the traditions that the game is built upon are a testament to that. Lords, the Long Room, the white uniforms, the long days and lack of results, the crowds in suits and ties applauding appropriately. We looked back at how it had been and sought to preserve those things, for it was those that made cricket unique. Australia looked forward to what it could be and sought to introduce improvements. Matches under lights, coloured uniforms, quicker games, guaranteed results, chanting crowds. Now that's not a story about cricket, it's a story of two different cultures, however linked they may seem to be when you look at flags, language, politics and law.'

Salamanca Place intertwines the roots of this country with the progressive mindset Dad was talking about. Rows of sandstone buildings that date back to the earliest settlement of the city. The buildings retain their early 19th-century look but have all been repurposed from their origins as dockside warehouses to modern restaurants, bars, craft shops and galleries. It is a trendy area that attracts the creative minds of the city. It's ironic that such progressive people are so determined to seek the oldest parts of a city to adopt.

It seems counterintuitive but the more modern a city is, the more it seeks to celebrate the older components of its history and Salamanca Place highlights this.

'That's balance,' Mum said as we came out of the Salamanca Arts Centre. 'When you use white paint on a white canvas there's little to see. It is the contrast of modernity set against an older backdrop that highlights the strengths of each.'

'Exactly,' Dad added. 'Australians have elements of history they're not proud of. They have the oldest civilisation in the world through their aboriginal population, but there are so many social issues that have arisen since white settlement that it forms a parallel history. The white settlement began through penal colonies scattered throughout the land, again not something you automatically reflect upon in a celebratory way. So, when you see wrong in the past, the motivation is to look to the future you want and get progressive today. The key to progress is to never lose sight of where you came from, and generally, the most progressive people will never forget the base from where things began. Acknowledgment isn't necessarily celebration.'

Little laneways directed us through to Salamanca Square where we were surrounded by modern apartment buildings on one side and Hobart's history on the other. The contrast Mum mentioned was so perfectly displayed.

'I want to come back here at night,' Oliver said which we all agreed to. Such a hub of creativity and hospitality would no doubt be a magnet for many at night.

'We'll have to come back because we need to get moving now,' Mum said. Despite being in the kind of place she loved, her eyes remained on our next stop as somewhere even more important to our trip. While Dad could romanticise and lose sight of the overall picture, Mum was always the wise head who ensured we remained on track. Oliver inherited more of that from Mum than I did. I didn't always admit it, but I seemed to be a more equal combination of each of them. I could get lost in fascination at seemingly insignificant things in just the same way as my father does. It was at times a blessing, but equally, there were times when this was a curse.

There was a range of sculptures in the square and some incredibly unique-looking buildings, but I didn't have time to work out what they were. For a small area, there was more to see and experience than I could have believed. If I'd doubted how we'd fill six days in Hobart earlier, I was beginning to see my doubts were needless.

7

14 November 1952

HELEN

While he got along well enough with everyone he came into contact with, Lucky never developed strong friendships. His parents tried to help the situation by organising a twelfth-birthday party for him. After he forgot to pass out the invitations at school, it ended up being just his family and mine that attended. With my sister and I alongside our two best friends, and both sets of parents sitting with each other, Lucky was once again the odd one out. He was a loner by nature, so this didn't bother him. It did seem ironic that an event planned to make him the centre of attention had highlighted his place as an outsider.

Seeing the guest of honour receiving less attention than anyone else had me feeling a little sorry for him. Having not seen him for a while, I went outside and found him lying on the ground having just fallen off his bike.

'Are you alright Luke?'

'Yes. Just fell off my bike. Happens all the time, so it doesn't hurt anymore.' Clearly, in time I would come to understand the significance of this, but at the time I thought nothing more of it and helped him up. He stayed off the bike, talked to me and made me laugh. Perhaps this was the real beginning. It may have been premature to call it a crush, but for the first time I stopped thinking of him as Jenny's brother.

When the new school year started, Lucky decided not to ride to school anymore, but to walk with Jenny and me. The two siblings weren't that close, and it seemed like at times they competed for my attention. I was in class all day with Jenny and certainly didn't want to lose that friendship, but as time passed, I was becoming closer to her brother.

Being in a lower-year group I didn't see too much of him at school, but when I did, he was usually on his own or wishing he was. It was part of the school culture that kids didn't hang around with people from other year groups, so spending lunchtimes with me would have invited more of the attention he sought to avoid.

The characteristic for which he would be remembered in adulthood was falling, but that reputation was already in place by the last year of primary school. It hadn't been horses he was falling from, but between the people in his classes, they'd witnessed him falling from many things in many ways. On the school oval, there were always people willing to assist him in falling. Although too small to be suited to football he had tried out for the school team but unsuccessfully, spending more game time laying on the ground than running with the ball.

Lucky began at Montrose Bay High School the following year. In the opposite direction from Goodwood Primary School, the walks together to and from school were now over. We'd see each other at home in the evenings or on the weekends but the dynamics of the friendship had certainly changed.

The walk to the high school saw him passing Elwick Racecourse twice a day. Often in the morning, he would see gallopers doing their training and it began to fascinate him. Progressively he began to spend more time in the vicinity of the racecourse, turning up on weekends and watching the races from various vantage points.

While most trainers were based around the old track at Brighton, a few trainers had small stables around Elwick. In time Lucky got to know some of these men and was always asking questions, trying to learn everything he could. While he never seemed interested in learning anything at school, he hung on every word he'd hear from a trainer, a stable hand or a jockey. While everything else in life seemed to have no purpose, he saw the level of detail that went into every aspect of each horse's preparation, and it all seemed to make sense. This was what he wanted to work toward in life, he just didn't know quite how.

One day I had gone for a walk to the local shop, and I ran into him.

'Helen, what do you think of the idea of me becoming a jockey?'

While I almost choked, I showed maturity beyond my years by not saying exactly what I was thinking. Lucky was so regularly criticised and victimised that he couldn't afford the hit to his confidence that he'd feel if I reacted like that. I couldn't in all good faith encourage his plan, but I was not about to destroy it straight off.

'Why do you want to be a jockey?'

'I love animals, especially horses. I love the excitement of the racing. Being small is an advantage. Plus, if you get good enough you can end up going all over the world. Imagine me riding in the Grand National in England.'

'I don't know,' I said trying to sound more neutral than I felt. 'I think most people who try it don't make a living out of it. And it's very dangerous. Heaps of jockeys get killed in races. Wouldn't there be other jobs you could get working with horses?'

'Maybe, but not as exciting.'

'Well, maybe you can. Whatever you choose to do, if you want it enough then I guess you could do it.' I was very philosophical at the age of twelve.

The level of support he took from my words seemed to have an impact on him. From that point on he was happier spending time with me, feeling like I was the only person who was completely supportive of him.

He had made comments to his family about becoming a jockey. They thought little of this, considering this to be his childhood dream in the same way most kids hope for some form of career that will bring them stardom. Children don't dream of becoming office administrators.

They dream of being a ballerina or a footballer. In the case of Lucky, the footballer was out of the question and a jockey was a legitimate substitute for childhood dreams, but his parents didn't appreciate this. Kathleen had wanted to be a dancer when she grew up and after a few years of dance lessons, she realised that she didn't have the ability nor did the less glamorous hard work sit well with her. A jockey's work in the early days was even tougher, and Patrick knew full well that his boy would never cope with that.

'Let him dream, there's nothing wrong with that at thirteen. He can't possibly get far enough to be let on a horse let alone follow it as a career. The lack of ability is only part of his handicap. He doesn't have the discipline to get anywhere near it.'

'I can't encourage him to waste energy dreaming of something he's not going to ever be able to do,' Iris replied.

'If you discourage him too much, you'll make him want it more. Then more damage will be done when the dream crashes. Just go along with it and watch the dream fade, faster than it did with Kathleen's dancing.'

'Kathleen got plenty from dancing. Friendships. Fun. Teamwork. Organisation. What is Luke going to get from horses? Killed?'

'He won't get close enough for that. Besides, he's learning about discipline and hard work, and that will take him a long way when he channels it into something better down the track.'

From that point, Lucky rarely got more than a roll of the eye from his mother when he mentioned the topic. Patrick was not outwardly emotive either way but would combine positive and negative comments about jockeys. 'Imagine missing out on ever eating things like this,' he would say in the middle of a decadent dessert, highlighting the discipline required to maintain such a light weight. 'Imagine the thrill of riding a champion like that,' would be his comment when reading an article in the Sunday paper about whichever racehorse was dominating the headlines, before bringing up a statistic about the proportion of jockeys in the country who ever win major races to gently discourage his son.

Statistics meant little to Lucky. He was always driven more by emotion than by any form of logic. He craved the joys that he felt winning the Mechanical Monkeys game at the show. He got so competitive yet in every facet of life he faced on a more regular basis he was never able to feel victory. He knew nobody else in his age group that idealised becoming a jockey and he figured that if he did, he'd be the best at school in something. He certainly wasn't going to be average, let alone the best academically.

It was late in 1952 when Lucky and I moved from childhood friends and neighbours to something more. I think we both always liked each other so much that it was the natural course, though I know that doesn't always happen. One night he asked me to go to the drive-in cinema that used to be on the inside of the Elwick racecourse. We didn't have a car of course, as we were only fifteen and fourteen respectively, but we watched from the side and the distance. To be honest we pretty much just talked, with little attention to the big screen in the distance, but every time we reached an awkward silence we could turn and watch Gene Kelly and Debbie Reynolds on the big screen. As the movie ended, he kissed me, and even though the moment was years in development, it confirmed what I already felt confident to be true. Lucky and I were meant to be.

The dynamic between the two of us didn't change too much, but it was enough for my parents to see that their little girl no longer saw the boy next door as just another child. While they liked Lucky and knew that he was gentle, respectful and harmless, they also considered him to be someone unsuitable for their daughter as a long-term option.

'Lucky is a very sweet boy,' Mum would say, 'but you need to think about the future when you start getting involved with boys. Lucky won't amount to much. You are better than that and you shouldn't get too involved with someone only to break their heart.'

'He is capable of more than you realise. He will be successful once he finds the right path for him. All I will ever want is happiness, whatever that person does. I am not that shallow.'

I knew my words implied that I thought she was. That wasn't the case, and it was natural protection that had driven her view. She wanted better for her children than she'd had in her life. She'd met my father when they were young and idealistic. My father worked for his family's business but came back from the war a shell of a man. The business hadn't survived, and he'd been a labourer ever since. Lucky's father was similar, but that was closer to his pre-war existence than was the case for my dad. Mum felt that life in her mid-forties had fallen a long way from her expectations. She failed to see that it wasn't my father, but the political landscape of the world that had been the cause of that.

I was never forbidden to see Lucky, but their opinion of him diminished as mine grew. The sight of my happiness and my continually improving results at school and in extra-curricular activities gave them no reason or opportunity to impinge on my choices. To them, I'd chosen to be with someone beneath me, but their opinions wouldn't sway me.

Lucky was every bit as happy as I was. I remember him telling me one night that after so many years of hearing the name, it was only now, through me, that he genuinely felt like the name Lucky was appropriate for him.

'Whatever other good and bad comes my way wouldn't matter. As long as I have you, I am Lucky.'

Even in love, Lucky fell hard, but this was the one time the fall seemed to be the perfect result.

8

15 May 2023

ZANIYA

Oliver had fallen hard. He had met Alice at university earlier this year and they'd quickly become a couple. None of us had met her yet, but it had become increasingly obvious he had met someone special. He wasn't entirely enthused about spending a few weeks apart from her, but he was obligated to be here for the wedding in Wynyard and it had been impossible for Alice to come.

In modern times, long-distance communication with a distant loved one isn't so difficult, and as we were walking to the pier, Oli was texting Alice and not looking where he was going. He managed to trip on the curb and landed on the footpath. From the moment I could see that he was alright, and his phone had avoided any major damage, I laughed harder than I had in a long time.

'That's it. From now on, you are Lucky Fergusson.'

'Wouldn't that need my falls to land me in hospital,' he said.

'I don't think that happened every time.'

Oliver was back on his feet. His phone was now in his pocket and his focus returned to the here and now. There was no sign of a limp from him as we started to move, so we continued onward.

There was an array of transport options to get to MONA, but after reading an article online, Mum insisted that the museum was designed to be approached by water, so the ferry was the option we were taking.

The Mona Roma was a special ferry designed to be part of the overall experience of a day at the museum, but the treat began even before boarding this. The departure point of the Brooke Street Pier was more than just a transport hub. The restaurants looked worthy of returning to visit. There was also an array of shops with interesting giftware crafts and various local products. We didn't have time to do it justice as we were just in time for the ferry.

I've had a bad record on the water. Anything too turbulent and my stomach does not cope well. In principle, I love the idea of being on the water, but after enough bad experiences, it took a lot of convincing from the rest of the family for me to agree to go by ferry.

'It's a river. It's incredibly smooth. You won't have any issue with it,' Mum said. I wasn't confident, but I wasn't going to ruin her day.

The ferry is painted in camouflage to stand out as much as possible from the standard Derwent River traffic. While eye-catching, the stakes were raised the moment we stepped aboard and started seeing what else was onboard. We may not have seen the best of it, for there was a first-class option known as the Posh Pit, but at more than twice the cost, we passed. The day was already going to be expensive enough, and we were sure the standard Mona Roma experience would still be memorable.

At the front of the boat was a row of seats that were supposedly pink torpedoes. Knowing that sex was such a significant theme amongst MONA's exhibits, I wasn't thinking of torpedoes when I looked at them. There was no way I was going to feel comfortable straddling one of them in front of my family and I was surely not going to feel anything but complete embarrassment watching any of them do the same. I insisted we move on from these as quickly as possible.

We walked through the ferry and at the back managed to get seats that surprisingly enough looked like normal seats. Other seats resembled sheep and cows, but we were all fine with going with the more traditional approach. I don't know the origin behind the ferry's obsession with farmyard animals, but they were less confronting than the penis-like torpedoes.

The wall behind us was filled with the brightest, most colourful and highly skilled examples of graffiti-style artwork. I never know whether the classification of graffiti is best saved for instances where the work is done without permission, after all, that is where it stems from. This was clearly part of the overall design. It's not necessarily my favourite thing, but it lifts the ferry more than a blank wall.

The ferry took a little under half an hour. As I had been assured, the trip played out exactly as my mother had suggested, with my stomach remaining perfectly settled on the calm river. From our seats at the back, we could appreciate the view of the city skyline which was more reminiscent of a European city than somewhere in this part of the world. The absence of skyscrapers in the central business district and the array of older buildings seemed far removed from the image I'm used to associating with Australian cities. Framed by the water of the Derwent in the foreground and the majestic Mount Wellington in the background, the city did look more impressive from this vantage point than anywhere on dry land.

Along the way we went under the Tasman Bridge, one of the city's most famous landmarks. In 1975 there had been a disaster that saw twelve people killed when a bulk carrier crashes into the bridge's pylons leading to the collapse of part of the bridge. The east of the city had been completely cut off, and the necessity of a second bridge became apparent. A few miles further along the river, we passed under this newer bridge, the less aesthetically impressive Bowen Bridge.

Of greater interest to me came a little closer to the end of the journey when I spotted Elwick Racecourse. A day ago that wouldn't have meant a thing to me, but after meeting Helen and learning the story of Lucky which centred so heavily around Elwick, it was a point of enormous interest. Not only was the racecourse his workplace and the home to his passion, but the surrounding suburbs were also home to him and Helen for most of their lives. I had a great desire to explore the area, but for now, had to content myself with the view from the back of the ferry.

I knew we were getting close to the Berriedale Peninsula, the small section of land that was home to MONA, but with only a view of what was behind us, my focus remained on Elwick. We were going there Sunday, but even now I couldn't help but think of the area and the stories of Lucky. I wondered just how accurately Helen had depicted his story to me.

9

4 November 1955

HELEN

'I'm going to be a jockey' he told his parents with the self-assurance common to teenagers across all generations.

'I've heard a lot of stupidity in my time, but never anything as stupid as that,' bellowed Iris. 'There are so many reasons why you can never be a jockey. You might be a bloody comedian with lines like that, but people will think it too ridiculous to even laugh at.' She had done as much as she could to discreetly discourage his dream, but now that he wanted to quit school to fully commit to it as a career plan, she was no longer going to be subtle in her disdain.

At a stage of life where we were all starting to choose the paths we wanted to follow in life, Lucky had been slow in finding anything that he found suitable for his future. Living near the racecourse, we saw horses quite a bit and he'd become increasingly more fascinated with them. There were occasions when racing was on that he would skip school to go and watch, often taking a place near the starting stalls. His interest began moving from the horse to the rider as he started seeing that as the ideal profession for him.

'Why can't I be a jockey? I love horses and that is the key.'

'There is far more to it than that,' Patrick said.

'Remember the Mechanical Monkeys, Dad? You told me if I persisted enough, I could do anything. I'm willing to persist with this.'

'Where do you want me to begin?' Iris was worried that her son had seized upon one of the very rare pieces of constructive advice that Patrick had ever given. 'The first thing a jockey must be able to do is stay on the bloody horse. You'd never get out of bed in the morning if you didn't fall out of it. You spend the rest of your day looking for other things to fall from. Bikes, chairs, merry-go-rounds. You have no balance, the first essential attribute of a jockey.

'I'm getting much better,' he said.

'What about your weight? You are fifteen and you are closing in on eight stone already. You are going to be far too heavy to be a jockey.'

'Not for a jumps jockey.

'Holy Moses! The word idiot doesn't do you justice, does it? Instead of needing a miracle you're doubling down to something more danger-ous, more unsuitable and with fewer opportunities. There isn't a hope in hell you'll be doing that.'

It was disheartening for him to hear the home truths from his mother, but she was only saying what everyone would logically think. Lucky didn't appear to be cut out for being a jockey however much there was to be said for following a passion.

'I don't understand Helen. They give me a hard time because they think I have no direction and don't know what I want to do with my life, then when I have a plan, they don't like it and want me to go back to before. I can't win.'

'You can win,' I told him. 'There's a couple of things to consider. If you love horse racing so much, have you considered all the different jobs there could be? Maybe a race caller?'

'No, I want to be a jockey, I'm sure.'

'If you want it enough you can make it happen. I believe in you.'

That was all he needed to hear. I'm not sure if it was the best or worst thing I could have ever said. It was certainly what he was desperate to hear, but it may have been the moment that sealed his decision. He agreed to stay at school until opportunities had come up within racing that demanded him to commit to full-time work. If a trainer needed someone part-time, there was every chance it would be before school hours. He didn't like it, but in getting my approval, and just a hint of acceptance from his mother, he promised that he wouldn't quit school just yet.

It's fair to say that Lucky's propensity for falling had removed the natural level of fear a person should have. Most people fear the potential negative consequences of an action, but Lucky was used to worst-case scenarios. He'd developed an ability to brush himself off and get up to fight again whatever happened. This ability was far less evident from any emotional falls he had, and he was more bothered by the fight with his mother than any recent physical injury he'd incurred in the course of being Lucky O'Shaughnessy.

Many jockeys begin in the industry through connections or through talent, but for Lucky, it was a combination of persistence and his often relied upon luck. As he was spending more time around the racecourse, he got to know more trainers and continually asked about any opportunities they may have. Somehow his reputation had preceded him and there was little interest from anyone in taking him on. Eventually, his time came.

Max Burton was a trainer who always seemed out of step with his peers. He had built his reputation on horses that had failed with other trainers and in time he'd had similar results with jockeys. He didn't have a big stable, nor did he train a big number of winners. As sure as a tradesman is only as good as his tools allow, Max worked with the lowest-grade tools to get his results. He was always happy to pick up a reject from bigger stables and develop them to win something, somewhere. The accumulated rejections Lucky had received made him the ideal material for Max.

Max's previous apprentice jockey had completed his indentures two years earlier. He'd continued to assist Max for some time but had now moved to Melbourne for a shot at the big time. Max also had a stable hand, Charlie, but after he suffered a serious injury inflicted by one of the horses, Max had been left performing every task around the stable.

The opportunity to utilise Lucky was perfect timing for Max, and he was hired initially to muck out the boxes and fill up the hay nets and water buckets. He was working a couple of hours of day split before and after school, earning a very meagre amount, but he made sure he learned everything he could from the experienced trainer.

Max couldn't help but be impressed with Lucky's enthusiasm. For the pittance it was costing him, he had someone who arrived early and left late. He never shirked a task however undesirable it was. He showed a desire for more advanced functions but displayed the necessary patience when he was knocked back. Whatever the kid lacked, Max was convinced he had every attribute that he wanted to see and agreed to sign him on as a full-time apprentice.

'I told you. I am going to be a jockey,' he triumphantly declared to his family.

Iris had retained her scepticism the entire time he'd been working for Max but was equally impressed with the commitment he showed.

'This phase will end,' I overheard her saying to my mum. 'But he has developed such a strength of commitment that when he finds the suitable thing to transfer that attitude towards, he will surely thrive.'

Patrick had always been less vocal about his son's path. Perhaps it was the disillusionment with his own life that had led accordingly, but he was in favour of Lucky doing anything he was passionate about. He was proud to hear the news of the apprenticeship and was in his corner when Iris reacted angrily to the idea of him leaving school.

'You know that he's never going to get anywhere out of his schooling. At least this way he's earning money and getting experience, discipline and responsibility while he's young. He mightn't get far in this line but there's nothing for him to lose.'

I was prouder than anyone. As awkward teens, neither of us had known how to progress our close friendship into something more, but both of us knew that our lack of interest in other people was because we already had the person we wanted in the house next door.

Lucky and I no longer had the daily walk each way to and from Montrose Bay High School together, significantly reducing the amount we saw of each other. As much as this saddened me, it proved to be the instigator of the change in dynamics in our relationship. We were no longer able to take our constant presence with each other for granted, and we then made more intent to make the quality of our time matter more than its quantity.

Before too long it was clear for everyone to see that I was his girl. His parents loved me, so were more than happy with that dynamic. My parents were sufficiently impressed with his character to be less focussed on their concerns about his future, so they too were happy with the burgeoning relationship. Happiest of all were the two of us.

Lucky was never going to put anything ahead of me, but work was certainly equally important. He developed a love affair nearly as special with one of Max's horses called Roy's Boy. While most of Max's horses weren't particularly talented, Roy, as he was known in the stable, made the rest of them look like superstars. He had one pace. Slow. Very slow. He wasn't ever cut out to be a racehorse, but his owner, a man named Clem McDonald, attended every race meeting in Hobart. He wanted to have a runner at every meeting so that he could take advantage of owner's privileges. He wasn't concerned at how unlikely it was that his runners were competitive. After fifty race starts, Roy's Boy hadn't ever won a race and had only a couple of minor placings, both of which had come in his younger years. Not even Max's renowned ability to improve ordinary horses had an impact on him.

Lucky and Roy proved to be a perfect match. Roy had a gentle nature and was the ideal horse for a fledgling apprentice to learn the basics on. He was also of little enough value that Max was happy to let him ride the old gelding for all his trackwork, safe in the knowledge that anything going wrong would not lead to the compromise of potentially good results. Roy would continue getting beaten out of sight whoever was aboard.

Roy had generally competed in flat races through most of his career, however he was going into the winter season with hurdles as his main target. Lucky had been riding him over hurdles in training and both horse and jockey were exceeding expectations, albeit expectations that were set incredibly low. Before being allowed to race over hurdles the horse had to complete a hurdle trial which was an important moment for the horse, but more markedly the biggest moment in Lucky's life to date as he would ride him in the trial.

'You're still a long way from riding in a race boy, so don't get ahead of yourself. You need to get through several of these to get licenced for races, so enjoy this experience but be careful with it. There's no prize for winning. Get him around the course safely. Clear the jumps. Keep his rhythm constant and steady. Do not ask him for anything more.' Max's instructions were like a trainer discussing a master plan with a jockey before the Melbourne Cup. All the other horses were legged up and trotted around to the start with little said.

'What are you doing?' Max asked as Lucky mounted.

'Ask him for nothing. Keep his rhythm constant. Clear the jumps. Stay safe,' Lucky replied.

'Good lad. Safe passage.'

Trials usually don't attract many onlookers, but this one had a few extra people on course. Both Lucky's family and mine were all sitting in the grandstand with various levels of fear and excitement within each of us. Max came up and joined us, but I know there were far more people whose focus would be on Lucky. He'd become enough of an identity around Elwick that many people were keen to see how he went. Few people had expected him to get this far, but he still had a long way to go before he could feel like he'd proven anyone wrong.

There were five horses in the trial, and it didn't take long before they settled into two groups. The three gallopers with some perceived ability drew more than fifteen lengths clear of Roy and fellow struggler Driscoll Street. A couple of the horses brushed into hurdles at different points, but Max kept commenting on how well Roy had taken every jump, and how perfectly Lucky was handling him. At the last jump in the back straight one of the leaders dislodged his jockey and around the same point Roy began closing a little ground on the two remaining leaders.

'He might catch them' I said excitedly.

'He'll get close' Max said. 'He better keep his head.'

Roy had closed the gap to 3 lengths by the final jump where one of the leaders crashed into the hurdle. Roy was close enough that it required quick evasive action from Lucky to steer him wide of the other horse. Losing momentum, Roy was then too far behind to end up winning the trial. There was, however, no doubt about the stars of this show from everyone watching. Not only was Roy's Boy the name on people's lips, but everyone was also raving about what a great ride he was given by Lucky.

Rarely would a jockey receive a better reception returning after a race let alone a trial.

'I didn't win it' he said, not appearing too disappointed.

'I didn't want you to win,' Max said in reply. 'What I wanted is what I saw. No, what I saw was better than I could have hoped for from you and the horse.'

Roy's Boy had secured his ticket to race in hurdles from now on. Lucky still had a long way to go before he would be joining him in an official race, but he had taken a giant step toward proving all the doubters wrong. The cynics from both inside the racing fraternity and the from other parts of his life were already fading into the background. Even Iris set aside all her previous misgivings, hugging him tight.

'Whatever happens next, I couldn't be prouder of you Lucky.'

10

15 May 2023

ZANIYA

Cynics had suggested that the plan to create a museum of modern art in Hobart was a waste of money, but these opinions disappeared once the vision had become a reality. Once the Museum of Old and New Art was opened, it put Hobart on the world's artistic map and generated a degree of interest in the city that nothing else ever had.

From New York's Guggenheim to the Louvre in Paris, from the Hermitage in Saint Petersburg to the Tate in London, we'd seen many of the world's most famous museums, usually housed in the world's biggest cities. If we hadn't known in advance that today was something more unique than all of these, it was apparent the moment the ferry docked at MONA.

Once we got off the ferry, we had to earn entry to the museum by climbing ninety-nine steps to get to the top. There didn't seem to be any other options, so I don't know what the elderly or the disabled would do. For us, it wasn't an issue, and probably the additional workout wasn't a bad thing in the middle of our holiday full of over-indulgence. At the top, we reached a courtyard area. Central here was a seemingly out-of-place full-size tennis court with all the trimmings. With all the people congregating in the area, I can't envisage anyone ever playing a match here.

Next was a trampoline, which unlike the tennis court, was being used in the manner you would expect. In all four corners were bells underneath that rang with the motion that each bounce on the trampoline caused. It ensured noise which added to the impact for the guest, but its repetition would probably annoy the hell out of the staff who heard it all day, every day. I could sense Dad was already feeling that after a few minutes.

We decided to focus on the outside of the museum first. For all of the controversies and mixed opinions that seem to exist about MONA, it's rare to find anyone speaking negatively about the grounds. Some of the art outside may not win the appeal of everyone, but also wasn't likely to offend or disturb. Several sculptures caught my eye, the most impressive being a miniature chapel. I was more interested in the view across to Elwick from a high point at the edge of the facility.

We made our way to the lawns at the back of the facility. Amongst the different options, I was keen that we get into the spirit of the place and sit on bean bags on the grand lawns. There is a main stage that is used for concerts, though as we walk through the area there is live music coming from the opposite side of the lawns. To be fair, the band wouldn't warrant the attention of a stage set-up to play for thousands; they were at best experimental and at worst just plain bad.

The MONA site has its own winery and brewery, so Dad and Oli had Moo Brews while Mum and I had a glass of the Moorilla Chardonnay. We lazed back on the lawns enjoying this while considering our lunch options.

'I suddenly fancy chicken,' Oliver said while looking just to my left. It soon became apparent to me that we had approaching company; two roosters were walking across the lawn just near us. Unlike the lifeless animals on the ferry, these were very much real and added to the surprising sights of the location. None of the other great museums I'd encountered had anything like these elements.

The restaurants within MONA had seemed a step above what we wanted. We agreed to eat on the lawns with lunch from the food vans.

There wasn't anything too exciting among the options, but we hadn't come here for the food. A quick bite and we were ready for the true main course, the museum.

For all the magnitude of the MONA site, the museum appeared as a relatively low-key, small and uninteresting facet. It was built into the side of the cliffs, and so rather than seeing a striking building like most great museums, we were seeing little to prepare us for what lay ahead.

Once inside we took the spiral staircase down three levels to the starting point of the museum. While most museums have you enter at the bottom floor, here you go down. The descent was probably the ideal preparation for what was to come, given the nature of the displays. At MONA you start at the bottom and ascend, and this point of the design is not an accident. There are no windows, and no natural light, which aids the work to shine at its brightest. It would have been a far more expensive way to build a museum, but the cost was not at the forefront of the owner's mind. He wanted the ultimate expression of his collection, and this was what he believed would achieve it.

At the bottom, the starting point of our museum experience is the Void Bar. Mum and I tried a cocktail while the guys opt for another of the Moo Brew options. More appealing than the drinks is the golden sandstone walls that stand around us. In addition to two large paintings on either side, the main focus of the area is the rockface; nature has ensured that whatever is on display here, there will be beauty amongst it. On completing our drinks, we began our journey through the exhibits.

What were the highlights? I think the standout memories for me were more lowlights. Two goldfish swimming around a knife. A man being raped by a dog. One hundred and fifty-one porcelain sculptures of life-sized vaginas. The poo machine. Fornicating skeletons. I'm not sure that any of these had any great artistic merit, but they were all ensured to create controversy.

It has been said that the works in MONA represent an obsession with sex and death, due to a belief that all human endeavour is based on the desire to have sex and avoid death. Perhaps my fundamental disagreement with this belief is the reason I didn't appreciate the experience like some.

Of course, there were highlights. The Snake, a composition of sixteen-hundred individual pieces that combine on the wall to form the image of a snake, is one of the more impressive works I have seen. At forty-six metres long it is a masterful idea that works perfectly, and this part of the museum was designed specifically to accommodate it. Another great piece was entitled *Bit.fall*, a device that pumps water that momentarily forms words. It appears as though these words hang in mid-air for a brief instant, where only those watching closely can read them. In a flash it loses shape and disappears, falling to the ground and leaving a memory unique to those watching at that moment. Immediately after, the next word appears, and the pattern continues. It becomes incredibly difficult to walk away when you know the next word is only seconds away. The words keep changing, and nobody else will have seen exactly what we did.

The layout of the museum is almost maze-like. There is always more than one way to turn, and while it all inevitably leads you toward the end of the road, it does so in such a way that it's almost impossible to see everything. Checking the app that showed us what we'd seen and what we'd missed, I knew we were only half-done as we got near the exit, but I'd seen enough. It is rare to ever see everything in a museum, and this was one where I was adamant we didn't need to. The strength here was the uniqueness, the architecture and the location. The individual pieces merely add or subtract from the equation, depending on your tastes.

'Wasn't that incredible,' Mum said as we walked out the door. It wasn't quite the word I would have used, despite finding it incredible in some ways. I found it more surprising that my middle-aged mother appreciated the cutting-edge museum more than I did, but she is broadminded enough not to be easily shocked or offended and enjoys having her horizons challenged by something different. I'd have thought that I was the same, yet the way most of MONA did this didn't resonate with me so starkly.

Art is rarely universally appreciated. Most of the best art is loved by some and hated by others. Nowhere is this more prevalent than in the collection held at MONA. I maintain that it is an incredible experience with a lot of awful art. I don't consider it the ultimate in love or hate but a combination. I cannot see how anyone can experience all that MONA offers without finding redemption within its failings or major negatives amongst its triumphs. I guess when people discuss MONA, they tell the story that they think sounds best rather than the complete picture.

11

22 April 1956

HELEN

When people discuss the statistics of Lucky's career, they tell the story they think sounds best rather than the complete picture. Forty-five career rides for forty-five race falls and zero finishes. More often they say forty-five career rides for forty-six race falls due to a 1971 race where he fell off a horse called Moravian at the first hurdle. Moravian was so placid he stopped and waited. When a trackman helped Lucky reboard, the prospect of prizemoney seemed worth his while. There were only five starters in the race and there was every chance one or two more horses would come to grief on the testing three-mile journey. The theory didn't have time to settle before horse and jockey approached the second hurdle and once again, they parted ways on landing. Now Moravian's patience had disappeared, and he continued without Lucky, who was sufficiently injured this time that he couldn't get up. This led to what could be described as his forty-seventh fall. Before the paramedics had managed to get him back to the ambulance, he fell off the stretcher and again tasted the familiar Elwick turf.

Fifteen years earlier, Lucky had reason to be feeling optimistic about all that was in front of him. Buoyed by the confidence gained in his first trial, Lucky's mornings at trackwork were becoming much busier. He was now working most of Max's horses, not just the hurdlers, and was getting additional opportunities to work horses for other trainers.

At over 8 stone, he had already committed to only riding in jumps races due to the higher weights that the horses were allotted, but on the training track, this was irrelevant. His ability to keep horses relaxed impressed everyone and led to further rides in trials. By February he had his licence to ride in races, but with few hurdles scheduled in Hobart at that time of year, he was forced to wait for his debut.

In April the opportunity arrived for him, and ironically it wasn't in a hurdle race. An occasional feature on the Tasmanian racing calendar were races known as 'jumpers flats.' These were races without hurdles but restricted to both horses and jockeys who usually raced over jumps. Max was planning to use this race to help improve Roy's Boy's fitness ahead of the hurdling races he was targeting through the winter. Although Lucky was yet to have ridden in a jumping race, his licence to ride in them made him eligible for the jumpers flat and so Max gave him this opportunity for his official first race ride. He'd been offered a ride in a hurdle race at Launceston the previous week but turned it down. His desire to begin his career on his favourite horse and for the trainer who had made this career a possibility meant that he was willing to forgo that opportunity for what he considered the perfect beginning to his career.

After all the promise shown in the trial, Roy hadn't managed to break through for his maiden win. He'd had eight races over the hurdles without managing a placing but had managed to complete the course safely on each occasion. There was no doubting his consistency and toughness, just the lack of speed needed at certain points in a race to become a winner. Now going back to a flat race after a short spell the expectations of victory would be low, but at this stage, Lucky was excited just to be competing.

'He's as tough as you are kid,' Max said. 'I just wish we had longer races on the program for him. Two miles is one thing, but he'll keep going three or four which most others won't cope with.'

As the sun shone on Elwick, almost everyone who knew Lucky was in attendance. In most cases, these were people who couldn't believe that the clumsy kid they went to school with was now a professional jockey. To be honest, even those of us who knew him best never really believed he would get to this stage.

The memories of that first trial seemed somewhat distant as we walked past the betting ring about twenty minutes before the race and saw Roy's Boy at 100/1.

'Don't worry, there is another one in the race that is 150/1 so he's a good chance to not finish last,' Jenny said.

'I don't care if he's last, as long as he's safe' I replied, a sentiment that Iris echoed. The smoothness of his apprenticeship had seen us become a little less focussed on the dangers of his job than we had originally been, but neither his mother nor I could ever completely let go of our fears.

Our excitement was progressively growing and as the horses came into the mounting yard, we were gathered around commanding the best viewing points. We let out a uniform cheer as the jockeys appeared from their room and we saw Lucky walk out towards Max and Roy. We didn't need to hear to know exactly what advice he would be giving him. "Keep him in a smooth rhythm, avoid getting cluttered on the fence, and don't be afraid to start pushing him as you enter the back straight the last time.

As the race began Lucky let him go at his own pace and worked him into a bit of space at the back of the field. For everything I'd said about not caring where he finished, there was naturally a part of me that was hoping for a fairy tale. Halfway through the race he began to lengthen his stride and got past a couple of rivals and for a moment I dared to dream. It was only a fleeting fantasy. At the half-mile mark, he was still third last and making no ground on the leaders.

Naturally, Max knew his horse well, and in line with his prediction, the horse continued to battle on and made a little ground in the home straight finishing tenth of the fifteen starters. It may not have been spectacular to the average track watcher, but both horse and jockey exceeded their trainer's expectations.

'Lucky rode him perfectly. Be proud,' he told us. 'When you ride a push bike in a race against motorbikes it doesn't matter how well you do it, you can't win. He gave him exactly the ride I wanted. His day is next month, and Lucky will get to show what he can do then.'

Lucky was a picture of disappointment as he came back in aboard the horse. There wasn't another person on the course who would have expected anything more than tenth for Roy's Boy, but Lucky was never one to have his opinion influenced by others. He was like a parent at a kid's talent show whose opinion was based more on a personal bias than an objective appraisal of ability. Whatever he lacked, Roy's Boy was enough of a star in Lucky's eyes that he'd have expected nothing shy of victory even if they were racing in the Melbourne Cup.

After the post-race discussions with the owner and trainer, Lucky got dressed before coming out to join us, now in a significantly better mood than straight after the race.

'It was amazing' he beamed. 'Not the result of course, but just the noise of the crowd and the feeling of adrenalin as the field surrounds you. Those are the things that are a whole other level on race day.'

'What did Max say,' I asked, knowing the answer but wanting to allow him to speak proudly about his performance.

'He was happy with the horse and even happier with the jockey. We're going to be back here in a few weeks for my first race over the obstacles and that's where you'll see Roy be more competitive.'

Over the years Lucky rode in more than a dozen jumpers flats. He never rode a winner but when anyone tells you he never finished a race you know they're ignoring certain facts to create their own version of history. Truth isn't always a big focus for people when there's a better story to tell than the right one.

Unfortunately, three weeks after his race-riding debut, the first episode of the more commonly told story began.

12

15 May 2023

ZANIYA

'I just don't see how you can call a poo-machine art,' Oliver said to Mum arguing the same point I'd made earlier. 'If I said I was making that for a school art project you would have been alright with it?'

'You'd probably have been expelled, but then middle school art projects don't usually offer quite that scope.'

As they continued to debate the definition of art, we again took seats on the back deck of the ferry for the return to the city. We'd gone later than the main rush on the way to the museum, so that was a quieter ferry. Now it was much busier, but we'd still managed a prime spot. Possibly it was too cold outside for most Australians, but such temperatures were normal enough for us. A couple of brave souls joined us outside, but most stayed in the comfort indoors. A true traveller will always choose the one-off experience over a little extra comfort. Given the calmness of the water, I felt more relaxed than I'd ever been on a boat, and so wanted to maximise the memory of the experience by taking in every moment with the best possible views of Hobart.

Arriving back at Brooke Street Pier, it was too early to think about dinner but too late to plan anything else beforehand. We decided to head back towards where we'd been this morning, the many bars around Salamanca Place seeming like the right spot to visit to talk about the uniqueness of the MONA experience.

'Some of it was alright,' Oliver said once we were all sitting down with a drink in front of us.

'Not much though,' Dad said. 'I think most of the works on display were only there because of the edge that controversy gives them. With time, that edge disappears.'

'The best measurement of art is time,' Mum said. 'Doesn't matter whether it's music, film, sculpture, or painting, the same thing applies.'

'Get real,' Oliver said. 'You're saying everything old is better than anything new.'

'Not at all. People revere Sargent Peppers, Pet Sounds, Like A Rolling Stone as much now as then, but there was a heap of rubbish that came out in the sixties which was incredibly popular at the time but has faded into obscurity ever since. Time has separated the quality from the rest.'

'Surely the quality was obvious even then?' I asked.

'Not really,' Mum said. 'Think movies. Compare Citizen Kane and Titanic. In the year of release, Kane was largely ignored in award season while Titanic won more Oscars than any other film ever. As time passed, Citizen Kane became renowned as the greatest film of all time while Titanic's reputation has descended to an overhyped commercial success with little more to it. If the Oscars were voted on now for their respective years, Kane would scoop the pool and Titanic would be substantially less successful. Something new could be better than either of them, but it will only become evident once it has had time to cast its influence.'

'130 years after he died, Van Gogh is the most admired artist in history. When he was alive, he was a nobody. Time saw the inferior works of other artists lose significance, and his work continually grew in prominence.' Dad loved Van Gogh, and it wasn't surprising that he'd find a way of bringing him into the conversation.

His focus quickly returned to the present day as he spotted a particular building across the square.

'There's the *Mercury* headquarters. Maybe you need to go in there and find the guy who wrote the article on Lucky and see what the prospects are of getting your piece in there to counter it.'

'I don't think a city's main daily is going to accept submissions from foreign journalism students, however relevant and accurate they may be,' I said. 'I think we'll stick to the plan of a letter to the editor from Helen and my article in the community paper. Between those two it should generate enough interest that the Mercury might then give him the tribute he deserves.'

'But will you get the credit you deserve?'

'It's not about me. Anyway, I'm sure when I'm back at Uni I'll be able to get some mileage from the experience.'

We stayed for another drink while deciding on a dinner option. We'd had multiple recommendations for a seafood restaurant on the wharf immediately opposite our hotel. We didn't make it that far after passing a cosy-looking restaurant named Harbour Lights. It didn't sound like it, but it was an Italian restaurant that went down well with all of us.

'I want pizza,' Oliver said.

'I want pasta' Mum added.

As it turns out it was a good call. I still had my seafood fix taken care of courtesy of a beautiful spaghetti marinara. Everyone thoroughly enjoyed their meals and for Dad and Oliver, complete satisfaction followed after further indulging in desserts of Tiramisu and Panna Cotta respectively,

'Don't worry, we can do Mures another night when we don't want to venture far from the hotel,' Mum said. I didn't bother voicing it, but I'd already worked out the chances were diminishing with our plans in place for Port Arthur tomorrow, Bruny Island Monday, and a couple of other loose plans through the weekend. If the substitutes were this good, missing the originals wasn't going to be an issue.

We wandered back along Morrison Street, passing the Mawson Hut Replica Museum.

'Something else for the to-do list,' Dad said.

Like our burgeoning list of restaurants to eat at, it remained to be seen how many items we would manage to tick off the list before we departed. At this point, the street connected with the harbourside walkway which got us back the rest of the way to the hotel.

'Imagine being here just before New Year's when the Sydney to Hobart finished,' Dad said. He explained that the Sydney to Hobart was a yacht race that generated enormous interest throughout Australia from Boxing Day each year. It finished just near this point and the huge number of competitors would swell the bars, clubs and restaurants in the vicinity.

'This really would be the place to be.'

13

30 May 1956

HELEN

In the 1950's the races were the place to be. A standard Saturday race meeting was an event that was always guaranteed to draw a crowd. For the first race meeting of May, the crowd numbers were swelled even greater by the fact that almost every person who had ever known Lucky was there to see him in action. Not only would he be riding Roy's Boy in the first race, but he was also booked to ride Parvo, one of the leading chances in the second race. Whereas last time my hopes were merely for his safety, this day had me hopeful for something more. A confidence-boosting placing, or ideally a career-defining victory. Naturally, with today's races being over jumps I wasn't taking his safety for granted, but knowing he worked horses over them every day of the week meant that I didn't consider this to be a substantial increase in his risk.

'33/1 with most of the bookies, but some of them have him at 25s' Dad said as he came back from the betting ring.

'You didn't bet on him, did you?'

'Just a pound each way.'

'You'll jinx him. We should all be happy enough if he wins that you don't need a profit from it.'

'I did too,' Patrick said. 'I probably won't bother with Parvo at his price, but just a little bet on Roy just in case.'

After being legged aboard, Lucky steered Roy around the mounting yard one last time, receiving not just cheers from our group of ten, but plenty of encouragement from other racegoers. Other than those who knew him closely, he would have been anonymous to most of the crowd, but for industry insiders based at Elwick, he'd become an identity through his incredible enthusiasm for even the most mundane task over the previous couple of years. There was nobody who didn't want to see him succeed, though of course most trainers hoped to see him do no better than second in this race, behind their own galloper.

'Go Lucky' I heard yelled from a group of people near the fence, roughly fifty metres from the finish line. I was able to make out a couple of people I'd recognised from his year group at school. I'm quite sure they never would have said a positive word to Lucky across all those years, but even the possibility of success had seen their memories become selective. Everybody loves a winner, and irrespective of the results from today's races, the fact he had made it this far had seen him perceived as a winner by people like these. I didn't mind. It was great to have that level of support, and I knew it meant a lot to Lucky.

The race was over two miles, starting far away from us at the end of the back straight and bringing the field back to the winning post and then another full lap of the circuit. With only one pair of binoculars between us we were battling to make out exactly where he was as the field was released, but before too long we could see the purple and green stripes he carried were near the back of the field on the outside.

'Good lad,' Patrick said, aware of the plan to keep him on the outside to avoid any trouble that may come. Max's plan was for him to settle near last and build a steady rhythm in the first mile and then make his progress as they passed the starting point having completed one lap. From there, the last six furlongs should see him passing tiring horses and hopefully getting to the front by the final jump at the furlong mark.

Lucky was impressed with the ease at which he'd found his position. He wasn't quite last, as one horse refused to take off as the field was released. With that runner fifty yards behind, he was as good as last.

Beneath him, Roy felt relaxed and ready as the first hurdle loomed. In an instant, he'd gone from perfectly placed to the last place he wanted to be – face first on the turf.

Roy's Boy had landed awkwardly, and Lucky ended up going right over his head. Fortunately, his position on the outside at the back of the field meant that he avoided the issue of other horses' hooves causing serious injury, but the impact of his fall had still been significant. He was taken to the Royal Hobart Hospital with concussion and a suspected broken collarbone. It was the furthest thing from the dream beginning to race riding, but as he would tell us all when we visited him in hospital it could have been so much worse.

It was some time before Lucky was made aware of it, but half an hour later the second race was run and won by Parvo. With Lucky's injuries, he was replaced aboard the horse by another apprentice, Michael Moriarty, for whom it was just a second career win.

Lucky always looked heavy-hearted at the sound of the name Parvo. In his view, everything that ever happened was the result of all the moments that preceded it. That wasn't just about his career, but life in general.

'If I'd just got through that race unscathed, I'd have been aboard Parvo for that victory,' he told me. 'From there I'd have kept the mount for his win at Deloraine the following week. Two wins from three rides over the jumps would have seen me getting aboard the better horses and the results would have followed. The results would have brought me the confidence to ride even better.'

The same conversation was replayed many times throughout his life. One time I asked if he could be sure that the same result would have happened if he'd been aboard Parvo, but that became a sore point.

'You think I'd have fallen off?'

'No, but any change to an event will change everything around it. If you were aboard, then maybe you'd have been one length closer to the lead or one length further back early. That may have led to two horses racing tighter, and maybe one could have fallen right in front of you.

Maybe by riding the horse better, you'd have ended up suffering more bad luck. I'm not saying it would have happened, but life is never so simple that you can be sure of any result staying the same if you change one circumstance.'

None of this ever impacted his feelings for Roy's Boy. The fall was not through anything Lucky had done wrong and was simply a matter of the horse landing awkwardly for no apparent reason. Perhaps if it was any other horse, Lucky would have been willing to blame his mount, but he refused to lay any criticism towards Roy. As far as he spoke about the fall, it was a one-off moment of misfortune.

Lucky was back sweeping out boxes in a couple of weeks, but it was far longer before he was back on a horse. Roy's Boy was given a spell to prepare for the more suitable dry tracks of summer. It wasn't until August that Lucky was back riding trackwork for Max, but with no other jumpers in his stable at the time there was no chance of another race ride for some time.

He did get a couple of opportunities to ride in trials and had no problems crossing the line first in these. Offers of race rides seemed destined to follow, but his second jumping race didn't happen until November. The horse was named Panamint, another real outsider. After the disaster from six months earlier, his mother was now too fearful to come and watch. The rest of his family came with me and my Dad, but this time both the men decided not to tempt fate by betting on his mount. At 100/1 it seemed like everyone else had avoided him as well.

While I was nervous, I still felt in control enough to be here unlike his mother, yet as the horses approached the first hurdle, I immediately understood her feelings as I looked away overcome by fear.

'Safely over,' Dad said, as Panamint landed in fourth place.

'Fifteen more to get over before I'll feel safe,' I replied.

As they entered the home straight for the first time he'd dropped back a couple of places, but Panamint had apparently been jumping very well. Naturally I looked away at each hurdle but the running commentary from my father was highlighting Panamint's performance beyond the on-course race caller's coverage.

There were three hurdles in the straight on the first lap, the last of them immediately in front of us. My confidence rising with each hurdle cleared, I had taken to shielding my eyes as he jumped rather than looking away. Although his position was deteriorating, now back tenth, his jumping was strong enough to feel that he'd probably make up places in the last lap. Already two other fallers had reduced the field from fourteen to twelve and whatever else happened Lucky had done better than them.

The proximity of the last jump in the straight had me unable to stop myself from watching. How foolish I was. Sure enough, the horse immediately in front of Lucky's clipped the hurdle and fell. Panamint attempted to take evasive action from the horse on the ground and in doing so, took control away from Lucky who was thrown to his left almost connecting with the running rail.

'Lucky' I yelled instinctively in the moment that seemed to be paused for minutes. Even now the second between the horse in front falling and Lucky hitting the deck seems to take an hour to occur in the replay in my mind.

It's impossible to explain how hard it is to watch someone you love in such a vulnerable position. You know the risks and it is a constant fear. Fortunately, I could see him moving and knew that although hurt, it wasn't anything too serious. He maintained that the most severe injury he incurred that day was to his pride based on the fall being right in front of the crowd. The doctors at Royal Hobart maintained that the bruising across his body and the broken wrist were probably more significant.

If only I knew then that this was one of his better results from a jumping race, then maybe I could have found a way to fight him harder in the pursuit of having him change careers.

Through his recuperation, we spent time away from Hobart, with the Tasman Peninsula becoming a particular favourite place of ours.

I yearned for Lucky to agree to move that way with me. Somewhere on the water with the amazing scenery and serenity that matched the fantasy I'd long held. Although only an hour from Hobart and manageable to live and commute from, it was more about the mindset and the decision to get away from what held him in Hobart. He was more at home in the tranquil surrounds I sought than I was, but it was purely the horses keeping him in the city. The same horses that I considered likely to be the death of him.

Oh for the day when we'd move down to the Tasman Peninsula, and all of this would be just a memory.

14

16 May 2023

ZANIYA

'Ok, the Tasman Peninsula it is, let's make some memories,' Dad said, as we drove out of the hire car establishments garage.

Nobody in our family enjoys driving when we are away. We avoid it as much as possible. Public transport, although dodged at all costs when home, is an invaluable way of experiencing the real city, and it's our main way of getting around when travelling. Unfortunately, it doesn't work everywhere and today was one of the days when we had to hire a car. There are many bus tours to Port Arthur, our main destination for the day, but we are equally as keen to see many of the great landmarks of the Tasman Peninsula along the way. Doing this, particularly with the flexibility to move at our own pace, was only possible by car. We didn't need to draw straws; Dad was always the one who would drive in these scenarios. He didn't necessarily like it, but he disliked being a passenger even more when anyone else in the family was driving.

We decided to skip breakfast at the hotel, partly because we wanted to get moving early, but more motivated by having an excuse to stop somewhere on the way for a small taste of semi-rural life in southern Tasmania. About three-quarters of an hour into our journey, we arrived at Dunalley. A dot on the map that was home to about 300 people, we wouldn't have been stopping here ordinarily, but we were glad we did.

A quick walk alongside the water was followed by a trip to the local bakery where we had a really enjoyable breakfast. We also got some advice on the best places to stop further down the peninsular, including one spot that we hadn't found in our own research. While our plan for the day had been built around Port Arthur, we knew there were a couple of places worth seeing along the way.

'Don't miss Remarkable Cave,' the woman behind the counter had said. 'It isn't quite on your way, as it's just past Port Arthur, which is why so many people miss it, but it's one of the real highlights. It might add half an hour to your trip, but believe me, it will be worth it.'

Once on the road again, our next stop was the Tasman Park Lookout. This was a small stop on the side of the road that gave a stunning panoramic view of Pirates Bay and the rugged coastline to the north of it. A short drive down the road took us to the Tessellated Pavement, a freakish geological formation where the rocky surface is split into rectangular blocks that look like tiles. There are other examples of this type of formation around the world, but nowhere is it as large and clearly defined as this spot. Oliver had explained it on the drive, but what I pictured sounded largely uninteresting, though as it wasn't taking us out of the way, I had no objection to stopping for a brief stretch of the legs. The reality well and truly surpassed my expectation. It looked like a stunning piece of artistic design, but it was nature at its finest. The blocks formed through the movements of the Earth. While that can happen anywhere, the particular salt crystals and the erosion by the Sea's waves caused sediment to fill tiny little gaps which over millions of years have grown into clear divisions and the amazing sight it is today. Dad's camera got a significant workout, though his photography skills aren't sufficient to have me confident he will have suitably captured the magic.

Some people spend a huge proportion of their time looking through a lens when they travel. Mum and Dad were never against the principle of photography but always instilled an attitude that had us using cameras less than most tourists.

'You only get these moments once. You can savour the essence of it, or you can miss it by looking through a camera trying to capture it. Sure, you can keep it forever that way, but only with the smallest impact. Over time you don't look back at the photos that often, but you relive the memories in your head far more frequently. If you've maximised the experience, those memories are far more powerful. Live the moment in the fullest sense and the memory within will be more powerful than any photo.' These were Dad's words on our first overseas holiday when we travelled to Pakistan. It was ironic to see him now, never travelling without his camera, though it's fair to say he did still use it sparingly.

Our next stop was a very quick one at Eaglehawk Neck. The neck is a narrow bit of land, no more than 30 metres wide with the ocean on either side. It became an important part of ensuring the prisoners of Port Arthur couldn't escape back in convict days. The Dog Line was established here, with ferocious dogs tied to a row of posts to warn of any escapees. It remained in use for several decades, so it achieved its aim. A life-size replica sculpture of one of the dogs was one of the few things to see here. After being asked to take a photo of a couple with the dog sculpture, Dad then insisted we had one too.

'I never said don't capture any moments,' he explained. 'Just don't miss the moment for the sake of capturing it. I don't think there is anything we have missed here.'

We rejoined the main road for little more than a few hundred metres before we were across the neck, and from there we headed around towards the lookout at Fossil Bay.

Before reaching this point, we passed through a tiny community known as Doo Town. Thanks to a whole lot of community spirit, every house in the village has a unique nameplate on it. Gunadoo, Xanadoo, Love Me Doo, Doo Drop In and Doo Little were among the names of the houses. It is the only feature in the immediate area, so we didn't stop, but we did make sure Dad drove slowly enough that we could take all these names in.

It turned out that there was one more thing to 'doo'. Doo-Lishus was a food van set up just past Doo Town in a car park that was used for a couple of nearby sites. We'd already intended to be stopping at this point, so it didn't change our plans, but it was an interesting additional sight. They weren't set up ready for business yet. We weren't too bothered, breakfast still having us fully satisfied.

We walked onto a lookout where we watched the waves crashing into the cliffs beneath. The lookout provides spectacular views along the coastline and gives a true appreciation of the power of the sea, something that became even clearer after a short walk took us to The Blowhole. This spot was originally a cave but after millions of years of erosion, it has turned into a spot where the water powers through from the ocean and sprays out at the far end. Unfortunately, the seas weren't heavy enough when we were there to see the best of it. Ideally, a blowhole will see water spout out high above the land. For our visit, it was more dribble than force. We had seen one in the United States several years ago that was incredibly powerful. With that memory, I'd hoped for more here, but our day ahead had enough planned that we couldn't wait here for more favourable conditions.

'It doesn't matter how well you plan any trip, you're always dependent on being lucky,' Dad said. 'Rougher and wilder conditions would make stopping here more rewarding, but it would also have made the rest of our trip less palatable.'

Our perspective comes from our own experience. The Blowhole will probably fade from my memory far quicker than much of Tasmania, not because it isn't an amazing site, but because fate was such that we didn't see the best of it. A day later and it may have been the greatest highlight of our trip. Many factors lead to our experience in any place. It is why I never take too much credence on other people's opinions regarding places to see or to miss. Another day, different conditions, different crowds. It all leads to very different experiences.

Walking a little further we got to a boat ramp, a short jetty leading to the calmer waters of Pirates Bay. While our first view of this came from near Eaglehawk Bay this very southernmost edge of the bay revealed a very different location. Protected by the edge of the land by Fossil Bay that extends further north, the boat ramp sees fishermen leave in calm waters in pursuit of their prey. We were just two minutes' walk from the thunderous waves by the cliffs of Fossil Bay yet seemed to be a world away with the stillness of the waters before us here.

We got back in the car and drove the short distance into the national park area, stopping at a car park near the Tasman Arch. The arch is a tall natural bridge in the sea cliffs, forming a frame on the sea from our vantage point. The sea crashes through underneath this arch against the shore. A great height above this was our vantage point. A short walk from here was another natural wonder known as the Devil's Kitchen, a deep trench carved out by the sea. Wandering between these points on a trail through the scrub was an enjoyable standard hike for a national park area, but to have such incredible natural wonders so close made this incredibly special. We ended up back at the arch and reading the information from the lookout point suggested that the constant force of nature would mean that over millions of years, erosion would see the arch eventually disappear. At that point, this would become another version of the Devil's Kitchen, which probably looked just like the Tasman Arch tens of thousands of years ago.

There were more places we'd missed, but we were already behind schedule and still had one more stop we wanted to make before going to Port Arthur. It was ten minutes past the famous site, but well worth it. Remarkable Cave proved to be remarkable in more than just name. Of all the natural phenomena we had seen on the peninsula, this for me was the standout.

From the car park, we had a ten-minute walk down hundreds of steps to get to the viewing point. The cave is unique, with two openings from the sea merging into one cave further along. At the end is the viewing platform. With the tide in, this led to a surge of water thumping towards us every few seconds. The water enters the cave from two wider points than it can leave, which results in an incredibly powerful surge.

Given the calm weather, the fact the water reached a level to get us wet highlights just how significant this would be in rougher conditions.

I'd love to see it then, or even better when the tide is out, at which point you could climb across and enter the cave. There are signs up to stop people doing that, but it doesn't seem to be patrolled so I think we'd get away with it. I probably couldn't do that with my parents around though.

After the best part of five hours from leaving our hotel in downtown Hobart, the myriad of attractions along the way had been completed and we were now just a few minutes away from Port Arthur. Whatever was in store for us here, I knew that the sights I had seen would probably stay with me longer than Port Arthur itself. So many tourists miss these, but they are among the great natural wonders I've ever seen. No wonder Helen was so keen to move down this way and escape the problematic life of Hobart with Lucky.

15

11 October 1957

HELEN

The problematic life that Lucky had built was made more difficult due to his courage. While admirable, this led him to continue to forge his career despite the obvious dangers he faced. His perseverance was second to none, refusing to allow any setback to stall his dream. His confidence, though at times shaken by all the negatives around him, never reduced sufficiently to step away from the belief that he would make it. There are fine lines between courage and foolishness, between perseverance and stupidity and between confidence and ignorance. Other than Lucky himself, it was hard to find anyone who used the more desirable adjectives to describe him.

By 1957 we were very much in love. For Lucky, life was little more than the job and the woman he loved. Not surprisingly he proposed at the racecourse. To be fair it was at the end of a movie at the drive-in cinema in the centre of the track rather than the stables, but it was telling that such a big moment should come at Elwick. Maybe the only more appropriate place would have been the Royal Hobart Hospital.

Our wedding date was set for January 1958. Lucky had just turned twenty-one and I was nineteen. We believed we were beginning an idyllic new life together. I was at teachers' college, about to begin my final year as a student, which meant Lucky was still the sole breadwinner. His apprenticeship complete, he was now a fully licensed jockey.

Making a living as a jockey was largely dependent on prizemoney from winning races or at least from losing riding fees by getting plenty of race rides. As well as three jumpers' flats, he had ridden in seven jumping races without managing to finish one of them. Ten race rides a week might see him earning a reasonable income, but ten rides in four years hardly augured well for his prospects. Bringing home a wage that at least ensured survival came from a range of tasks he did for Max and occasionally getting to ride trackwork for other trainers at Elwick and the odd morning at Brighton.

Iris had never really accepted his career choice and Patrick was warning him that once he had a wife and children, they would need to be provided for in a more secure way than he could as a struggling jockey.

'What job can I ever do where I can earn the kind of money I can make as a jockey?' Lucky asked.

'Almost any job' Patrick replied. 'It's fine for the likes of George Moore. He can make a fortune riding in all the big races and winning most of them. That sort of salary depends on a few factors – firstly getting rides in races, secondly staying on top of the horse and thirdly winning some of those races. You've spent nearly eight years following this dream, five years getting to your first race and now three years later there's nothing.'

"This is my passion. And I have a talent. Max isn't the only person who has said it."

"You've got a talent alright; nobody falls like you," he said.

Lucky pointed out how happy everyone was with his trackwork riding, which showed his ability to judge pace and work with the horses. He'd won trials on the flat and over jumps. It was merely bad luck that had seen so many bad results follow him on race day.

I often talked to Lucky about the future in more than just the romantic notions that everything would work out for the best in time.

'I can get by on the work I do at the stables and my trackwork riding. The race rides are merely the cherry on top, which at some point will start becoming more regular.'

'I'm more concerned about your well-being than the money,' I said.

'Workers compensation insurance covers my well-being.'

'No. Workers compensation insurance only covers the financial aspect, which is not what I am talking about. My interest is your health and safety.

'I'm getting all the bad luck out of the way while I'm young enough to bounce back quickly.'

Bouncing back quickly seemed to mean something different to Lucky than it did to most people. Riding in races is pretty much the standard day at work for a jockey, but each time Lucky had one of these days at work, it was followed by a trip to the hospital, weeks or months of recovery before the slow build back to another day at work when the sequence began again.

Lucky first really questioned his career choice after a race meeting at Brighton. Two jumps' races were on the card this day, and he was there early despite only having a ride in the latter race. Twenty minutes before the first race the news came through that a couple of jockeys had been caught in major congestion due to a major car accident on the road from Launceston. Jockeys were needed for two of the top fancies in the first race and there were only two licensed jumps jockeys available. Michael Moriarty got offered the favourite, Grogan. Lucky was unbelievably excited to get the ride on White With One, one of the better hurdlers in Tasmania.

When the news was announced on the public address system there was a range of groans from punters who had fancied the horses' chances. Already, Lucky had a reputation. The impact on the betting market was substantial. White With One had been at odds of 6/1 before the announcement, but within moments the bookmakers all started putting his price out. By race time he was at 16/1, with few if any punters willing to concede that Lucky would be capable of winning his first race. I wouldn't have expected confidence from people, but this seemed over the top. That said, I was not concerned about the prospect of victory, just that he would safely complete the course.

Lucky rode him perfectly in line with the trainers' instructions. He sat just behind the leaders, and while some of the other jockeys had their whips out, he remained sitting calmly as they were approaching the bend towards home. He was passing others and had moved into second place, just a couple of lengths behind the favourite and closing the gap with every bound. His horse looked fresher and with the momentum he looked the one to beat. Lucky later described his adrenalin levels at this point as being something beyond anything he'd ever experienced. Even as a spectator, I could understand why.

The last jump loomed as he was drawing to the quarters of Grogan. Under pressure the favourite hung out badly as he jumped, heavily obstructing White With One who clipped the top of the hurdle. The horse fell and for the eighth time in eight jumping races, Lucky ended it on the turf. Not a person on course could have suggested the fall was anything to do with Lucky. He was a victim of circumstance after having done everything right.

The race club's doctor looked him over and said he would be fit to ride in the second race. I was disappointed, having thought we'd escaped the day with nothing seriously wrong, but was going to have to endure another spell of anxiousness.

Max's mare Clementine wasn't going to be highly fancied by punters whoever was riding. Even my eternally optimistic husband had said he didn't expect to get through this race.

'She has a mind of her own. She's very hard to settle and while she jumps fantastically at times, she is just as likely to get into a mood and throw it all away going straight through a jump,' he said.

'Why are you risking your life on a horse like that?'

'It's my job. I have a responsibility to give her the best possible chance. And anyway, I don't see her hurting me. The most dangerous falls don't come from horses like this. She'll be at the back staying out of danger for most of the race. The trouble comes when the chasing pack gallops over you, and that won't be happening.'

Whatever his record as a jockey, Lucky was looking more effective as a predictor based on this. Clementine dug her heels in and refused to gallop as the field was released. After giving the field a furlong head start, she finally consented to Lucky's strong urgings, but then once starting she wanted to sprint. She was running significantly faster than any of her rivals, quickly eating into the large deficit she had. She impressively cleared the first jump and by the second she'd almost halved the gap to the rest of the field. Her headstrong nature had gotten the better of her though, and she didn't want to consolidate her stride coming to the hurdle, going straight through. She tumbled and Lucky went flying off her. It may have been a less embarrassing fall than some he'd had, with nobody noticing as they were focused on the field half a furlong ahead and didn't see what happened. The horse was back on its feet and sprinting on as before, while Lucky was not looking anywhere near as spritely. To my relief, I could see through my binoculars that he was moving, albeit gingerly.

***

'Lucky O'Shaughnessy. I know you love seeing me but there has got to be a more sensible way of going about it,' said Matron Carol McKay as she came to see him on her rounds. Once again it was the Royal Hobart Hospital where he'd be spending Saturday night.

'It's been several months now Matron. I'm not that much of a regular.'

'How many races have you ridden in since I last saw you?'

'Other than today? Um, well none.'

'Sadly, he seems to consider you and your colleagues as more regular acquaintances on his days at work than the other jockeys,' I added.

'And to think they call you Lucky.'

While sitting with him until the end of visiting hours two other nurses attended him, both of whom entered the room exclaiming his name like a long-lost friend despite not knowing him in any other capacity than through the hospital.

On this occasion, his injuries weren't serious and though he stayed in overnight for observation he was released home the next day. Courtesy of cooperation between his parents and me, we got a guarantee from him that there would be no more race rides before the wedding which was just seven weeks away. That was a negotiated settlement that started with us all requesting no more race rides ever. It didn't take long to see that was a battle we couldn't win, but at least I now felt confident that I would be walking down the aisle to a man who wouldn't be sitting in a wheelchair.

The wedding was a small affair, based partly on our wishes but equally due to the limited financial resources within our families. The ceremony was held at St Marys Cathedral, just a few blocks from the Royal Hobart Hospital. Matron McKay and colleagues Sally and Angela were true to their word and attended the ceremony to see us in better circumstances than they were used to. Max was one of the few people from racing circles to attend. Lucky wanted him to be his best man, but it didn't quite fit having a seventy-year-old man alongside our respective teenage sisters as my bridesmaids. There was racing in Launceston on the day which kept a few away, but many of the jockeys and trainers who weren't up north still chose not to attend. I found that surprising considering how popular Lucky was, but I guess sometimes the perception of popularity is different to the truth. Perhaps through it all, Lucky was as much of an outsider as in his youth. All up there would have been sixty people in the church, roughly two-thirds of whom came to the reception which was held on the property of family friends. There were no frills, but it was what we wanted. A celebration of our love surrounded by the people we loved. Some brides want everything, but anyone that needs more I had really should re-evaluate why they're getting married at all.

We had our honeymoon on Bruny Island and fell in love with the place. It was only a few days but that was enough to feel a connection that ensured we'd feel linked to the place forever. When we returned to Hobart, I moved into the rental house we'd leased back in September.

Lucky had already been there for a couple of months but as was the way in those days we'd have offended too many people if I'd moved in before we were married. The house was small, but it was all we needed. We were just a few blocks from both family homes and Lucky had just a five-minute walk to the racecourse, so the location worked well. It was a longer trek for me to University at the Domain but with only one year to go, this seemed like a lower priority. Who knew where I would find work the following year, but we knew we could reassess things later.

Lucky was back in the stables and looking ahead to making greater strides career-wise.

'It used to be passion that drove me but now it is responsibility,' he said. Not that the passion had diminished at all, but it was now alongside the committed responsible man he purported to be rather than the renegade youth.

What impact this would have on results wasn't going to take long to see as he was booked for Max's youngest jumper, Ghost Tour on his hurdles debut in March. When the program came out, I was disappointed to find that Ghost Tour's race would be the last on the card. The anxiety of a race day was bad enough. Going through that much of the day before the main event was not what I wanted.

16

16 May 2023

ZANIYA

Going through so much of this day before the main event was just what I wanted. We'd entered the Port Arthur Historical Site seeing very few other people arriving, but a few people already leaving at the end of their visit. As much as I had enjoyed the coastal sites of the Tasman Peninsula, the rest of the family was quite resolute that this was what our day was all about. Port Arthur certainly warranted our time, for it wasn't only a significant part of Tasmania's early history, it was also home to one of the most tragic parts of recent Australian history.

In a country that was so dominated by its use as a penal settlement, Port Arthur was designed for the worst offenders. People were transported from England to Australia for sometimes minor crimes, but those who reoffended on arrival were then sent to Port Arthur. From here, escape was impossible, or at least it appeared to be inconceivable. Those who escaped only had one possible destination to seek, Hobart, and that meant passing through the Dog Line at Eaglehawk Neck where we'd been earlier. Proven or not, the belief was that the waters surrounding here were shark-infested, so nobody tried that option.

For all the reminders of the penal colony, our first stop was the tribute to the victims of the 1996 massacre. A gunman killed thirty-five people and wounded twenty-three more in the worst act of its kind in Australian history. Even small children were targeted by the gunman.

The massacre was so horrific that the nation's gun laws were changed with bipartisan support soon after the event. It was poignant for Mum and even more so for Dad.

'There was just so much symmetry between the tragedies here and at Dunblane.'

Dad had spent two years with the Central Scotland Police, stationed in the city of Stirling just near Dunblane. The Dunblane massacre occurred in the two weeks between his move back to Newcastle and his wedding. He felt closely connected to the massacre; not only did he know many of the investigators, but also the families of the victims. Most significantly he had investigated the perpetrator of the massacre on another matter the previous year.

'It didn't overshadow our wedding, but it had an impact. Some of your fathers' colleagues that were meant to come down, couldn't,' Mum said.

'We got back from our honeymoon in Spain and the following Sunday we woke up to the news of the massacre that happened here. It appeared a copycat attack, coming so soon after with such similarities. Heavily populated location within a remote town. A loner known to police but never thought of as capable of such an atrocity. Dunblane was the biggest death toll of any gun rampage in Britain and then this was the equivalent in Australia.'

'Both events then got clouded by conspiracy theorists who suggested in each case that the events didn't happen in the way officially reported,' Mum added. 'Gun legislation was changed in both nations after the events which is what prompted the theories.'

The tribute was in the form of a memorial garden on the site of the former café where many of the murders took place. It was a small and sombre reminder of one of the world's most senseless acts of violence. By keeping the memorial discreet it avoided the Port Arthur site being noted more for the massacre than its rich older history.

Even without a connection, it was impossible not to think about what had happened and feel moved to be standing in this exact spot.

The victims would most likely have been just like us; tourists without a care in the world, enjoying the experiences of this beautiful spot with such positive expectations only to find the most unimaginable horror awaiting them.

The string of murders occurred in the on-site café, the gift shop and the car park as well as further murders beyond the boundaries of the historic site. Initially, some people moved towards the gunman as they believed it was part of a historical re-enactment. After a suitable time reflecting on the tragedy of 1996 and the fine line that can separate the best and worst of life, our focus was now ready on the Port Arthur of the 19th century.

Moving onto the older history, we began with the harbour cruise. Included in our admission cost, the cruise gave the most spectacular view back across the water to The Penitentiary. Most memorable was seeing and hearing about the Isle of the Dead, a small island just a short distance across the water from the penal colony sight. As its name suggests, the island was the resting place for those who died at Port Arthur between 1830 and 1877. More than eleven hundred people met this fate. Approximately two hundred of the graves on the island are marked, a tribute reserved for prison staff and military personnel, while the convicts who accounted for most of the dead were buried without tribute. Considering how small the island was, it seemed apparent that there would have been no spare inch of room to allow anything more ceremonial. It was not surprising that any settler of importance in the colony was buried elsewhere, avoiding the indignity of being laid to rest on the island. There was an option to do a tour of the island, but we'd earmarked sufficient else to ensure a busy day and chose to bypass this.

Back on dry land, we made our way to the Penitentiary, the visual centrepiece of the historical site. The structure was gutted by fire after the penal settlement had been closed, but the remaining ruins provide an insight into what had been home to more than five hundred people at a time. Looking through the prison bars I know that the views look far more scenic to me than they would one hundred and fifty years ago.

Perhaps such an outlook was deemed to be appropriate punishment by ensuring those inside knew what lay so close, yet so far from their reach.

Behind the penitentiary, we made our way through the law courts, the guard's tower, the hospital and the police station before viewing a separate prison. It wasn't *a* separate prison, but *the* separate prison, so named because all the prisoners in here were on permanent solitary confinement. There was no talking allowed. There was a chapel, because in the day prayer was essential, but each prisoner was brought in separately and placed in a closed-off section where they could see no other prisoners. It was no coincidence that right next to the separate prison was an asylum, as the treatment imposed on people here drove most to insanity. The separate prison was reserved for only the worst prisoners, not based on their crimes, but on their failure to adhere to the behavioural demands placed upon them in the penitentiary. At the time, the British were still evaluating the most effective means of punishment, and Port Arthur was at the edge of experimentation. Humanity was insignificant. Rehabilitation wasn't considered relevant. Submission was all that mattered.

The asylum was now a museum but with so much visual history right before our eyes throughout the site, we spent little time here, moving on to something different. Most places in the world have good and bad areas, but there are few places where the division is as strong as a penal settlement. Moving from the domain of the convicts to the homes of the esteemed free settlers saw a very different look. Spacious houses with well-manicured gardens provided a welcoming escape from the nature of most people's existence in the colony. Life may have not been the trauma for the free as the imprisoned, but with little else around them, comfort in the home was essential.

As dusk fell, we went inside to the restaurant for a quick meal before we were due back amongst a greatly dwindled crowd for the ghost tour. We were more than a little apprehensive that we'd be experiencing something overly cheesy. I imagined that we'd be seeing dressed-up staff appearing in the distance at the appropriate moments to make things

appear paranormal, but this was far more professional than I'd anticipated. Our tour guide, Jenna, told us that she had never seen a ghost,
so while it was possible, and many people had previously claimed to
see ghosts, we shouldn't expect to see one during the tour. Jenna did
add that she had experienced a vast number of strange and inexplicable
events that made her believe that spirits were involved. She emphasised
that she wasn't going to try and convince us of any presence and nor
would there be any special effects used. She would merely tell us events
from the history of the site, all of which were true, and allow us to make
up our own minds.

There may have been no special effects or manufactured stories,
but the tour managed to leave most of the twenty people feeling more
than a little anxious at times. Carrying our lanterns as the only light
in amongst very dark surroundings contributed, but mainly it was the
skill of our guide. She was a brilliant storyteller, allowing a hushed tone
to build suspense when talking of mystery and murder before hitting
us with a loud noise that had our heartbeats accelerate having not seen
it coming.

With each area we went to, there was another story and a different
method used to put us all on edge. Some of the tour went through
places we'd seen during the day, but more of the highlights were different spots, such as the Parsonage which served as home to the various
ministers who had been sent to attend to the spiritual needs of the
settlement.

Jenna spoke quietly and calmly in the darkened room. She explained
that she did not want to be disturbing any ghost on the off-chance that
there could be one present.

'One of these ministers, the Reverend George Eastman died in his
upstairs bedroom. He was placed in a coffin that was lowered out of a
window. During this process.....

Everyone in the room jumped as the previously quiet Jenna stomped
her foot loudly on the floor. She continued, now speaking at a louder
volume, her job of terrifying her audience done.

'.....*the rope snapped, the coffin crashed and broke open and the body fell out onto the road. Ever since, there have been ongoing accounts of doors opening and closing with nobody around, unexplained footsteps and the sight of the reverend's ghost.*'

'What happened to being quiet and not disturbing any ghost that may be present,' one of the tour group asked.

'I felt sure there wasn't one here right now,' Jenna said, clearly prepared for such a question. The technique of drawing an audience to a point where they are vulnerable to such a sudden noise is an old one, but that hadn't stopped it from proving effective.

Next door was the accountant's house. We were told there have been many unexplained sightings of someone known as the 'Blue Lady.' She is thought to be the accountant's wife and died in childbirth. Her soul apparently inhabits the house still looking for her child. A century and a half after her death, there have been numerous accounts of people seeing her with outstretched arms. Jenna explained one of these.

'*In 2011, a woman was on this tour with her very young daughter. The daughter suddenly ran off from her mother and was on the veranda with outstretched arms as though she was hugging someone. Nobody could see anyone else there but the little girl. When her mother caught up to her, she asked the child what she was doing, and the child said she was hugging the woman in blue. The child was too young to have had any knowledge of the story, and there were enough people on the tour to verify this as true.*'

At one stage, I fell behind my family, looking more in-depth at the frighteningly named 'Dissection Room.' I talked to a young couple who seemed to be genuinely scared, and truly believed in ghosts. I didn't question or judge them, for I felt that the tour had done an exceptional job of selling the concept. I didn't feel the presence of ghosts, but I believed I'd been in the presence of an entertaining guide performing a clever script. I don't doubt that she only told us about true accounts of sightings, but I suspected most of these accounts had come from people open to belief. It may be based more on imagination than science, but if ghosts were to exist anywhere, this would be the place.

Probably the scariest moment of the night was more than half an hour after we left. Dad was driving, with Mum and Oliver both sleeping while I was focussed on my phone, scrolling through my social media. As it turned out Oliver wasn't asleep and had spent ten minutes lulling me into that belief in order to make me jump.

'See you didn't need a ghost tour,' he said.

'Trust me, you're not going to make a career out of that as that tour guide can. She was brilliant.'

It would take us nearly two hours to get back to the hotel. I wanted to do a bit more work on the story of Lucky and Helen on our return. It's amazing how everything I am seeing down here seems to connect to parts of their story and it helps me shape how I want to write it. I loved today's journey. With each step, it kept getting better and even what I feared may be the tackiest part of the day turned out to be a highlight. I would recommend that everyone should do the ghost tour.

17

27 February 1958

HELEN

Ghost Tour had been an expensive yearling bought in Victoria in 1952. After showing potential in his first campaign with a placing at Flemington, he failed to deliver on expectations. He was sold at a loss and transferred to a trainer in the Gippsland region, and after failing for him he was then sent to a Launceston-based trainer. Despite winning one of five starts for him, the owner decided to cut his losses at the end of his previous campaign and sold him to Max for 50 pounds. Max had then gifted us a 25% share in the horse as an additional wedding present. For regulatory reasons, it had to be in my name and not Lucky's, but in essence, it was to be an extra special horse for both of us.

'He won't dare dislodge me. He knows he must look after me to get looked after back,' Lucky said.

'Did you look after Roy's Boy any less because you didn't own him? He didn't remember any need to look after you on race days.'

'Whose side are you on?'

'Rationale.'

Lucky probably considered Ghost Tour the third member of our marriage. As much as a role as racing played in our marriage, I had no great love of horses, so he wasn't that close to us in my eyes. As Lucky worked his backside off at the track, I was happy that he had a horse that helped make the days pass faster and easier for him.

He was a striking grey horse who stood out from the crowd. Not only was he distinctively coloured, but he was a tall, big-striding galloper. Never would a horse like this have been expected to be a hurdler, but the sale and transition to Tasmanian jumper had come as a result of his ordinary performances. Horses, particularly those who'd had his price tag, would never be given up on too quickly.

'Today's the day darling,' he said bouncing out of bed like a kid on Christmas morning. It was his first race ride as a married man and our horse's first hurdle race in Hobart. Max was confident he'd run well, and Lucky was convinced that this could be more than just his first finish. He was thinking of nothing less than victory.

'Maybe you should put a bet on too,' he suggested.

'No way,' I bellowed more insistently than he was used to hearing from me. 'We do well enough if you win without that. 25% of the prize-money as owners, plus your cut as the winning jockey, not to mention the emotional high. I'm not jinxing things with a bet. Not with our funds so limited.'

As determined as Lucky was to take the mantle of a responsible adult, it wasn't a role he was suited to. Like his career choice, everything to him was what felt right rather than what he'd analysed as such. I was always going to be the voice of reason within our marriage while he would remain carefree. We could be out on the street, and he would just shrug his shoulders and tell me that we'd just make the best of it.

Lucky never showed great nervousness on race day, but he'd never shown this level of confidence either. That feeling wasn't shared by punters and bookmakers as he was priced at 20/1. A couple of comments suggested that he'd be less than half those odds with any other jockey on board.

'Weight stops trains,' I heard one punter say to another as I made my way from the betting ring towards the mounting yard. 'O'Shaughnessy is a bigger handicap than any amount of weight.'

'Lucky would stop planes. I wouldn't want to be on the same aircraft as him. He'd probably find a way to bring that down too.'

Tempted as I was to defend him as I heard them laugh, I knew the best option was to ignore it and keep on walking.

Once Lucky had seen me in the yard as he mounted Ghost Tour, I was free to escape. It may be overly superstitious, but I really couldn't bear the thought of watching the race. Whenever he fell, I hated the moments of helplessness when I couldn't do anything and knew nothing. Sometimes it only takes a second before there were signs of movement and I could relax slightly, but other times the wait was much longer. I decided to go inside the stand. I would be able to hear the commentary without watching. If he made it to the finish safely, I'd be back in the stand before he returned to the weigh-in area. If he fell, the distraction of making it back downstairs should hopefully reduce my time standing around waiting.

'They're just about set. Racing. It's a great start for all the runners. Hot Pockets is the first to show up from Four Hats. Let's Go Home is moving forward alongside Ghost Tour. Volarchi is next from Duntroon, Precious Pat, Homer's Odyssey, Clifton Heights, See No Evil and Premiers Pride is at the rear. Entering the home straight for the first time and Lucky O'Shaughnessy has taken the grey Ghost Tour to the front....'

I think this was the first time Lucky had ever been in front. I remembered the time that he told me that there was more to fear from a fall when the rest of the field is behind you, from the hooves connecting with you as they gallop on. Of course, to counter that, there is less chance of falling when the horse is in the lead as there aren't the potential obstructions of horses falling in front of you.

'...from Homer's Odyssey out wider, two lengths back to See No Evil and Premiers Pride is still at the rear. Oh, and there's a fall at the third jump.'

My heart rate surges as I wait for who has gone down. I expect the inevitable, only to have the ultimate relief immediately follow.

'Duntroon is down and Premiers Pride's jockey has come off trying to avoid the fallen horse. A lap to go and Ghost Tour is still in front for Lucky, can he stay on until this point on the next lap? Volarchi has closed

the gap and moved to his outside. Hot Pockets is next in a line with Let's Go Home and Precious Pat, Three lengths further back to Clifton Heights then Homer's Odyssey. Four Hats has put in a couple of ordinary jumps and is back alongside See No Evil at the rear. Into the back straight and the first of the treble coming up. Volarchi is up alongside Ghost Tour and they've moved four lengths ahead of the field.'

Rather than feeling positive about how the race was going, I was feeling more anxious than normal. The longer he remained a winning chance, the more crushed he would feel if he didn't finish.

'...and Four Hats has sold out at the next, McGregor is on the ground but he is moving. Volarchi has now moved clear in front with 5 furlongs to go from Ghost Tour. Still many lengths back to Homer's Odyssey and Hot Pockets. See No Evil has made good ground on the outside and is still closing on the pack. Let's Go Home is under pressure alongside Precious Pat and it looks too big a task for Clifton Heights. Inside the half-mile they approach the next and oh no Ghost Tour has come down, Lucky O'Shaughnessy has fallen again......'

It just feels too predictable. When his horse is struggling or when his horse is going well. When it is his fault or when there's nothing he could do about it. The fall is always just a matter of time.

I made my way outside as Volarchi crossed the line in front and focused my binoculars on the hurdle at the top of the back straight. I'd already heard the race caller comment that he was conscious, but I wanted more reassurance. He had paramedics gathered around him. I could see he was sitting up but with the attention he was getting, I suspected he was far from unscathed.

I moved downstairs to wait outside the jockey's room. As the other jockeys made their way back to the room, each of them acknowledged me and either shrugged their shoulders or offered a 'bad luck' message. None of them really thought it was bad luck. Without seeing what had happened, I honestly didn't know if it was his fault, but that would be the perception purely because of who he is.

He was in the back of the ambulance and heading towards his regular race-night accommodation at the Royal Hobart Hospital. I followed talking to the club doctor. Lucky had a suspected broken collarbone and a broken nose. He'd landed shoulder first before his head hit the ground front-on. The horse was fine and got straight back to his feet chasing the winner.

He wasn't in too bad a way in the evening while I was there keeping him company when Max joined us.

'What's your verdict boss?' Lucky asked.

'You did nothing wrong. Taking him to the front was the right move. Just a shame the winner came up and pressured him that early. He was a class above everything in the field. We probably could have run second if he'd been able to stay relaxed a little longer.'

I asked why the fall happened.

'Just happens sometimes Helen,' Max said. 'The more tired they get the more likely they are to jump a little shorter and lower. He smacked the hurdle and lost his balance on landing and at that point it was unavoidable. Four other jockeys didn't make it through the race either, so it was not only Lucky that didn't finish.'

'So, you think he should continue riding?'

'What are you talking about?' Lucky said.

'I just want an opinion.'

Max explained that it wasn't for him to say.

'He's a capable jumps jockey. He has had plenty of bad luck and the reality is he could continue to have bad luck. It's a dangerous job and I wouldn't encourage anyone to continue unless they truly believed it was for them.'

'It is,' Lucky said.

'I'm going to be training until I'm eighty and I'll need someone riding trackwork and doing other jobs around the stable for me if nothing else, so he's going to have work as long as he wants it. I'm sure that isn't your biggest concern though, is it Helen?'

I hadn't really anticipated Max being on my side in encouraging Lucky to give the game away. To be honest, I don't know what we would do without his income, and I have no idea what else he would do. I did at least want him to start considering other possibilities. You can't be a jockey until the age of eighty, and he wasn't going to have the resources to move into training. Eventually, the time would come that he was going to need something more in life. I would prefer it to be sooner but felt that at least he should be at the point of analysing options.

Lucky's recovery was expected to take four months before riding trackwork again, and six to eight months before he'd be able to ride in a race again. During this time, he had plenty of opportunities to evaluate whether continuing as a jockey was worth his while by following the path of Ghost Tour. Three weeks after dumping Lucky at Elwick he raced at Brighton and completed the course, finishing second. Next start he went to Deloraine and finished third before winning his next start at Elwick. By the end of the preparation, he'd had ten races with his only failure to finish being the day that Lucky rode him. He won three races in this time, two at Elwick and one at Deloraine. Our 25% ownership – well legally it was all mine - proved to be quite lucrative, with his earnings for the season topping 200 pounds. Lucky considered the fall was due to a lack of fitness at the start of the preparation rather than a consequence of who was riding.

'If only I'd not been aboard that day, I would have had nine rides on him since that time. Maybe a result would have been different somewhere along the line, but that's just as likely to have been the other way. That day at Launceston he would have won if the jockey didn't wait so long before taking off. I know him better and wouldn't have made that mistake.'

'You can never know. Maybe ability is irrelevant and it's all luck. Maybe your share of that is all used up everywhere except the race-track,' I said.

Lucky was always able to make a reasonable argument to justify his position, but the more times he lay in pain, the more likely it seemed that he'd look from a different angle.

While the prizemoney had been an unexpected bonus, money was manageable with me now teaching Year 3 at Glenorchy Primary School. Lucky also received small workers' compensation payments, and when able he was back at the stables doing the work of an apprentice for Max, on minimal wages. To further ease the financial pressures, and to hope that Lucky could see that sometimes one had to move beyond their dreams, I started working on Saturday mornings helping my sister run a market stall. While it earned me a few extra pounds each week, the main highlight was being in that environment. I loved markets.

18

17 May 2023

ZANIYA

I love markets. Hobart's Salamanca Market has a reputation for being the best in Australia. When this trip was first planned, each of us did our standard research to get as many ideas of the must-see and must-dos of the destination. This was immediately near the top of my list, but as it turned out, everyone else was just as keen.

The Salamanca Market has been an institution in Hobart for 50 years. It is held in Salamanca Place at Battery Point in the shadows of the old sandstone buildings that housed the warehouses for the port in Hobart's early history. More than 300 stalls operate each Saturday, and they usually get more than 30,000 people attending. In a city this size, that is a remarkable number.

We didn't have breakfast at the hotel. We were all a bit slow-moving this morning, and it was nearly 8.30 before we left which is opening time for the market. We meandered slowly, taking advantage of the nice day to walk along by the water, debating whether or not to stop along the way for a coffee.

'I'm sure there'll be coffee stalls there Zaniya,' Dad said.

'I'm sure there'll be insanely long lines for coffee there. One now to allow us to feel alive then one a bit later there so you can feel like you've supported the small local.'

Dad was a strong proponent of supporting local small businesses. I completely understood and agreed but hadn't managed to make him understand that the small local café was just as small and local as the market stall. When we were passed by someone carrying a cup of insanely good-smelling coffee, I knew I was halfway to winning the argument. The sight of a reasonably quiet café across the road completed the deal for me.

We all arrived at the entry point feeling somewhat more awake and alive than when we'd left the hotel. The entry point we'd taken seemed to be about halfway along the line of stalls. One of the first things we saw was a coffee van which already had a line snaking inconveniently past a couple of other stalls.

'Good call Zaniya,' Dad said. He was never too proud to admit he was wrong.

'Let's make this our meeting spot if we lose each other,' Mum said. 'Central, and if anyone's lost, they can join the queue and get coffee while they wait.'

We decided to go down away from the city end first. The first fifty or so stalls contained a random mix of handmade jewellers, second-hand books, gin tastings and fresh produce. At this stage, I was keenest on the idea of something for breakfast, but nothing suitable had yet presented itself. The first genuine option appeared moments later. The smell was incredibly Australian. Sausages sizzling on a barbecue accompanied by onion being grilled. It wasn't what I felt like, but the smell had made me far more conscious of my hunger. Dad and Oliver both stopped and grabbed a sausage and onion in bread, Whether or not this is officially recognised as such, it must be the national dish, such is the frequency with which it is on offer. Possibly the only more traditional Australian food is the meat pie, and it is a pie stall that we pass next. I give brief consideration to a scallop pie, as this is a particularly famed Tasmanian food that is rarely found anywhere else. It seems a step too far for me, but Mum is brave and gives it a go. I can't deny how good it smells, but it just isn't what I wanted. I will give it a go before we leave Tasmania.

We'd reached the end of one row of stalls but had still three-quarters of the market to see when we turned and I immediately saw my breakfast. The sign saying French Crepes was hardly the authentic piece of Salamanca that my family had gone with, but the stomach and tastebuds want what they want. Served with strawberries and a chocolate sauce, it was far more decadent than I'd intended, but I have no regrets.

In typical irony, now that we were all fed, we saw a procession of food stalls offering all manner of options. I remained more than happy with my choice but still took heed of the reminder that it's usually best to survey the whole scene before committing a choice. I did stop and buy a freshly squeezed juice to compensate for the earlier indulgence.

As we progressed further through the market I was impressed by how little repetition there was. Many markets like this have you seeing the same things over and again, but at Salamanca, there was great variety among the stalls. There were multiple woodworkers, but their products were greatly different. There were handmade jewellers, but each of these was distinctive in its style. Photographers, old movie prints, clothing, honey and jams, leather goods, spices, wines, unique giftware, there was always something to capture your attention that you didn't feel you'd see again if you passed it by.

We'd spent nearly two hours wandering through before we'd done a full loop taking us past every stall. We all wanted to go back and get certain things we'd seen, so we agreed to split up and meet back at our original meeting point of the coffee van at midday. We couldn't leave it too much later due to the afternoon's plans and the hope of dropping back to the hotel briefly first.

I went straight to my target; a stall selling old Tasmanian photos and memorabilia. I hadn't held the family up by sorting through them all in the hope of finding something of Lucky, but I was going to peruse what I could now.

'I don't suppose you know if you have anything featuring Lucky O'Shaughnessy?'

'Who?' the stallholder asked.

'He was a famous jockey here many years ago. Just recently passed away.'

The man looked at me, somewhat miffed about a 19-year-old woman who looks Pakistani yet speaks with a broad English accent, asking about a Tasmanian jockey from half a century ago.

'There are a few horse racing pictures in amongst it but I don't know all of the details,' he said, giving me some semblance of hope.

I flicked through the various collections. The closest thing that stood out to me was a picture of a horse going over a hurdle. It said the horse's name was Genghis and it was ridden by Kevin McGregor in the Cup Day Hurdle of 1967. I continued and found another photo, this one of the entire field taking off at the start of the Glenorchy Hurdle of 1963. There were about a dozen horses and riders but no mention of names. Could Lucky be in among it? It seemed unlikely given the scarcity of race rides he had, but with no other better options in the stall, I decided I had to buy it. I would take it with me to Bruny Island on Monday and ask Helen if he is in the photo. If not, she may be able to identify some of the others in the photo who would no doubt connect to some of the stories.

I ended up last back to the meeting point despite being five minutes early. To be fair, we are a punctual family so I shouldn't have been surprised. We exited via the parliament gardens, and just before reaching that point, stopped and looked through the range of fresh produce stalls set up just outside the market proper. Turning to leave I notice something on Dad's upper back.

'Um, someone's left their mark on you Dad.'

He looked at me confused.

'You've got bird-shit on your right shoulder.'

Pulling forward on his shirt he could just make it out, though Oliver's laughter would have been all the confirmation he needed.

'That's good luck, right,' Dad said.

'Not so lucky.'

19

13 August 1964

HELEN

Not so Lucky

The nickname Lucky appears to have been given ironically to Elwick-based jockey Luke O'Shaughnessy. Eight years after his first race ride he has not only failed to ride a winner, he is yet to finish a race. Every form of misfortune has befallen O'Shaughnessy throughout his career. Twenty-one race rides have resulted in twenty-one failures to finish. He has fallen near the start of races and fallen near the end. He has fallen when his horse has jumped poorly and fallen when it has been other horses at fault. O'Shaughnessy continues to be the living testament to "Murphy's Law," as it seems that anything that possibly could go wrong for him, has.

'It's hard to understand,' leading jumps rider Michael Moriarty said. 'Lucky has been in the states jockey ranks for a similar time as me. He has won many trials and is a great track work rider who many trainers are happy to trust their horses with at work. For some reason on race day, it all seems to go wrong for him. In many of the falls he has had, it has been through nothing more than sheer misfortune. When a horse immediately in front of you falls there is sometimes nothing you can do. It has happened to me a few times, but it just seems to happen to Lucky continually. On average you expect to fall maybe one or two times in twenty races, but for him to have fallen in all twenty defies belief.'

O'Shaughnessy's falls have led to injuries that would frighten anyone. Broken leg, arm, collarbone (twice), nose, wrist and many concussions would make most people reassess their career, but O'Shaughnessy continues to defy logic as he aims to break through with a maiden success.

'This is all I know and it is what I love so there is no chance of me giving the game away. Plenty has gone wrong for me but I know that if I continue to work hard then eventually things will work out,' he says.

'Of course, there are moments of doubt. Everyone has them, even the most successful people in any walk of life. At some point we all hit hurdles – I guess in my case quite literally – but you get back on the horse. At that point, you reflect on why it is you are in that position. The rides I've had have been earned based on my ability and that silences the doubts within.

While many would suggest his career objective should be centred on winning a race or at least finishing one, O'Shaughnessy says his aim remains to ride in the English Grand National at Aintree.

'I realise now it is looking less likely, but I don't believe in giving up on dreams too quickly. Why aim for anything less than the ultimate in your field?'

When asked what it would take for him to give up on his chosen career, he shows the resilience that he has become renowned for on the local racing scene.

'The day that I believe a horse's chances are reduced when I'm aboard, is the day I will stop riding in races. Results, nor the opinions of others will tell me that, just the feeling I have on top of the horses.'

Can O'Shaughnessy make it twenty-second time lucky? He rides outsider Von Puttkamer in the Aston Hurdle at Elwick tomorrow.

That article appeared in Hobart's daily newspaper on Friday, August 13th, and the superstitious could be forgiven for seeing a connection between the date and the story of luck about a man named Lucky. It was the first time that anyone outside the racing fraternity had noticed him and his record. To be honest I am not sure that too many people in the industry had realised his record was quite like this.

Completing, and even winning trials while also having completed several jumpers' flats had taken the spotlight off his hurdle race record. Nobody considered him to be an asset to a horse's chances as the betting moves always showed, but people hadn't focused enough to notice the facts behind his career. Most would have considered him as the last-choice jumps jockey in the state without knowing that he'd never finished a hurdle race. Once this article was published, he was no longer the uncompetitive battler, but now the source of humour throughout Tasmanian racing.

Lucky was good-natured enough that he'd provided quotes for the journalist expecting an article that highlighted a hard-working battler. Not for the first time, his expectation of the intent of others was far better than the reality that accompanied it.

'I'll be a laughing stock,' he said.

'It's not going to be the first time others have laughed at you, and you need to do as you've always done. Retain your belief and know that those who laugh are merely showing their ignorance.'

'But what they laugh at is true.'

'It is an interpretation of the truth.'

'What?'

'The article says you've never finished a race. What about all the jumpers' flats?'

'Yes, but I haven't finished a jumping race.'

'The article didn't specify that.'

He never won arguments with me and was struggling to see the best way to attack this one, eventually accepting his best option was retreat. Despite this, I knew the essence of his argument was true. He would be a source of jokes but not for a reason of his own doing. He needed to know not how to avoid that, but how to understand it for what it was.

We'd had some more good fortune with Ghost Tour, but not in the way we would have most wanted. Three of Lucky's rides were on him, and all three ended in the standard way. To be fair, the horse did also dislodge three other riders, so it wasn't a fate that was reserved for Lucky.

Over the last three preparations of his career, he did win an additional four races. By the time Max retired him after a sequence of poor performances, he had amassed nearly a thousand pounds of prizemoney just from our share. Through the years, with Lucky unable to earn much, the good from this horse far outweighed the bad.

Von Puttkamer was less significant for us. We weren't part owners, but more significantly he'd been a source of frustration for Lucky. He showed ability over the hurdles, but only when he was in the mood. He'd thrown Lucky twice at trackwork, injuring him and delaying his comeback to race riding. Eventually enough had come together, and Lucky would be aboard him in a race, two years after his hurdling debut for Max.

I arrived on course with him, making sure that everyone saw the pride I had in my man. There may be more talented jockeys on course but there wasn't a man amongst them who had Lucky's fight, his courage and his passion. Winning strike rates may mean a lot on a racecourse, but through the course of life, it wasn't a characteristic that mattered so much. Lucky's strengths were attributes that would stand the test of any of life's real hurdles, and I wouldn't have swapped that for anything.

I took my place in the grandstand. While Dad or some of Lucky's family still occasionally turned up, today I was on my own. I knew most of the other jockeys' wives, but the majority of them had formed a clique that I wasn't a part of, nor did I wish to be. Several of them were sitting just near me and they began giving me the same sort of treatment that Lucky got in the jockey's room.

'So, I see that Lucky's ambition is to ride at the Grand National in England. I think you need to get his passport cancelled Helen. He'd probably fall at the water jump and if he's true to form, he just might drown.' The comment from Harry Mortimer's wife Susan earned the laughs of her friends but I didn't take the bait. I looked at her with a slight raise of my eyebrow.

'Sorry Helen' she followed up with. 'No malice intended. Maybe this will be his race and he'll have the last laugh. I won't hold my breath.'

'Like Lucky at a water jump you mean?' added Sarah McGregor, wife of the reigning Tasmanian premiership-winning jumps jockey, Kevin.

I ignored them and opened the race book, pretending to read what I'd already read several times before. I heard the sniggers continue before eventually the topic changed and both Lucky and I were forgotten about.

As the horses left the mounting yard, the one wife who I had become friends with, Rebecca Sinclair, came and took a seat next to me.

'Good luck Helen.'

'Good luck to you too.'

Her husband Paul was another battler, far older than Lucky, but similarly, he didn't fit in with the inner sanctum. He rode track work at Hobart's other racecourse at Brighton, so he hadn't got to know Lucky too much in the early days but saw enough similarities to himself in the younger man that they developed a bond in time. When Paul was around, Lucky never felt alone in the jockey's room. He may be the butt of jokes, but Paul ensured that there was always a comeback for anyone who chose to deliver those lines. His career didn't have the notoriety of Lucky's, but neither did it have the successes of the likes of Mortimer, McGregor and Lucky's old nemesis Michael Moriarty.

At forty-five, Paul knew his days were near the end. He'd started as a 17-year-old in 1935 on the flat, but after spending two years at war, he returned to the sport riding over jumps. In the following two decades, he'd written about fifty winners from roughly two thousand rides, a mediocre strike rate but enough to get by with. His reputation as a battler gave perspective to Lucky's career; Lucky averaged two or three rides a year compared with Peter's hundred. Admittedly Lucky was averaging nine months a year injured, but that fact further emphasises the uniqueness of his record.

As the race began, Von Puttkamer and Paul's mount, Johns Harvest, were both racing near the lead. Coming around the turn for the first time, Johns Harvest had gone to the lead while Lucky was right behind him. As promising as this looked, I knew not to think too much of it.

At 100/1 and 20/1 respectively it was a sure sign that they'd be feeling the strain before too long. In itself, this made me nervous, and it did so for good reason.

At the first of four jumps in the back straight it happened. Johns Harvest fell and broke a leg on landing. Lucky had nowhere to go and both he and the horse came crashing to the ground. With so much of the field behind him, the real danger was not the initial impact, but being trampled by any of the oncoming horses. While most dodged him, one hoof came down and connected. I may have been more than half a mile away in the grandstand, but I could genuinely feel the impact, and instantaneously the fear that had the bile rising inside me.

Most trips to the racecourse finished with me waiting at the jockey's room for the information to flow from the paramedics to the club doctor before coming to me. Today I'd reached the room downstairs well before the ambulance was back. It was at least five minutes before I heard second-hand that he appeared to be conscious. No doubt like most race days, I would be home alone tonight with my husband in hospital.

Every career has peaks and troughs and I always expected Lucky's to be dominated by the latter. Maybe it was foolish, but I did always retain hope that we would see a peak.

20

17 May 2023

ZANIYA

We are going to see the peak. Mount Wellington, Hobart's omni-present feature. Wherever you are in Hobart, the summit can be seen and there is something commanding and powerful about that for a newcomer to the city. It is so common to see Hobart framed pictorially by its mountain and its river. After spending time on the river Thursday, it was now time to experience its other great natural feature and the stunning aerial views it would provide us.

There are a couple of ways that most tourists make it to the top. A range of companies run bus tours up here, however the convenience of being able to stop off along the way leads many to prefer to drive. A very small number of possibly mad tourists decide to walk to the top. Courtesy of my over-enthusiastic parents, I find myself in this company.

'The summit may give you spectacular views, but you only get a snapshot. Hiking up on the trails, you're constantly turning and seeing different perspectives,' Mum said.

'Plus, you can appreciate anything far greater when you've earned it,' Dad said. 'The view at the top always appears more spectacular when you've faced a challenge to get there.'

I knew he was right, though I doubted I would be willing to admit it at the steepest points of the trail. For some, the symbolic nature of dipping their toes in the Derwent and taking off from there is ideal.

We've skipped that, and got a bus to the lower reaches, shaving off half of the distance, though probably only a very small percentage of the difficulty. Mum and Dad would both have liked to devote more time to the mountain and explored some of the many other spectacular trails across it, but as always on our trips, compromise was at the forefront of our planning. Between Mum's desire to go to MONA and Dad's wish for our trip to Port Arthur, they weren't going to get more than a few hours on the mountain; enough for Ollie and me to appreciate the beauty without being destroyed by the physicality. We may be a generation younger and fitter than them, but without the same level of desire and enthusiasm, we were the ones who were going to be pushed harder by the difficult stretches.

We walked the Pinnacle Track which was meant to take us about an hour and a half from our starting point halfway up the mountain. Dad tried to convince us to take the Organ Pipe trail, one that would extend our time to the top far longer than we could afford. The Organ Pipes were a spectacular geological formation that had a walking trail pass right beneath them. We'd seen the dolerite rock formation from the distance, and at this time we couldn't get any closer.

Though it had seemed like a nice fine spring day in Hobart, the temperature was getting progressively colder as we got higher. This didn't impact us too much due to the intensity of the exercise we were doing, but when we got close to the top and we encountered snow on the ground, we fully appreciated the climatic difference that comes a kilometre above sea level. At 1,271 metres, this wasn't one of the world's highest summits, but most giant peaks aren't so close to a city. To transition from normal suburbs to a sudden climb like this isn't something I've done anywhere else. The comfortable conditions in the city were very different to how it felt here.

The views at the top are great, but some on the way were possibly better than at the summit, for you could see as much, but from a closer distance. That still didn't diminish the feeling of satisfaction as we reached the summit.

'That is breathtaking,' Mum said as we got to the platform that gave the best view. We were fortunate that there was little cloud, and certainly not at a low enough level to impact us. The mountain is visible from most parts of Hobart, yet in our time here there had been plenty of times when we couldn't see the summit.

The combination of the mountain's height and its proximity to the city means that the eyes are drawn down more than out, unlike most mountain tops. Hobart was straight out below us, and after looking to the right and seeing the city's tallest building, the Wrest Point Casino, I looked to the other side and focussed in on the Elwick racecourse. Such a large parcel of land as a racecourse always makes for an easy landmark to identify from a distant lookout, but this time I was more drawn to it than would normally be the case.

Mum and Dad both pointed out different landmarks that we'd visited and there seemed to be a family challenge about stating the obvious. Dad was guaranteed to win this, as he'd never let anything pass without a mention. The cold was starting to impact me, so I went to the indoor lookout. The views were of similar quality inside, and there was also plenty of information about the mountain, its history and its significance to the city.

Oliver was already there, looking out the other side at the broadcasting tower. The tower is a one hundred-and-thirty metre concrete structure, that cloud cover aside, is visible from anywhere in Hobart.

'Makes you wonder why people would care about the aesthetics of a cable car, when they already have this,' he said. Plans have been in place for a cable car to be installed taking people up the mountain, but it has been an issue of great contention amongst the local community since the installation was first proposed.

'I think that was to do with far more than how it looked,' I said. 'Then again, I think a cable car would actually look pretty impressive. For what it's worth, I like the tower too.'

There were many other reasons for the community objections to the cable car, as we overheard in conversations at the markets this morning.

Progress always faces obstacles. It needs to, as without checks and balances in place to ensure that change is actually for the better, history and culture are lost. Hobart is more globally famous for MONA than anything else. A museum that ignored the rules and rewrote them. Beyond that and nature, its greatest selling points are the history of Port Arthur and places like Battery Point in the city.

Changes can give cities a new lease on life, but some change needs to be stopped. Clearing every hurdle and reaching the finishing line should never be taken for granted.

21

14 August 1964

HELEN

'I think we will have to put him down, Ken.'

'Sure, I'll get the rifle.'

'NOOOOOO,' Lucky screamed, as he tried to get up despite the severity of his injuries.

'Calm down Lucky, we were talking about the horse.'

Lucky collapsed and was soon in the familiar surrounds of the back of an ambulance on his way to the even more familiar Royal Hobart Hospital.

Rebecca had helped comfort me despite her fears for her husband. To be fair, the painful clique behind us showed every sympathy after the accident. I wasn't in the mood for forgiving and forgetting, but I was grateful that their attitude had changed from earlier, for I wouldn't now have coped with a single bad word.

Lucky had three broken ribs and a punctured lung as well as a concussion and a broken wrist from the fall.

'How much longer can you do this Lucky?' was my first question when I saw him after surgery.

'How is Paul?' In the midst of all he was suffering, his character shone through, focussing more on what someone else was enduring than his pain.

'He is home already. Bruised and battered but not broken. Once again you copped the worst of it even though you and your horse weren't the cause.'

'How about the horses?'

'Von Puttkamer didn't have a scratch on him. Got straight up and followed the field. Paul's horse didn't survive.

'It's the weirdest thing. I had a dream that they said they were going to put me down and when I panicked...'

'They told you they'd been referring to the horse,' I said finishing the story for him. 'That wasn't a dream Lucky – Ken and Trevor told me about that while the paramedics were attending to you.'

'Another joke for the jocks to throw at me next time.'

'Next time? When is this going to end?'

'That wasn't much of a way to end things. I had him placed perfectly. My skills are getting better but my luck is getting worse. That can't continue. Skill is controllable while luck balances out and I'm getting more and more overdue for it to turn my way.'

'It could turn the other way.'

'My luck in races could get worse?'

'A fraction worse luck and that fall would have killed you.'

The hoof that struck him did serious damage but compared with the possibilities that could have happened, he got off lightly. A week later he was home and three months later he was back on light duties at the stable. If the hoof landed on his head, we'd have been burying him. Despite this, it seemed equally inevitable as foolish that he would continue.

His next race ride was more than a year later in the north of the state. Longford, just out of Launceston, was the venue, and it would be the first time Lucky had ever seen the track. Max was trusting his veteran jumper Grand Amnesty to Lucky for the first time in a race. Lucky had ridden him in trackwork regularly, but the timing of his injuries didn't coincide well with Grand Amnesty's racing timetable. Finally, they would be united on race day for Lucky's debut at the northern track.

Max also had Von Puttkamer, Lucky's previous race ride entered in the same race, with Harry Mortimer having the ride on the more fancied stablemate.

'Longford's a very different track to Elwick,' Harry explained at trackwork the day before, 'so you need to ride it accordingly.'

'What do you mean?'

'Well, don't fall off,' Harry said.

'That hasn't been working for me anywhere else. But is there anything else that I need to know about the track there?'

'It's smaller than here. They make their runs when you come down the side, and that means a lot of jockeys move too early and occasionally you can swoop over them in the straight. The home bend is tight so they often come a fair way off the fence in that last furlong and you can slip through inside them. Of course, if you're on the ground by that point it's all irrelevant.'

Lucky was never going to fail through a lack of planning, researching and learning. Staying aboard was all he needed to focus on, but that wasn't sufficient for him. He wanted to maximise his chances of victory, not just of completing the course. He could live with the mocking that he'd received throughout his career, but he was equally determined to win respect as to win a race. He believed that his best prospect of doing this was showing professionalism in every way. If moving through on the inside would save ground without fear of running out of room in the straight, then it may be his move that would be the difference between victory and defeat. The one thing better than a win would be a win purely due to his ride.

Whenever he rode away from Elwick, he always travelled with Max and the horses, so I usually tried to convince someone to make the trek with me. Dad agreed to drive to Longford which not only spared me the boredom of a long trek on my own but also saved me from a longer drive than I ever liked doing. We ended up getting delayed and only just managed to arrive on course as the jockeys were being legged up.

I didn't get to wish him luck. Maybe the absence of a good luck kiss would change his fortunes.

Dad insisted on stopping in the betting ring and opened his wallet to put on a bet.

'Don't jinx him, Dad.'

'I'm not backing Lucky, I'm backing Max's other horse. Max does train quite a few winners. Once you eliminate the ones my son-in-law rides, his strike rate is pretty impressive.'

Dad did have a point. On both of the previous times Lucky rode one for Max when he had two horses in the race, the other one had been successful. I'd never really thought about it until Dad mentioned it, but maybe he was on to something. I was more hopeful that he was now jinxing it the other way, with Lucky now winning and Dad losing his bet. With Von Puttkamer at 10/1 and Grand Amnesty at 100/1, it didn't appear likely.

We only just managed to find a vantage point to watch the race from amongst the large, festive crowd. My eyes automatically were drawn to the familiar purple and green silks only to initially look at Harry and Von Puttkamer before remembering Lucky was wearing a white cap to distinguish him from the stablemate. Not surprisingly I had to look several lengths further back to see him, but at least he'd cleared the first two obstacles.

And he's down again, Lucky O'Shaughnessy has come off his mount. No, sorry, it's the stablemate Von Puttkamer who has lost the rider, my apologies.'

For all the standard panic I endure in every race he rides in, mistakes from the commentators don't help. My binoculars had been focussed on Lucky and ignoring everything else. I didn't know what to think in the few seconds before the correction was made. The caller had them the right way around when both horses were jumping well, yet the preconceived notions of Lucky seemed to come straight to the fore once a fall occurred.

The original field of fifteen was down to twelve as the field passed the post with a lap of the Longford track to go. Approximately one mile from home and another eight jumps, my hopes were slowly building with each obstacle cleared. Victory had never been a serious part of my consideration. Completing the course would feel as much of a triumph for Lucky as any other jockey would experience when winning a race. I always felt that once getting that monkey off his back, actual race wins from better opportunities would become easier to envisage. Today, victory was a forlorn hope, as he was three lengths behind the second last horse and more than twenty lengths from the leader, but he was jumping soundly.

Seven, then six, then five. Approaching the half-mile, the horse's form over the hurdles remained strong. Two more rivals had fallen, but Lucky had no problems navigating around them.

He cleared the fourth last, and at this point had caught up to another runner, and past him on the outside with a strong leap. Turning onto the side he was closing on others as well, and while a placing was unlikely, he was only a couple of lengths off the horses in sixth and seventh. Another fall perhaps? Was the impossible becoming possible?

Optimism again proved futile. Once a jockey has been dumped, it is anybody's guess what a horse will do. Without the weight of a jockey on its back, a horse can run faster, but it isn't confined by the vagaries of the track. One riderless horse had jumped a couple of hurdles of its own volition but decided that was enough. A few strides before the next hurdle, he veered at right angles to avoid the hurdle. Billy Dawson aboard Kane is Abel initially copped the brunt of this and fell before the interference further spread to Nigel Harris, riding Calliope, who also hit the deck. With Grand Amnesty racing just behind and outside of this pair, it was seemingly unavoidable for Lucky to face the same consequences. Somehow, he used his rarely appreciated skills to manoeuvre the horse out of trouble. A sharp tug on the right rein had the horse deviating out of trouble with a sharp movement wider on the track.

While this saved both horse and jockey from trouble, it also meant they went around the hurdle and would therefore be disqualified.

'At least they can't say I have fallen in every hurdle race I rode in now,' Lucky proudly stated to Max as he dismounted.

Max didn't share Lucky's enthusiasm. He knew full well that the official results would show that Grand Amnesty had failed to finish, the same comment as would be shown if Lucky had fallen.

'You could have taken the horse back a furlong and gone over the jump then finished the course. That's all we wanted today.'

'I would have looked a fool if I did that and then fell,' Lucky said.

'A few people think I look a fool putting you on my horses in races,' Max said. Both men knew that it was a comment made in jest, but there was an element of truth underpinning it. Lucky had ridden perfectly aboard the horse, timing his moves perfectly in line with Max's intentions and then showing brilliant reflexes and skills to evade the trouble on the side. For all of this, the result was the same as always. Experts knew that Lucky had ability, but none of them bar Max wanted to take the chance. They weren't afraid to use him for trackwork or trials, but on race day he was only an absolute last resort.

Max let Lucky leave with Dad and me. 'It's not often you leave in something other than an ambulance. Your wife deserves the pleasure for once,' Max said.

'Thanks Max,' Lucky said. 'It's a good thing I didn't fall. They don't know me at the local hospital like they do at the Royal Hobart.'

'I think the staff at any hospital near a racecourse are made aware when you've got a ride,' I said. I rarely contributed to these jokes, but sometimes I couldn't help myself. I still harboured the belief that eventually, common sense would prevail. Of course, my husband was one of the greatest examples of proving that common sense wasn't so common.

22

17 May 2023

ZANIYA

My family love to prove that common sense is not that common. After covering so much ground on foot through the day, it would be ridiculous to plan a long evening walk as well. They did though, and we were walking to the restaurant and nightlife hub of North Hobart.

'Some people take holidays and lay back on a pool lounge in a resort, relaxing and feeling great until they return home with their time away nothing more than a blur. Others experience as much as possible and return home richer for the experience.' Dad couldn't have been any more predictable. Of course, I do agree with him in theory, but in practice, I am too damned tired.

The North Hobart precinct is centred around the continuation of the city's main shopping mall. There is the odd restaurant that we pass soon after the end of the mall, but it's a kilometre later when we hit the main area. There was a diverse range of options. Korean, Greek, Chinese, Mexican, Italian, Seafood, Steak, Vegan, Vietnamese, Burgers – there is a seemingly endless choice. While the array of cuisines mightn't rival the melting pots of London or New York, it is impressive for a city of this size to have this diversity. Having them all so close together gives people the opportunity to pick a destination without having to commit to a cuisine. We'd done this out of hope more than expectation, but now here we could see that this had not been in vain.

Naturally, we'd seen more than a dozen options that I would have settled for, but which hadn't won unanimous support. Not that my choices weren't suitable, but Mum and Dad weren't stopping until the end of the main strip. Only once they'd seen everything would they commit, and most likely to something I chose far earlier. While getting all four of us to agree wasn't always the easiest task, our semi-random approach to these decisions always tended to favour those who dared to speak up first. In doing this as we went, I'd already set the parameters that should narrow down the choice. When Oliver stressed that he wanted a steak, it connected to one of my choices, and both parents offered little objection. We were heading back to the Roaring Grill.

With our dinner decided, we kept our eyes open to what else the area offered. Pubs, cocktail bars, a micro-brewery, a wine bar and a karaoke bar. I wasn't sure that it was the perfect place to be out with my parents, but I liked the area and thought how cool it would be to live nearby. When looked at in conjunction with the rest of the city, it gave a level of vibrancy that I never would have thought would be associated with a city of this size.

Given I picked the restaurant, I wasn't just keen to enjoy my meal but felt invested in everyone else's too. Fortunately, I had nothing to worry about there. Between us, we had steaks, lamb shanks and sea-food, with everyone raving about their meals. While Oliver stuck with local beer, the rest of us shared a bottle of Tasmanian Pinot Noir that I thoroughly enjoyed despite not usually being a red drinker. Given all we'd done through the day, none of us felt guilty ordering dessert. My sticky date pudding was superb, while everyone else seemed equally as impressed by their cheesecake, crème brûlée and tiramisu respectively.

'Still upset we didn't stay at the hotel?' Dad asked. I'm sure he chose the moment of taking out his card to pay the bill to make a point that the sacrifice I'd made walking here wasn't so substantial.

'I never said that was what I wanted. I was as keen as anyone to be coming here, I just would have been a whole lot happier if you'd let me pay for a taxi,' I said.

We moved across the road to Republic, a bar that had a live band playing, and where I was reminded again of how fortunate I was to have parents who weren't out of place in such an environment. Growing up, there was always such a divide between most of my friends and their parents, yet it didn't exist in our household. Mum and Dad always treated us with an extra level of respect and maturity. By treating us as adults, we behaved as adults. Few people of our age would go on overseas holidays with their families and not feel inhibited by the presence of their parents, but for us, that wasn't the case. As a family, we were all equals. We all could seek the experiences we wanted, but as a close-knit family, most items that appeared on one person's bucket list turned into a yearning for all of us.

'One more?' Oliver asked the moment he had an empty glass in front of him. The band were on a break and just about to come back for another set, and having only caught the last song of their previous set, I was keen to stay. I knew I was going to be asleep the moment my head hit the pillow tonight, so I wanted to keep going while I could. That's how I like days on the road to be. Squeeze everything out of every day so that you sleep soundly, and wake refreshed ready to go bigger and better the next day.

'Not for us. We're going to call it a night and walk back to the hotel,' Mum said after a conversation with Dad that seemed to take place entirely through facial expressions. 'But you two stay. Get a cab back if you're too worn out.'

'We'll be leaving at 9 to walk down to the Botanical Gardens if you decide you want to join us,' Dad said. 'If not, then we'll meet you in the lobby at midday to go to the races.'

As they left, and Oliver's glass was still empty, I got up to get the next round of drinks. The bar was busy, and as well as several people trying to get served, there was a group of people congregating inconveniently close to the serving area. Fortunately, someone noticed my difficulties and got the barman's attention on my behalf.

'Thank you,' I said to the attractive stranger before ordering the drinks.

'Where are you from?'

'The UK. Newcastle.'

'Beautiful place,' he said.

'Really, you've been there?'

'No. Sorry, just making conversation.' He looked embarrassed that his attempts at the smooth-talking Aussie hunk had failed. He hadn't failed on the Aussie hunk part though, so I made sure I quickly put him at ease.

'You haven't missed that much. It's not as memorable as your hometown.'

He laughed and told me that I wouldn't say that if I knew his hometown. 'I'm new to the city. My hometown is actually a dot on the map an hour away from here.'

'Well, your adopted hometown then. Where's true home?'

'It's called Dunalley.'

'Oh my god, we were there yesterday.'

'Small world. Well, small island.'

I'd become oblivious to Oliver impatiently waiting for me to return with his beer, until my distraction, whose name was Toby, asked if my boyfriend was going to be angry about waiting for his drink.

'My *brother.*' I emphasised the word strong enough to ensure that Toby knew he had the all-clear. Moments later Oliver came over. He'd probably seen me chatting and had wrestled with the idea of whether to give me space or to save me from an uncomfortable situation.

'Toby, this is my brother Oliver.'

'How ya doin' mate,' Toby said in his accent broader than most I'd heard down here.

Oliver knew straight away that I was more than comfortable with Toby and didn't stay too long before moving on to prop up another section of the bar. Shortly after I excused myself to go to the bathroom and made a beeline for my brother on the way.

'You won't say anything to the olds if I don't come back with you?'

'As long as they're not sitting in the hotel bar and see me return alone.'

'They'll be asleep by the time you get back, so that won't be an issue.'

'Just make sure that you're in the lobby at 12.30 tomorrow and nobody will need to know a thing. You sure you know what you're doing?'

'No, but that's half the fun. Look, this mightn't go anywhere, and I could leave with you in half an hour, but I just want to cover my bases.'

'Cool. Well, I'm gonna have one more, then I'll go. I'll make sure I let you know when I'm going, but I won't get in the way.'

I kissed him on the cheek and thanked him. I couldn't have a better relationship with my brother. Older brothers usually are one of two things: over-protective or inattentive. He is there for me anytime in any way. He will jump in to save me from anything but will also let me do what I please if he knows it's my informed choice. I can trust him completely, which in that respect makes him one step closer to me than my parents. I love them as much, but I don't think I could envisage the situation with Toby working quite the same way if they were still here.'

'You didn't leave,' Toby said when I returned to the bar.

'I don't know my way around the town enough to be leaving on my own,' I said.

He looked at me and smiled. I knew he was thinking the same as I was, and I wondered if I should have been more subtle. I didn't care. Squeezing everything out of each day meant avoiding wasting time. Tonight wasn't something that I ever considered would be part of a Fergusson family holiday, but that just added to the excitement.

'Well, I'm happy to save you from the dangers of the city. Show you some of the better things it offers. We'll find somewhere a little quieter, ok.' He took me by the hand and led me towards the front door. Oliver had spotted us, and I gave him a nod and a smile as my way of saying 'See you tomorrow.'

23

29 May 1966

HELEN

In February 1966, Australia changed to decimal currency. Tasmania was far less inclined than the mainland states to welcome significant change, with our state Labor Government continuing to lead the state as had been the case for more than three decades. Premier Eric Reece was developing a more autocratic style of government and took greater control of the state's administration. He began focussing on a range of smaller issues within various portfolios, and within the racing industry, it seemed that Lucky was drawing unwanted attention. Reece had appointed a new racing minister and a new management team for the sport in the state. From all we could see, the first initiative on their agenda appeared to be eliminating Lucky from the industry.

In an industry with a high public profile, participants can be seen in very different lights by various groups. Lucky had become a sideshow to the serious punter, a novel attraction to the casual observer but a drain on the industry's coffers to the powerbrokers of Tasmanian racing. Horse racing is a high-risk industry and there are enough injuries to ensure that the workers' compensation fund is regularly sourced. Lucky was a participant known primarily for his injuries, so when this budget line became a major focus, his name was front and centre in the eyes of the administrators.

Tightening regulations around the licensing of jockeys was said to be about improving the professionalism of the industry, yet the proposals that had been raised would only impact one jockey: Lucky. The changes had been set to take place from the beginning of the next racing season on August 1st, despite pushback from numerous parties who saw this as a deliberate attack on one man. With time, the proposed changes became a debate about people's attitudes towards Lucky.

The first meeting at Elwick in May saw Lucky with his first race ride since breaking his leg on Jaybo the previous year. In the wake of the issues that were playing out in the industry, it was understood that this could be his last race ride. It wasn't only Lucky and I who were conscious of this, but the entire racing public and this was evident by the size of the crowd who turned up. It was an inconspicuous meeting without the highlights that would normally see such attendance, but the focus that was on Lucky at this time was so great that there were now masses who turned up to see him.

'There is no way we'll let them stop Lucky,' Marty Johnson said to me in one of the rare moments he had a break from selling racebooks. 'If it's all about money then they need to look at this. Thanks to Lucky there's an extra couple of thousand admission tickets; an extra thousand race books sold, thousands more drinks, pies, sandwiches, and betting turnover. With the extra money his appearance brings in, they could afford to pay a lifetime of medical bills for him for every time he rides.'

'I'd rather there were no medical bills,' I said.

'You want them to ban him?'

'I want him to finish the race safely today. Stop the injury cost from being relevant. Probably then you stop having the masses turn up, so maybe you wouldn't want that.'

'The one day he rides doesn't keep us afloat when he misses the next fifty,' he explained.

Lucky's mount today was Loch and Quay for local trainer Mervyn Nicks. Lucky regularly rode trackwork for Mervyn, but this was the first time he'd be aboard one of his horses in a race. Mervyn admitted that he'd given the ride to Lucky out of principle; he believed that he'd earned his licence and had done everything necessary to retain it. He'd been interviewed for the local newspaper and discussed Lucky.

'Lucky isn't the most natural jockey out there, but he isn't to blame for the record he has. When I look at his falls, most of them have come from sheer bad luck. He has put horses into perfect positions only to have others fall right in front of him, where no jockey in the world could have escaped the aftermath. The falls that have come through his mistakes are no more numerous than you'd find from any jockey. Despite his name, he hasn't been lucky when it comes to race day, but he has consistently proven his capabilities, and I am more than happy to be legging him up on one of my runners.'

For all that he'd said, Mervyn hadn't trusted Lucky with an elite performer. Loch and Quay had been a winner in two of his fifty-three races. One of those wins came from his twenty-one starts over the hurdles. It was more than twelve months since he'd been placed in a race and there was no reason for confidence that today would be any different. The reassuring thing for me was his relative safety as a jumper. He had finished all but two of his hurdle races. On one occasion he was pulled up by the jockey when out of contention before the home turn, while the other occasion saw the jockey fall on the flat section of the course. Had it been Lucky who fell in such a way, plenty would have been said about his performance, but it was Albert Morgan, a high-profile visiting jockey from Melbourne, and it was accepted that it was merely a one-off mistake.

While Loch and Quay was a comparatively safe jumper, this wasn't the first time that Lucky was riding a horse with that sort of reputation. Often the greatest dangers came not from being aboard a horse that fell, but through being immediately behind another who did. I'd seen Lucky ride often enough to know that nothing was safe. Enough different things had gone wrong that I would feel equally nervous before any race he was riding in. I knew well enough not to pay too much attention to the bookmakers, but they were offering odds of 33/1 about his chances.

Initially, I was surprised, for this was one of the shortest-priced horses he'd ridden, but my confidence was fleeting. Howard Turner was a neighbour of my parents and worked for one of the bookmakers. When he saw me, he explained that so many of the small casual punters were putting bets on Lucky's horse as a form of support. Even though the bets were small, there were so many of them that the bookmakers were protecting themselves.

'The boss said he has virtually no chance, but the people backing him will do so whatever price we offer, so we keep him at a price that won't cost us excessively if a miracle does happen,' Howard said. 'Mind you, we'll still be paying out a fortune if he wins. Usually, we clean up when a roughie wins, but this horse would cost us substantially more than any other runner at Elwick all day. But good luck,' he added, knowing I needed to hear something a little more positive before making my way to the grandstand.

In most respects, the size of the crowd was irrelevant to me, but with the jockeys aboard their mounts and headed towards the starting line, I now regretted the lack of space in the grandstand. Naturally, I had my seat, but I would have far preferred to have more space around me. As it was, the emotional turmoil that undoubtedly was to come would be exposed to far more people than I would like. Equally as difficult was having so many voices so close to me talking about Lucky in very uncomplimentary ways. It may all have been meant in good humour, but it doesn't sound that way when it is directed at a loved one.

The race was two miles which would take a little under four minutes. The heart rates of the horses would progressively build through that time, but mine was already through the roof as the starter released them. Without binoculars, it was difficult to be too sure of how Loch and Quay had settled in the first couple of furlongs, but with all horses still on their feet after the first two jumps I was relieved that Lucky had got further than in his worst race.

There was a jump just before the winning post that we had a perfect view of. One of the favourites for the race, Aintree Dreaming, fell from near the lead. Lucky was several places back and vulnerable, but he was able to get around the trouble unscathed. Aintree Dreaming picked himself up and began to chase the field. His jockey was also on his feet, though not moving with quite the unimpeded freedom of the horse.

No more falls occurred through the next few jumps, but a new problem looked set to emerge. Riderless Aintree Dreaming had caught up to the rest of the field. While each horse in a jumping race can be a threat to the safety of every other jockey, the unpredictability of a riderless horse maximises this threat. Sometimes they run around the hurdles. Sometimes they race off in front of the field. Unfortunately, sometimes they move to the most inconvenient possible spot. Aintree Dreaming had stayed out of harm's way for a mile, but after going around the field, he moved back towards the inside, impeding the leaders of the race. Highly fancied Mister Caesar threw his rider, while Mayflower, sitting on his outside, just escaped the trouble.

Aintree Dreaming continued towards the next hurdle before suddenly deciding he didn't want to jump it. He came to a sudden stop before turning to the right to go around the hurdle. Horses close to the inside were able to avoid him, but two horses on the outside of the field had no real chance of clearing the jump courtesy of the riderless horse. Naturally, Loch and Quay was one of these runners, along with another roughie in the race, Workmanlike.

Maybe this was the moment when Lucky's legend really escalated. A poor horseman may not have reacted quickly enough and continued into trouble. A jockey for whom this was just another race may have been so focussed on self-protection that he'd have got his steed around the hurdle and pulled him out of the race. Lucky was neither of these things. He had shown brilliant skill to get the horse around the riderless runner, but by not going over the hurdle, he would be disqualified from the race. While Workmanlike's jockey pulled his horse up, Lucky turned the horse backwards and galloped him a hundred yards backwards before turning and heading back to the missed hurdle.

The awareness Lucky showed could have been considered ingenious. Although he'd lost a few hundred yards to the four horses remaining at that stage of the race, he knew that by finishing the race, Loch and Quay would earn prizemoney. Any other falls later in the race could see that prizemoney boosted further. Beaten margins didn't matter. Finisher or non-finisher certainly did matter. It would be quite fitting if his first finish in a jumps race had been after performing two such brilliant feats, both by escaping Aintree Dreaming, and by getting his mount over the line in such unusual circumstances. It would have been, but it wasn't.

When a horse is running at 30 miles an hour, jumping a three-foot hurdle comes reasonably easy. Unfortunately, after turning Loch and Quay back to face the hurdle without enough of a run-up along the way, the horse wasn't able to accelerate up to that speed. The horse realised this more than the jockey, and one bound before taking off he immediately stopped. Lucky, out of the saddle and throwing the reins at his mount, didn't stop, flying right over the horse's head. He landed head-first on the edge of the hurdle and was out cold.

As with every fall he had, I felt sick in the stomach. The fall was near the top of the back straight, sufficiently far away that I had no idea of how serious it was, or what damage he may have done. I rushed downstairs to the mounting yard where officials let me through so I could be as close to the news as possible. When he was placed in the ambulance, the news was radioed across to us that he was unconscious and was going to be taken straight to the hospital without coming back through the jockeys' room. They clarified that he was breathing, no doubt in an attempt to keep me as composed as possible, but I felt far from that.

I collected his things from the jockeys' room and was driven to the hospital by an assistant steward, Des Fowler. We arrived within a quarter of an hour of the ambulance but were waiting far longer before we got to hear anything. Eventually, a doctor came and saw me, delivering news. I couldn't decide whether this was relief or not, as the doctor told me first that Lucky would be alright, but that he had broken his neck.

'Broken neck. How can he be alright?'

'We will operate tomorrow. He will be alright, but it is major surgery and he will have a long recovery and need extensive rehabilitation. He will be here for several weeks. There is no reason to believe he won't make a complete recovery, though I shouldn't think he will ever return to riding horses,' the doctor said.

Lucky recovering completely yet not riding horses again seemed to be contradictory to me, but now wasn't the time to focus on that. After every fall I wanted him to say that was it. I wanted him to accept that he wasn't cut out for this career and that he would give up. Every time we had the same conversation and every time he gave me a whole set of other reasons why he needed to continue. I can't deny that I admired his willingness to overcome every possible obstacle, but amongst courage, there is always a need for common sense. I know that he will reflect on this race as an example of how he proved his great horsemanship in avoiding potential trouble during the race, but I couldn't get away from a different view. However good he was in certain moments of the race, he still ended up in hospital at the end of it.

Just like every other time.

24

18 May 2023

ZANIYA

Oliver had sent me a text an hour ago to say that he'd gone to the Botanical Gardens with Mum and Dad. He'd told them that I was staying in the hotel to do some more work on Lucky's story, so as I got into a taxi from Toby's place, I knew my secret was safe. I got myself ready well before the rest of the family got back, and then opened my laptop to do some more work, thus ensuring Oliver's story was truthful.

'How was last night?' Oliver said on his return. 'I hope it wasn't too ideal.'

'Why?'

'Meeting someone in a bar is one thing, but when that person lives on the other side of the world you're limited. You only have a couple more days in the city, most of which is time that's already committed, so there's little chance of anything more than last night. If it was all too perfect, you wouldn't want to leave it at that.'

As close as Oliver and I are, there was a line that our conversations wouldn't cross. Without further details, I told him that I'd had a very good night, but that he need not worry. I wouldn't be seeing Toby again. He may have been everything I wanted last night, but that doesn't mean he is everything I want. Far from it.

Last night was completely out of character for me. I was being true to the woman I want to be as opposed to the girl I've always been.

There is a cloak of anonymity that comes when you travel. You can take chances; you can seek new experiences and you can act on instinct rather than analysis. It might not usher in a new me, but it's shown me that I can take control and follow through on what I want to pursue. I don't have to stick to a particular definition of who I am but can be whoever I wish to be.

'Thanks,' I said as we waited for the elevator.

'For what?'

'For being the perfect brother. Letting me be me. Running interference when needed, and always having my back.'

'You've had the same upbringing as me. We travel to experience life. To make memories. That's what Mum and Dad have instilled in us, so while they may never have done quite what you did, the spirit behind it is consistent with what they want for us.'

'I don't think they'd be quite so approving.'

'They wouldn't. But they found each other so young they've never been twenty and single. Seeking an exciting experience is who they are, but that wouldn't be what they'd consider your choice last night to have been.'

It's reasonable. Attitudes come from experience. I shared so many attitudes with my parents, but there was enough unique in my life experience that obviously situations arose where we saw things very differently. After the event, I am sure they wouldn't be overly judgemental or negative towards me, but at the time they'd no doubt have taken the protective parent approach and reacted very differently.

We met Mum and Dad downstairs and after avoiding any details of last night, we got into a taxi out the front and I ensured the conversation turned on to the time ahead rather than what had passed. Oliver must have said the right things this morning that they never felt the need to mention last night.

I had been to the races twice in England. Neither day was sufficiently memorable to justify going on the other side of the world. Circumstances change mindsets though, and I was excited by the prospect.

The meetings I'd been to were major events that attracted big crowds. On those occasions, many people attend purely for the party and the atmosphere, with the horses being almost incidental, and the jockeys barely noticed. Today would be very different for me. I just hoped that I would find someone who could add a little more to the legend of Lucky O'Shaughnessy.

'Oh my God, Goodwood Primary School' I called out as we passed the school that Helen and Lucky had attended nearly three-quarters of a century earlier. I'm sure our taxi driver couldn't understand the fascination that a northern English family was showing to an ordinary primary school but hearing the strange curiosities of different people would not be unusual in his job.

Just before turning right to get into the racecourse, we passed the Hobart Showgrounds, and I thought back on the stories of him falling off the merry-go-round and the lessons in persistence that came from the Mechanical Monkeys. This for so long had been his part of town.

There had already been a couple of races run when we arrived, but the day was more about observing people than watching races, so this didn't concern me. I'd hoped to find a group of small men in their eighties as if each of his peers congregated at this shrine to Lucky. The reality was naturally not so convenient. The fact that Lucky continued to return here as a guest for decades after his career finished did not mean the same applied to everyone. People moved. People moved on. People passed on. How much I would learn from this day was questionable.

We watched one race from the lawns in the home straight and then another from the grandstand. There were maybe a hundred people scattered throughout the stand and they were a real cross-section. Young guys out with their mates who were going to ensure the bar staff were kept busy. Mug punters who couldn't be distracted by their surroundings, such was their intent on securing the best possible odds on the horse that their individually tailored criteria had assessed as the one to beat. Children who were enamoured with the horses and spent their time getting as close to the stars of the show as they could. Old men reliving days of yesteryear when this was the centrepiece of a Hobart weekend. There didn't seem to be too many of these around, but I had to pick my mark.

'Excuse me,' I said after finding an elderly-looking man sitting in the stand, fifteen minutes after the previous race. People rushed to find seats a couple of minutes before each race, then disappeared to various parts of the track a couple of minutes later. When someone was still in their seat at this point, it appeared to be an open invitation to chat with them. At least, I hoped my interpretation was reasonable.

'Do you remember a jockey named Lucky O'Shaughnessy?'

'Well yes. I am a local. I've been coming here for the past 60 years. You couldn't be from these parts and not know who Lucky was. He used to be known as Autumn Leaves because he was certain to fall.'

'I'm writing a tribute to him on behalf of his widow. Would you mind if I asked you a couple of questions about him?'

He introduced himself as Vic and told me that he became something of a casual acquaintance of Lucky in later years when they were both regulars sitting in this grandstand. Before that Vic hadn't known him personally but was all too aware of his on-track exploits.

'They say he used to trip over the moment he walked out of the jockey's room.'

'How did he keep getting race rides if he was so bad?'

'Trainers aren't always trying to win races. Sometimes they play the long game with their horses and are more than happy to have a few failures in the form guide to help inflate their odds for when they're ready to win.'

I started to suspect that Vic was more eccentric than a credible witness. If everyone was so convinced that Lucky was the issue, it would hardly inflate odds at later starts when people saw the horse had failed when he was aboard.

'But you know, there weren't many jockeys down here that rode over the jumps. If we had a big field, any available jockey could get a ride. All the trainers scrambled for the dozen or so jockeys that were any good.

Any additional runner was forced to take whoever was left. In some cases, this meant Lucky.'

'So, he was as bad as the stories suggest?'

'If you ignore the one minor problem of staying on their back, he was quite masterful with horses. One day he was riding in a race here and both his horse and another fell at the hurdle right in front of the stand. The horses got back on their feet but while Lucky had been completely dislodged, the other jockey's foot was stuck in the stirrups. The only time I ever saw something similar the jockey was killed. It could have happened this day if not for Lucky who risked his own life jumping in front of the horse and calming him while assisting to dislodge the jockey's foot. Could any other jockey have done that? *Would* any other jockey have done that?'

'Why didn't that get more attention than his record?'

'It did. But it's not like today where you can see it all on the television. Back then, an incident like that happens, and by the time you shake your head and ask if you're seeing things, it's all over. Once this happened, he forever had the respect of the other jockeys but once a bit more time passed it was just an old tale that lost a bit more of its impact every year. Meanwhile, his career statistics looked one step worse with every race he rode in, which meant that story kept growing. I can't explain it all, you're the journalist, right?

I tried to get a bit more information about the man Vic got to know in Lucky's later years, but it appeared that the connection was minimal. I thanked him for his time and moved inside where my family was gathered around the bookmakers' boards, considering placing a bet on the next race which was only a couple of minutes away.

'How can I resist number ten,' Dad said referring to the name St James Park. Reasoning that a horse in Australia is likely to win a race because he is named after your English football team's home ground made no sense to me, though for the $10 he was willing to lose, who was I to tell him he was wrong?

Oliver was less daring, but in proving he was his own man, chose to go against Dad. He was putting $5 on a horse named Being Earnest because he said it had looked the most impressive when the field was in the parade yard.

'Not that I have any idea about horse fitness, but from my untrained eye he looked like a man amongst boys. Maybe he's an old lazy man who can't run very fast, but I don't have too much to work with, so that will do me.'

Rather than the various odds, I was more intent on the old guy taking their bets. He looked like he'd been a fixture here for many decades, so when the time was right, I would make sure I had a quick word with him. Clearly, in the last minute before the race, the flood of last-minute punters was going to have him occupied at this point. I joined the rest of the family back out in the grandstand just before the horses jumped. The race was over 1200 metres, starting at the end of the back straight with the Derwent flowing right behind them and a clear view across the water towards MONA. The outlook was picture-perfect. As the starting gates sprung open and a dozen equine athletes exploded into stride, I felt that it was more than picture-perfect; it was a moment not to be captured but to be fully experienced as it happened.

The excitement built alongside me as the runners turned for home. St James Park had been leading from the early stages while Being Earnest had been right at the back. The big strider had begun a powerful final sprint that looked likely to win the major prize until the race favourite, Bytheway, came through on the inside to forge clear. Oliver's horse was second and Dad's horse finished third. They had both bet each-way and ended up making a dollar on the race.

'At this rate, we only need to stay for a year, and we could pay for a bus fare back to town,' Dad remarked.

I was racing back inside to get to the bookmaker before he did. He may be keen to collect $11, but I was far keener to get any possible insight from someone who'd known Lucky.

'I remember him well,' the bookmaker Jimmy Hughes said. 'In the latter part of his career, there were huge numbers of small punters putting something on him. It was easy money for us, but to be honest we would have gone broke if he did end up winning a race. I didn't know him so well personally, but the fellows you need to speak with are Harry Mortimer or Gordon Lang. They rode against him so rather than telling you the stories they've heard, they can tell you the stories that they're a part of. They are both here today. Hang around and I'll introduce you when they come back through.'

25

3 June 1968

HELEN

It had been ironic that Lucky's most serious injury was the one that saved his fate from the Tasmanian racing authorities. After his fall from Loch and Quay, the debate continued into proposed licencing changes, but the race clubs across the state had united to push against this. Lucky's last race had seen the Tasmanian Racing Club earn revenues many times higher than a normal meeting, thanks to the masses of people that had come purely to see him ride. They didn't anticipate such a windfall repeating, as the chances of another comeback seemed remote, but the outcome from that day had reminded the clubs' officials that the issues at stake were far more complex than what the bureaucrats were implying.

To other race clubs across the state, the issue of jockey licensing had been a smokescreen. To them, the aim of the government was overreaching into control of their industry. While it may have originated with Lucky, it could be anything that was targeted next. The industry was determined to be setting its course, not being directed by external forces. It was rare to find such unity within the industry. Lucky seemed to be the only person capable of getting everyone on the same page.

While the state-wide authority bemoaned the impact of the financial burden that Lucky created, they were eventually compelled to step back from these plans.

'What is the point of a new set of regulations to drive one person out of the industry when that person is unlikely to ever ride again anyway?' The statement from the racing minister to the head of the state's racing board signified the balancing act he faced. Good government meant getting the best results. Good politics meant avoiding decisions that would upset the electorate. Legislation that was clearly targetting an individual was never popular. He did advise that the government was losing goodwill on two fronts, and backing down now would save greater damage.

'The industry is angry as they think you're fighting them for control of their sport. The public is upset because they think you're attacking a defenceless man with whom their sympathies lie. Stepping away with a carefully worded press release will restore your position amongst both groups.'

Eventually, the government signed off on a counterproposal from the industry. Any jockey who had been seriously injured would now have to complete an increased number of trials before they could ride again in a race. This compromise would ensure that Lucky had some scope to make it back, however unlikely that was. It also ensured the public could see that no individual was being targeted, but the safety of all participants was to be the focus.

Lucky recovered slowly and after a long period of rehabilitation, he was back to light duties at the stables by the spring of 1967. Max knew that it would take little time before Lucky was demanding to be back aboard the horses at trackwork and from there, the urge for race riding would soon follow. Fortunately for me, there were few enough jumping trials in Hobart that it would take quite some time before he was able to meet the necessary criteria to be able to ride in a race again. Lucky wasn't afraid of obstacles, but he would face many before I had to deal with the trauma of watching him race again.

He was back on a horse for the first time by December, just walking some of Max's horses. By the new year, this had advanced to gentle trackwork and by March he was riding in trials. These were not over obstacles and would therefore not count towards his requirements for eligibility to ride in hurdle races. Each of these was, however, a step in the right direction for him, gaining confidence riding tight amongst other runners.

In June he had his first jumping trial, aboard a horse of Max's called High Talent. If the name Lucky was ironic for my husband, this horse's name made him the ultimate companion. Seventeen starts without a placing, he was a horse that Max considered unlikely to ever achieve anything, but his friend and loyal client Clem McDonald insisted on his horses being persisted with beyond futility.

In theory, the difference between an official trial and a race wasn't great. All the dangers of a race were still present in a trial, yet whether it was the different level of pressure or something else, nothing had ever gone wrong for Lucky in a trial. Others had fallen around him, but he never did. This trial was no exception, and although he finished last on High Talent, he was around safely.

Max gave Lucky another two opportunities in trials the following week, and having come through those successfully, he was officially cleared to ride in jumps races. Before this, he had a ride in a jumper's flat at Elwick, and just like two years earlier for his previous race ride, the crowd numbers swelled with his appearance. Aboard a mare named For Our Benefit, Lucky rode the perfect race bringing her down the outside to run into third place, her first placing from twenty-three starts. While gentle applause greeted the winner as he returned to scale, the crowd gave Lucky a hero's reception.

'I feel guilty,' Lucky confessed to me. 'They think I've overcome something special by finishing that race. It's only the hurdles that I haven't finished.'

'I think they're reacting to you coming back from a broken neck. To have made it to any race is a miracle. It wasn't that you finished, or that you placed, it's that you defied limits that few people ever would,' I said.

A fortnight later the races were at Brighton, and Max had High Talent entered for a hurdle race.

'I will never find a field slow enough for him to keep up with. To say he is ordinary would be too kind. He is at least a safe jumper though, and if Lucky refuses to stop then this is the right horse for him,' Max told me to calm my nerves. 'He won't have anything behind him to cause a problem, and he'll probably be far enough behind that Lucky will have time to take evasive action if there is trouble ahead of him.'

It defied logic to me. The passion that drove Lucky's desire to be a jockey was the thrill of the competition, yet the lifeline his career was given was a ride on a horse that couldn't genuinely compete. I had tried to talk him out of a return to horses for months during his recovery. When I failed in that quest, I worked on keeping him away from race riding, but now I had failed on that count. I couldn't bear to watch but equally couldn't bring myself to stay away. For all my attempts to talk him out of this madness, once the decision was made, there was no situation where I wouldn't stand beside him.

As had become normal for any race day where Lucky had a ride, the crowd was substantially greater than at a standard race meeting. I couldn't help but wonder if Max may have received some sort of incentive payment to put Lucky on one of his horses. The Brighton Racing Club would be making thousands of additional dollars today courtesy of Lucky's appearance, so maybe something was going on under the table to make this happen. I believed Max had too much integrity to be part of such things, but somewhere over the years, I'd developed enough cynicism to remain wary. It was beginning to feel like Lucky and me were the only people not benefitting from his appearance.

The race was not just the return over jumps for Lucky, it was also the last day of race riding for his colleague Harry Mortimer. Mortimer had been both friend and inspiration to Lucky, and he would have been at Brighton to be part of his day whether riding or not, but it meant so much more that they'd be sharing words aboard their horses on the way to the starting line. My main hope was that Lucky would still be able to be talking to him at the finish of the race as well.

The betting market was offering no false impressions about High Talent. The odds of 100/1 were not a complete reflection of his chances, for they were probably even less than that. The profile of Lucky attracted enough small punters wanting to put a bet on him that the bookmakers didn't want their book too far out of balance. A miracle victory would have destroyed them. Macbeth, the horse Harry was hoping would give him a fairy-tale finish to his career was also not fancied too highly, starting at 25/1.

Like every horse in the field, High Talent cleared the first jump in style, albeit already a couple of lengths behind the second-last horse. Clearing the second, the gap had grown a little greater, but his jump was equally as good, and I began sensing that Max's plan may come to fruition. A long last, but a safe finish.

The third jump was located just before the turn out of the back straight. With my eyes focussed on Lucky, I missed how the drama started, but a false stride from one runner led to four others being brought down. As Max had predicted, Lucky had High Talent far enough behind this carnage that he managed to manoeuvre his horse to the outside and get around the stricken jockeys and horses.

Through one incident, the field of fourteen was now down to a field of nine. High Talent continued to jump well and as they passed the post with a lap to go, Lucky was still aboard, albeit several lengths behind the second-last horse.

With the field hitting the bottom turn, they were less than a minute away from the scene of carnage by the top turn. Often when a fall occurs the field is redirected around that particular hurdle. In this instance, it appeared impossible. Two of the fallen horses were too severely injured to get up, while two jockeys were unconscious and receiving urgent attention from the paramedics. So much of the width of the track was restricted that was going to make it impossible for the field to avoid the mayhem. Stewards sought to stop the race immediately and the clerks of the course were sent to try and alert jockeys.

The circumstances, though rare, were not unprecedented and most jockeys had their horses pulled by the second of four hurdles in the back straight. Lucky hadn't ridden in an abandoned race before and didn't realise why jockeys were pulling their horses up. As the others slowed and trotted wide around the hurdle, he accelerated on High Talent, believing for a fleeting moment that he was moving into the lead. Landing the jump, he knew something was wrong when a look to his right revealed no rivals, but a clerk of the course nearby. He began to slow his horse and heard the clerk yelling 'Race abandoned, pull-up' and cursed. Hitting the lead was too good to be true. High Talent was slowed to a walk after going outside the next jump from where part of the drama ahead was visible. He didn't want to look any closer. Having been part of so many terrible falls it was too confronting.

'What else can happen?' he said returning to scale. 'The one time I was going to finish, and the race is abandoned.'

'There was no alternative,' Max said.

'It's never happened when I've fallen.'

'Lucky you, eh.'

The most disturbing sight on a racecourse is when a sheet goes up alongside a stricken horse. In this instance, it was apparent that both fallen horses were being euthanised. I was grateful for the fact that it was in the back straight, far enough away to not be too exposed to the horror, but still the hearts of everyone on the course sank dramatically. Everyone was also concerned for the two jockeys. At that stage, nobody knew how much worse the news would become.

Kevin McGregor and Colin Walters, the two leading jumps jockeys in Tasmania for the current season, were both taken to hospital. Walters, one of the veterans of the local jumps scene suffered significant injuries, including a broken neck, just as Lucky had overcome. Given his age and the more sensible attitude he had, it seemed almost certain that this would bring an end to his long and successful career.

McGregor's fate was far worse. After 14 hours in a coma, he was pronounced dead at 4.17 am the following morning.

26

18 May 2023

ZANIYA

'If you want to know all about Lucky, you're going to need a lot of time because there's a lot to tell.'

Harry Mortimer had to be ninety and looked every day of it. The sharpness of his introduction made it clear that his mind was more spritely than you'd expect from his weather-beaten face. The fact that he was still making it to the races and wandering the facilities here without too much trouble, suggests that his body is holding up reasonably too.

'You just better not be one of those people looking to stitch him up as they did in the paper the other day, or you'll have us all chasing after you.' The threat of a group on walking sticks chasing after anyone wasn't likely to strike great fear. In this case, it wasn't relevant, for I was on their side, but as I visualised the chase he mentioned, it became a little difficult to focus on Harry's words for a moment.

'What absolute garbage that was. Lucky was a great man, and you can't tell his story without that being at the heart of it.'

He briefly referenced Lucky's lack of success but referred to it as an element of his story rather than the story itself.

'I'd achieved more in my career than Lucky did by the end of the first race I rode in, but for all the races I won, I was guaranteed to be forgotten quickly. Lucky will never be forgotten. He was a legend.'

'That's what I hear,' I replied. 'The problem is knowing how much of the legend is the real man and how much of it is just a good story that people keep embellishing.'

'Nobody re-tells a story by glossing over the highlights and focussing on the boring moments in the middle. Good stories get embellished but that doesn't mean the essence of them is untrue.'

I reflected on his apt words. We had been at the track for two hours and seen three races that had taken an aggregate of four minutes. 97% of the time here had been the moments between highlights. This was how life tended to work.

'You're a journalist, right? Well, what matters? Telling the truth or selling the story.'

'The truth,' I said.

'The truth doesn't matter unless you can sell it.' True as that may be, I didn't want our discussion about Lucky to be hijacked into a debate about the profession I was working towards.

'So, what's your version of the Lucky O'Shaughnessy story?'

'No doubt he was one of a kind,' Harry began. 'The legend states he was the world's worst jockey but that is definitively wrong. He was the jumps jockey with the world's worst record. That's indisputable, but it is a different statement altogether. In any field of life, a person's record is a measure of numerous factors. The best batsman doesn't necessarily score the most runs. The best singer doesn't necessarily sell the most records. The best jockey doesn't necessarily win the most races. Not that I'm suggesting Lucky would ever have been close to the best, but his record wasn't a reflection of his ability.

'Forty-five rides for forty-five failures to finish speaks for itself. Note that I didn't say forty-five falls. He pulled some up, he rode in an abandoned race. Sure, most times he fell, and if you include the day he remounted and fell twice or the time he fell out of the ambulance, then he probably did have as many falls as he had rides. You know, if he really was that bad, he wouldn't have had forty-five rides. If he had been a stone lighter and riding in flat races, he probably would have been a top-class jockey. He had a good sense of judging pace which is a key attribute for jockeys. Some of the things he did in races were incredible, they just didn't turn out to be enough.'

'So, despite his name, he was just unlucky?'

'Partly. You get unlucky once, twice or three times, but not forty-five times. Like any profession, your success is based on your ability across all aspects of the job. There were things he did brilliantly and there were other aspects that he wasn't so good at. For him, balance was one of these.

'When you go back to England you can watch hurdle races and you will see horses land awkwardly several times in a race. Good jockeys stay aboard in most of these instances. The average person wouldn't and when it came to balance, Lucky was more like the average person than a skilled jockey. In trackwork and trials, horses weren't under the same pressure, so their landings were generally smoother. This helped Lucky look good. Even after the reminders of all the previous failures, each comeback would see him make such a good impression at trackwork that he'd earn one more try on race day.'

We were approached by another man, older and smaller than Harry and as I suspected it was Gordon Lang, another former jockey from Lucky's era.

'You're from England, are you? That's a long way to come to follow a story like Lucky's'

'Well, it's a family holiday. I hadn't heard of Lucky, but by chance, I met his widow and heard a little about him. I became intrigued.'

'How is Helen?'

'She wasn't happy about the article in the paper the other day?'

'I saw that article. What didn't she like?'

I explained that the article made him out to be a figure of parody which she thought was inappropriate in an article that was meant to be a tribute after his passing.

'Well, that is who Lucky was. He was far more than that of course, but that is what made him an identity. That's why they wrote the article.

They won't write about Harry and me when we go. In time Helen will be proud that he is so well remembered.'

'What else was he?' I asked, hoping for more insight to round out the picture of him. 'Away from his obvious lack of success and his incredible persistence, what would you say about him?'

He paused briefly, no doubt having talked about Lucky in the same standard way so many times and now confused at the thought of going deeper.

'He was a hell of a guy. He was the butt of jokes all through life, but he laughed along. People would laugh at him, but as he laughed along their attitudes changed. There was always so much banter in the jockey's room.

Harry then jumped in. 'We all called him Autumn Leaves as he fell with that reliability.'

'And then he said that wasn't fair because he can fall in any season, not just autumn,' Gordon added. 'That's the point. He knew the best way to keep the jokes in check was to join in, rather than hide from it. But there was another side.'

My eyebrows raised wanting to know where he was heading.

'It all hurt him. When you're copping ridicule left, right and centre, it has to have an impact. He laughed along as self-protection but I know it hurt him. Not the jokes, but the fact they had a valid basis. He wanted to achieve as much as anyone. More actually. He worked harder, he gave everything he had and walked away with the reputation of being the worst. It's one thing to be the worst in a field where you didn't try so hard, but when you have been so devoted to something and still failed, how can you possibly retain any self-esteem.'

'I couldn't,' I acknowledged.

'Nobody could,' Gordon said. 'Despite that, his drive to follow his dream, albeit a reduced version of it, was more powerful than his fears. He once dreamt of winning the Grand National in England but by the end, he just dreamt of finishing a race. Outwardly at least, his determination didn't reduce in the same way that the size of the dream did.'

'Back in those days,' Harry said, 'a man didn't let anyone see his emotions, but it doesn't mean he didn't have them. I saw him one day in the showers after another losing ride – it was one day he didn't end up in the hospital, I can't remember quite what happened, but he still didn't finish. He thought there was nobody else around as the jumps jockeys had all gone, and the flat jockeys were out for the next race. I walked in at the wrong moment and saw him. He looked genuinely broken. There was nothing anyone could have done to lift him, yet he would never willingly have let that be seen. The next day he was back at trackwork, his head down, bottom up, working to improve and get better.'

Gordon explained that as a flat rider, he was never in direct competition with Lucky. They'd become reasonably good friends over the years, in no small part because of the admiration he had for the so-called loser.

'He had personal characteristics that I couldn't match. Every jockey has courage that most people can't believe. Do you have any idea how many jockeys are killed doing their job? The numbers are huge. For most of us it's a threat we know exists but feel a little removed from. Lucky saw the dangers at very close hand. He broke every bone in his body throughout his career. Most people were sure that one day he wouldn't be so lucky, and it would be all over. It never stopped him.'

Gordon lived a block away from Lucky and Helen for a few years in the 1960s. He said he would have done anything to see him ride a winner or at least a finisher but knew it wouldn't happen. Harry added that for all of the jokes that were directed at him, everyone was always united in their hope that he'd be alright.

'We loved the idea of sending him home with a bruised ego and we always hoped that would be the extent of any bruising or breaks. Unfortunately, come race day there was always something more.'

'Not riding in the jump races,' Gordon added, 'I would always be watching from the sidelines, uninterested in who won and just focussed on Lucky's fate. I kept imagining what it would be like if he finished. The crowd would have given him an ovation greater than a Hobart Cup winner.'

The men were distracted by the next race being close to the start time and said they'd be back to me after the race. I noticed that none of the races were over hurdles and as I went to the shop, I asked someone about this.

'No jumps racing in Tasmania since 2007' the man said. 'There were so few trainers, jockeys and suitable horses that it wasn't viable to continue. Most of Australia is the same, barring a small number of participants in Victoria.'

'What would Lucky O'Shaughnessy have done today?'

'Who?'

I then realised that as legendary as the man's exploits had been, they were from a long bygone era. Australians revere their great sporting heroes a century after their careers, but their culture doesn't quite react to the battler finishing last the same way we Brits celebrated someone like Eddie The Eagle. Australia had a famous speed skater named Stephen Bradbury. He won an Olympic gold medal after all his opponents fell over. He remains a national hero for his unlikely win, but it still comes off the back of that same reality. They only want the story of the winner. He'd been a national champion for fifteen years yet retained an anonymous profile until the day that a lucky Olympic win made him a major identity.

I made my way back just as the barriers opened for the race. I didn't want to be in the way of the two gents, so I watched from behind their prime vantage point, noticing my family on the lawns below us. Dad appeared to be getting excited as the runners got towards the finish line, so he must've decided to participate in the action in the betting ring.

'I told you Six Pacs was the one,' Harry said to me as I came back. I was confident that the topic of today's races never came up but rather than create an unnecessary issue, I nodded my head, smiled and took my seat with the two men.

'Lucky used to come to every race meeting for many years after his retirement,' Gordon told me. 'It's probably 30 years ago they moved to Bruny Island, and in those days they became a little less frequent, but we'd still see him here several times a year. I can assure you, his ability to tip horses was worse than his ability to stay on top of them.'

'He once put a multi-leg bet on and had every horse in the first race except one,' Harry added. Because I knew him well enough, I ran down and put a bet on the one he said couldn't win. Easiest money I had ever made.'

'Hard to believe he was called Lucky after all these years,' I said.

'Down here we call redheads "Bluey" and bald guys "Curly." Calling him Lucky was pure irony or it seemed that way at least.'

I knew the origins from what Helen had told me the first day we met, but I felt these guys were less interested in listening than talking and that suited me fine. They were almost in competition now with the different funny stories of Lucky.

'You know he didn't just fall off the horses', Harry said. 'We didn't have ambulances behind the field when we started, just a couple of medical staff with a stretcher and a car. More than one time they'd put Lucky on the stretcher, and he fell off that too!'

Gordon said it was fortunate that he and Helen never wanted to travel by air, because nobody would have been willing to be on a plane with him as he'd fallen from everything else. He went on to state that the Tasmanian Racing workers compensation fund nearly sunk into insolvency as a result of Lucky's career.

'It's a shame he was married. If he was on his own, he could have sold the house. He didn't really need it because he spent most of his nights in the hospital.'

My family made their way towards us, and I did the full set of introductions. Gordon was too far into his reminiscing to deviate from his course.

'In recent years we didn't see him on course, and we missed him. I spoke to him over the phone from time to time. We always said we'd catch up soon but isn't that the way life works? You always plan to do things when you get the chance until the time comes when the chance is gone.'

Harry nodded. 'There was a group of us here at every meeting – maybe 10 or 12 ex-jockeys from the 1950s through to the 1970s but he always seemed a bit out of place. Helen and he often sat away from everyone else. Understandably she had always wanted him out of the racing game, and I think she became resentful of everyone else in it. She still came with him to the meetings for decades after he retired, but she always seemed a little difficult to warm to. Everyone who knew her away from the racecourse said it wasn't like her at all.

'He enriched so many lives,' Gordon continued. 'It mightn't have been in the way he wanted to do it, but he had a powerful impact on a lot of people. You can take a snapshot and call him a loser, but when you look at the picture in detail, he was a hero.'

I felt a tear in my eye hearing this. Any thought that Helen was skewing the story of her late husband had disappeared. I thanked the men for their time and the thorough picture they'd painted of the man, wishing them the best for the rest of the day.

27

10 June 1968

HELEN

Everyone in the racing scene was impacted by the tragedy at Brighton, but resilience is a built-in characteristic of all participants. The following Saturday saw a race meeting with two jumps races at Mowbray in Launceston. Lucky wasn't engaged for a ride, but we attended as spectators, supporting Harry Mortimer. Harry had chosen to defer his retirement for one more ride in honour of McGregor. He was unsuccessful but completed the course safely as did all of his rivals. The dangers and risks were once again in the back of the minds of all riders, and the sport carried on exactly as before.

I had the foolish notion that Lucky would have reconsidered his plans after the events of Brighton. If anything, Lucky felt more compelled to work harder.

'There weren't that many jumps jockeys in Tasmania and with three less now there is guaranteed to be more opportunities.'

'To do what? Fall? Get injured? Killed? Or be fortunate and stay safe yet just not finish races?'

'That's how much faith you have in me?' I could see I'd hurt him, which I hated doing, but I couldn't understand how he failed to see how torn apart I felt watching him risk his life.

'It is not about faith in you. Kevin was a champion and look at what happened. If it could happen to him, it could happen to you.'

'Sonny Dawson was killed driving to work. Should I not drive? Helen, this is who I am. It is what I do. I do it because I love it and despite everything that is said, written and joked about me, I am good at it. It's the only thing I am good at. Take this away and what am I?'

'My husband and my world.'

'Yes, but your world and your husband includes all of who I am. The jockey is a big part of that.'

There was nothing more to say or do. Nothing was going to change, and it was an anxiety I would be living with.

This period became the most active of Lucky's career. Having never previously ridden in more than three races in a year, he had four rides in the next month. The first of these was at Elwick the following weekend, once again aboard High Talent. After jumping so perfectly at Brighton, it was a significant turnaround this day as he put in a poor jump at the first hurdle and then raced ungenerously from there. Lucky was dislodged at the third hurdle, roughly a quarter of the way through the race. On this occasion, he sustained no significant injury, though he was taken to hospital for observation. In the standard jockey room banter, some of the other jockeys suggested he was only going there to reacquaint himself with the nurses.

'Who do you refer to as your main work colleagues Lucky – us or the nurses at the Royal Hobart? You spend more time with them than us.' Banter like this circulated around the jockeys' room as they kept looking for new lines to put him in his place.

A week later, he rode an outsider named Lord Cheong for Elwick trainer Glenn Higgins in a jumpers flat. A brilliantly executed front-running ride saw him finish second, the best result of his riding career. He followed this the next week with a rare trip to ride at Launceston. Back over the jumps it was the familiar story of another fall, again one that led to no significant injury. Back at Elwick the following Saturday, he was aboard High Talent again. He made it through the first lap with solid jumping but was several lengths behind the second last horse. A horse fell turning into the back straight which Lucky was able to avoid, but High Talent crashed at the third jump in the back straight. While he picked himself up and slowly chased the field, Lucky hit the deck hard enough to be concussed and transferred to the familiar surrounds of the Royal Hobart Hospital. No further serious injury was found and he was released home the next day and was back riding track work a couple of days later.

Opportunities were curtailed for a period as High Talent had suffered a minor setback that meant an interruption to his preparation. Max had no other jumpers at the time despite Lucky trying to persuade him to find a suitable horse from the mainland who was just below the class needed to win there.

'When they're too slow to sprint, they try them as stayers. When they're too slow for staying races, they race them over jumps. If they're too slow to win jumping races the connections give up, but they may still be good enough to win here, especially if we can add a couple of lengths to them.'

'Whose money are we buying these budding stars with?'

'If Mr. Moore can afford to keep paying the bills for uncompetitive horses then surely he can afford to buy a couple that can make him some money.'

'He does not like hurdlers. He's only ended up with a couple because they were bought for the flat but couldn't measure up.'

'High Talent was meant to be something?'

'We didn't expect too much, but a lot more than he's got.'

Every person has good and bad components to their jobs. Lucky had long since accepted the reality that his career as a jockey was about riding trackwork. Every race ride was a bonus to him, but the opposite to me. When he excitedly came home from the track one Tuesday morning telling me about his upcoming ride this weekend on a horse named Aristotle, I was equally despondent.

'I'm not going to be there,' I told him.

Initially Lucky seemed hurt. I had been there throughout each step of his career. I had witnessed every positive and every negative moment.

I had reached a point where I couldn't do it to myself anymore. I accepted he wouldn't give the game away, but I was no longer going to be endorsing this decision by standing on the sidelines.

'Is this going to turn into a choice for me?'

'No. I understand you. I understand why you make the foolish choice to continue taking these risks. I don't know if you understand the horror it puts me through,' my voice quavering as the tears began to accompany my words. 'It's not going to be easier at home, but maybe, just maybe I can be slightly less impacted than by seeing it unfold. One day you won't be able to ride any more. Today is the day that I can't watch any more. I will pack your bag. I will drive you there. I will pick you up. I will nurse you. I will soothe you. I will cook for you. I will heal you. I will do anything else for you, but I cannot watch you ride again.'

'I thought we were in this together,' he said.

'We're in life together,' I replied. 'Every part of life connects us, but you are not in the classroom when I teach. You're in my heart, but you aren't physically there with me. I will be in your heart at race time, but I cannot and will not watch.'

Lucky looked pensive as he contemplated my words. He understood and in time it became apparent that this moment had done more to make him question his choice than the pain of any fall he'd ever had. The questioning wasn't quite enough, as he continued to stand his ground and pursue his dream.

'Thank you, Helen,' he said as we arrived at Elwick on Saturday morning. 'I know you believe in me, and that's not the cause of this. If the roles were reversed I couldn't watch either, and I never would have made it as long as you did. People think I'm strong for continuing after all I've been through, yet I think I'm not fit for that term alongside you.'

He kissed me and got out of the car. I told him I was proud of him, and I looked forward to being even prouder in a couple of hours.

I turned the radio on as soon as I got home, hoping to keep abreast of all that was happening on the course. Naturally, Lucky's name was destined to come up with an inordinate frequency for a jockey with only one mount for the day, and that on an extreme outsider. When the race caller did his preview of the meeting a half hour before the first race, he made particular mention of the combination of Lucky and his horse Aristotle. The caller suggested that Lucky's chances of finally finishing a jumps race didn't seem that great. Aristotle was somewhat the opposite of High Talent; an inconsistent performer whose best form would make him a serious contender in this race, but also a horse renowned for putting in poor jumps at times. This was the last thing I wanted to hear.

I tried to keep myself occupied with housework but naturally couldn't concentrate on anything else and was relieved when the broadcast returned to Elwick 10 minutes before Lucky's race. Not surprisingly there was little mention of Aristotle amongst the leading chances until the race caller again brought up Lucky's career stats in jumping races. His colleague, Brian Mawson, a man we had the displeasure of knowing, gave a rather unkind response. He suggested that Lucky was a sideshow and had no place in the seriousness of a horse race. With every word he said, I became more accepting of my husband's choice to prove people like this wrong. I hated the fear, but I adored his determination and courage.

I moved closer to the radio as the horses were ready to start and the call of the race began.

'The starter would like a photograph of that, such was the clean beginning of all the runners. Painted Rough was smartly into stride with Mansab, from the outside Trafalgar was well away with Road to Rome, Grand Amnesty was getting back in the field along with Lucky O'Shaughnessy's mount Aristotle outside of Merriman as they approach the first hurdle. All over safely and a big leap from Road to Rome sees him move to the front of the field a length clear of Mansab and Painted Rough, King of the Stars sits fourth from Grand Amnesty and Trafalgar out wider, Merriman next on the rail from Aristotle, Kenmax Star behind that pair along with Lawman and then a gap back to Marlborough, Lady Tess and last of all is Currency Lad. Road to Rome continues to lead, two lengths *clear going over the last hurdle in the back. Mansab is pulling the rider's arms out of their sockets on the inside now just being shaded by Painted Rough who put in a big leap at that jump and oh one has gone down back in the field....*

Instantly my heart skips a beat. I feel certain I am about to hear something that will prove every bit as stressful as what watching it would have been.

....it is Kenmax Star who has parted ways with his rider, Glenn Morphett, but all the other horses have got around him safely. Coming into the home straight and approaching the first of the double with just over a lap to go. Mansab has forced his way off the fence and gone up to challenge Road to Rome. Mansab nearly sold out at that obstacle, the rider calling for a cab and that's lost him some momentum as King of the Stars joins him out wider on the track. Three lengths back in fourth is Painted Rough who also put in a poor jump at that one, and as they come down to the next hurdle Marlborough is making good ground around the outside from Aristotle who has jumped well for Lucky O'Shaughnessy so far...

I now realised how painful listening to a race broadcast was when the caller continually singled Lucky out.

......and further back to Lady Tess, Currency Lad and Lawman who is now detached from the second last horse by several lengths. Over the last with a lap to go and oh no, wouldn't you know it, Aristotle has fallen at the hurdle by the winning post and O'Shaughnessy is down again...

Now I felt ill. I did not know whether to run to the car and race down to Elwick or wait until the end of the race to hear what the caller had to say. If I was there I could at least have some idea of how serious it might be, but at this stage, he could be up on his feet ready to laugh about the incident or he could be unconscious and fighting for his life. I have no idea.

After two more run-throughs of the field, a riderless Aristotle had caught the rest of the field and when the caller mentioned this he said that Lucky was still on the track with paramedics around him. I wasn't wasting another second and ran out the door, started the car and raced the two-minute journey to the racecourse.

Darryl on the gate knew me well enough that the sight of me running towards him had him ready to usher me through. I was out the front of the jockeys' room standing at the edge of the mounting yard before all the horses from the race had made it back, such was the efficiency of my movement.

'He's alright,' jockey Jimmy Lunn said as he returned.

'Are you sure?' I asked.

'He is conscious. He's moving a little bit.'

This was the first indication of anything I had. A steward came over and reiterated what Jimmy had told me before getting further word that he was being taken to the hospital for X-rays.

'Suspected broken collarbone,' he told me.

'Again. That is a familiar one,' I said.

Having now dismounted, Jimmy was headed back to the jockeys' room, and I asked if he could grab Lucky's bag and bring it out to me so I could take it into the hospital for him.'

'Sure Helen,' he said. 'You know, there was a bit of laughter when he opened the bag earlier. His pyjamas fell out and he copped a real ribbing about you being so certain he'd be spending his night in hospital that you had to pack the pyjamas.'

'He never comes home the night of a hurdle race. I never even contemplated the idea of a jumps jockey spending the night of a race anywhere but the hospital, but I guess the rest of you do.' I realised I was now caught up in the jokes about Lucky but between us, we'd learned that playing along a little limited the extent to which these things got said. Treating the realities with a touch of humour earned greater respect.

'You can't ride hurdles and avoid hospital forever, but for most of us, it's more exception than the rule' Jimmy chuckled. 'Lucky just has that reversed.'

28

18 May 2023

ZANIYA

We were introduced to Judy, Gordon's wife, and chatted about our trip, our chance encounter with Helen and the circumstances that had led to us being at Elwick.

'It's a good thing you've met me then, as I probably knew Lucky better than the other jockeys did.'

'Really?'

'Maybe not better, but differently. When men get to know each other through locker room talk, they only get to see a small part of the real person. I probably saw more of the person within, even if I didn't spend as much time directly with him.'

'How would you describe him?'

'Ahead of his time. Probably what you'd now call a sensitive new-age guy. Maybe that's not quite the Lucky of 60 years ago, but he was very sensitive, very loyal and very caring. I think he'd rather have had a child than win a race. As much as the horses meant to him, it wasn't a shadow of what Helen meant. He took the pain of his losses hard, but most people who hurt that badly, hide away from the potential of suffering more. He would just push harder to make things happen better, yet it still didn't consume him and remained very much secondary to the people that mattered. It mightn't sound like such a special story, but it's the man I remember.'

I was incredibly appreciative of getting a female perspective other than Helen's. In truth, it's less a gender issue than just hearing the opinion of someone who knew him without that being based on racing.

The conversation turned to the coming days, and she insisted we give her love to Helen and told us to pass on that she would call her during the week. Like the gentlemen, she referenced how intentions are all too often put off too long. She knows she must not any longer.

Mum mentioned that we were keen to go out for a good meal tonight but that we hadn't worked out where at this stage.

'You should go to Da Angelo's,' Judy said. 'It has been our favourite restaurant for many years.'

'No, go to Wrest Point,' Gordon said. 'It's more of an iconic part of this city than any restaurant.'

'Da Angelo's is a much better meal.'

'A revolving restaurant with the best views of the city cannot be beaten as a once-off experience. You must go Wrest Point.'

'Dinner for four there would be more expensive than their trip home. If they want a good meal, Da Angelo's is the best restaurant in Hobart.'

'They can eat good meals all around the world, they can't replicate Wrest Point anywhere else.'

As entertaining as a pair of octogenarians bickering can be, Dad was keen not to be the source of divorce and jumped in, suggesting we might go to Da Angelo's for dinner and then move on to Wrest Point later in the evening for a wander. It didn't completely achieve his aim as Gordon still suggested we'd be missing out not eating at the revolving restaurant while Judy implied that we'd already seen the best views of Hobart and would be wasting our time going there at all.

After saying our goodbyes, we ended up replicating the Langs by disagreeing on where to go. I'd never been to a revolving restaurant and was keen to try it. My parents had told me about one they ate at in Karachi many years ago. I had believed that the top floor of the building must have been rotating, which seemed like an engineering miracle.

Shattering my delusions, Dad explained how the circular platform that the tables sat on revolved while the building itself was stationary. Although the reality may not have been as exciting as my childish imagination had envisaged, it still seemed that 360-degree views of Hobart from its tallest building would add to any meal.

'How much did you win on that last race Dad? You can go the extra money for Wrest Point,' Oliver said.

'Ah, Six Pacs. He may have won me enough to pay for an entrée there rather than dinner for four, but I'm happy enough to go there.'

We decided to get the bus back into town and then another to our final destination at Sandy Bay. In many of the cities we visit, we travel extensively by public transport, not so much for the cost or convenience as for the experience. The network in Hobart reflects the smaller city and so not only have we used it less, but it doesn't provide the same exposure to the soul of the city that you can see in the transit networks of bigger cities.

Seeing the major sites of the city on a tourist bus is like looking at a person dressed in their finest with a stylist having done their hair and made them up. Public transport is a glimpse at that same person the morning after; hungover and dressed in their most comfortable trackies. It is often a less appealing look, but generally a far more accurate reflection of the real person. When visiting London, I celebrated the spectacle from the Eye, but I felt the real city more when travelling by Tube. Here, sipping champagne on the Mona Roma while looking back at the city underneath the mountain was a special memory, but as we took our seats on the 510 bus, alongside the cross-section of Glenorchy and its surrounds, I felt a little more connected to the average Hobart resident.

It was only about fifteen minutes into the city. We got off in Elizabeth Street and walked just around the corner to a bus stop on Macquarie Street, and two minutes later we were aboard a bus for Sandy Bay. One suburb past Battery Point, Sandy Bay is one of the more exclusive parts of Hobart. It is a large suburb, stretching much of the way up the hillside towards Mount Nelson as well as down to the River Derwent. When picturesque waterways meet the views from elevation, expensive property is guaranteed, and there are many million-dollar houses in the suburb.

As the bus takes us on the main thoroughfare of Sandy Bay Road, we see what appear to be designated sections that each had a unique character. There was a section for professional services followed by an upmarket shopping section, another with the major retailers and takeaway food chains before yet another filled with old mansions. As the road twisted, the Royal Hobart Yacht Club was to our left and the playing fields of the University of Tasmania were to our right. The next bus stop and we'd arrived at Wrest Point.

Wrest Point had a hotel built on it before World War II, but a generation later there was a belief that an attraction to draw people to Hobart was more important than a facility to accommodate the tourists. A referendum saw the granting of a casino licence, and the old hotel was replaced with the 17-story dodecagonal structure of today. It is the tallest building in Hobart and in its early days, became the symbol of the city.

We confirmed the availability of a table upstairs for later in the evening before starting in the casino area of the facility. It certainly didn't prove to be anything like the experiences I've had of casinos, though to be fair the only one I'd been in was the famous Monte Carlo casino. While the races had a combination of desperate punters amongst a range of other types, the casino tables seemed to have only the diehards and a few out-of-place tourists like us.

It appeared that the method of choice for gambling here was poker machines. Every table game required human labour to operate, which didn't suit the standard business model of the modern casino. The staffing requirements for poker machines meant each staff member could supervise a large volume of machines. There was no risk that a skillful player could dent profits on a machine like they could on some table games. It didn't need multiple players to justify operating the game.

The machine was perfect for the casino, and despite this being obvious, the large number of people on the machines seemed oblivious to these realities and kept pumping their money through them.

Wrest Point markets itself as an entertainment venue. Like in Las Vegas, the business plan is to attract people through the door with entertainment and hope to keep them here playing the machines. There is an array of bars, theatres, and function rooms as well as restaurants. Several big names were playing in the entertainment centre here coming up, so the main venue must have been fairly sizeable. Some of the smaller bars had free gigs on different nights, and one of them, the Birdcage Bar, had a duo performing later this evening, so we planned to come back after dinner.

We had a quick walk outside along the boardwalk to soak in the view of the river up close, before making our way to the top of the tower and the Point Revolving Restaurant. Our table by the window gave us a view of the south, though naturally, that was going to become all the more appealing over time. Between this and the menu, the words of the Langs had been proven. This was an experience, but it came with a price tag. The menu was French-inspired and Tasmanian produce dominated.

Between us, we enjoyed oysters and scallops for our entrees before a vast range of mains. I chose gnocchi which proved to be exquisite, and I wondered how good the other restaurant Judy had mentioned must have been if it was superior to this. Perhaps it was purely a more appealing price. Everyone seemed equally as impressed with their meals, and the views were as spectacular as we'd expected. It mightn't be as memorable as dinner at the top of the Eiffel Tower, but it still got top marks from all of us, especially after having Crepes Suzette cooked at our table. We just shared a serving between us but would have liked to have had the capacity to eat more. It was amazing.

We reneged on the plan to go back to the bar downstairs, sufficiently stuffed at this point. We all knew the best option at this point was walking but given the unfamiliarity of the area we got straight into a cab, but only took it as far as Salamanca Place, then walked back from there.

While everyone else was keen on a nightcap downstairs, I had no time. There was so much from the day that I wanted to go over in my notebooks. As detailed as I'd been, I needed to work through what I could while it was fresh in my mind. I was destined to be getting a whole lot more information on Lucky tomorrow, so I wanted the accounts I received today to be filed and understood before adding the next chapter.

29

11 October 1968

HELEN

The Tasmanian Racing Club honoured the memory of their recently departed star jockey with a new race, the Kevin McGregor Memorial Hurdle. It was the first time I had seen his widow Sarah since the funeral. I'd felt so sympathetic to her situation, but after the way she and her friends had always been with Lucky and me, I was trying to keep my distance. It was Sarah who sought me out, apologising for the cruel words she'd often used in the past.

'I never meant anything by it. I was always such an anxious mess when Kev was riding, I did what I could to shift my focus to cope.'

'Think nothing of it. I know the anxiety as well as anyone.'

I had always considered Kevin and Sarah to have been the opposite of Lucky and me. The humanity that transcended this moment and the events that led to it highlighted how wrong this was. The differences that were so pronounced in superficial ways, hid realities that saw us connected deeply. Drawn together in the same small city, the husbands pursuing the same dreams, us wives sick in the stomach with the same fear. We may have come from different sides of the track, but we ended up at the same place. Kevin, who was so assured throughout his career, was gone in a way that seemed more likely to be Lucky's destiny. Sarah had taken the role of the grieving widow that I'd spent years preparing to play.

Twenty-two horses were contesting the feature race which meant a ride was available for almost every jumps jockey in Tasmania, even allowing for three visiting jockeys from Victoria being down for some of the favourites. With few other available options, Lucky was able to secure a mount. Not a great one, but the 500/1 outsider Prince of the Stars. Most horses Lucky rode had their chances written off based on his engagement, but 'Prince' had been failing at long odds in easier races than this, with more successful jockeys aboard. He'd had three different riders in recent times but all of them had passed up the mount today for better chances. The horse was only in the race due to its owner having had a connection with Kevin McGregor and he felt it reasonable to give Lucky the ride.

When the race started I thought this may be the day he avoided falling. Not finishing, just not falling. Prince refused to gallop as the rest of the field took off. He gave away a start of a furlong before he consented to run. Given the futility of the task, a more sensible option would have been to call it quits immediately, but sensible had never been part of Lucky's vocabulary. He pushed the horse hard trying to catch the field. As they got close to the first hurdle, Prince again decided he wasn't in the mood. Now when the horse should have taken flight over the fence, he pulled up so quickly that Lucky had no hope of staying in his stirrups. His head went forward as fast as the horses pulled back and when horse and jockeys heads meet in such a way, the consequences are inevitable. He was unconscious before hitting the ground.

After the sombre mood before the race when the club had paid tribute to Kevin, the atmosphere seemed to lighten with Lucky's fall. The crowd seemed to view his presence as comic relief rather than a serious participant in the race. With the fall, he'd delivered the punchline and they were now ready to focus on the race proper. The fact a man was unconscious in the middle of an event honouring a jockey who died in a race fall didn't seem to resonate. When there was no sign of movement from Lucky, the joviality of the masses seemed to pause as the crowd feared the worst.

Rather than rushing downstairs, I remained in my elevated position with my binoculars fixed on him. It took more than a minute, but I saw movement. At that stage, the medical staff focussed on moving him to safety. He was placed on a stretcher and moved away from the hurdle. Thankfully this time he didn't fall from the stretcher. I could see him trying to sit up, almost tempting fate while they moved, which reassured me about his condition. By the time the field was back to this point of the track on the next lap, Lucky was safely sitting well inside the rail, though still looking far from alright.

As insignificant as it seemed in the scheme of things, I did notice that a big outsider, Eternal Faith won the race with Paul Sinclair aboard. Paul was one of the few jockeys who showed genuine friendship to Lucky, so I was always happy to see him have one of his rare successes. In his fifties, it would have been a couple of years since his last win. He didn't get many more opportunities than my husband these days. His wife Rebecca was as keen for him to retire as I was with Lucky, though in the Sinclair case, it was more to do with financial necessity than misguided dreams.

'What do you think it is?' she asked me before I had a chance to offer my congratulations. I shrugged my shoulders and acknowledged that he was conscious.

'Please pass on our congratulations to Paul. Couldn't have been a better result for Kevin's race. Well, aside from Lucky winning, of course.'

'I'll be in touch. Let me know if there's anything we can do,' Rebecca said. She left to go down to the jockey's room which was where I too was headed, but I waited. She may be a friend, but at this moment I didn't want friendship or conversation. Unless it was definitive good news, I wanted to be alone in my thoughts, even if being genuinely alone was impossible in amongst the crowd.

The ambulance took him straight to the hospital without any further observation on course. I initially hadn't realised the ambulance had left the track, so by the time I made it to the car and drove into town, he'd gone through the admission procedure and was on a ward sleeping. As well as the concussion which stemmed from the head clash, he'd broken his collarbone on landing. Both of these were common enough injuries for him.

The collarbone operation was not done until Monday, and for the following few days, I let him recuperate with nothing but my support. By Friday, it was time to bring up topics he mightn't want to hear.

'I want to move to Bruny Island.'

30

19 May 2023

ZANIYA

I can't wait to get to Bruny Island. A few days ago, I didn't know it existed. I have to confess that in all of my planning for our trip, I centred completely on the city without looking wider. Since meeting Helen on Thursday, I've spent quite a bit of time looking into the island and feel so blessed that circumstances have led us there. It looks beautiful.

I'd spoken to Helen on the phone briefly yesterday and we worked out a plan. She gave me some ideas of what to look out for on the way, particularly the lookout at 'The Neck.' She then gave me directions to her house where we need to be around 11.30. She'll then give us a tour of the southern part of the island including a tour of the Cape Bruny Lighthouse after lunch at the local pub.

I had intended to present Helen with a draft of a tribute article to be sent with her letter to the Mercury. At this stage there was still too much missing in my knowledge of him, so I was going to be sending her that tomorrow once we'd left for Cradle Mountain. Of course, I was also planning a more in-depth article that delved into the legend of Lucky O'Shaughnessy and getting more detail for that was my main mission for today.

Perhaps my focus wasn't quite where it should have been last night. I had looked at my phone every ten minutes wondering if I would get a message from Toby. I'd made it clear that I wouldn't have the opportunity to see him again based on our itinerary, yet there was still a part of me that wanted to know that he would if he could. I guess that's insecurity shining through, and something I would like not to be so beholden to. One way or another, the impact of getting lucky had inhibited me from writing about Lucky. I didn't want to be letting Helen down, so I was up early this morning to make up for it. I did wake up to find a message on my phone from Toby, but it didn't do anything to make me feel better. Or worse for that matter.

'Hey, last night was great. Wish we had more time 2gether. If ya plans change u no where 2 find me. Enjoy the rest of ur trip.'

I know my standards are completely unrealistic, but even in a text, I can't stand that sort of spelling. *Ur, 2gether, ya.* Even if it had been possible, there is no chance that I would have retained interest in someone like that. Nevertheless, it was reassuring to hear that he would have been.

Years ago, one of the boys from Oliver's school had a major crush on me.

'Seriously? Matt? He is disgusting. There must be something wrong with me if someone like that likes me.'

'A compliment is a compliment whoever it is from,' Oliver said. 'It doesn't require you to requite his interest but don't be insulted by it. He may be the least appealing guy you know, but it doesn't make his taste in girls any less valid than the best-looking man in the world.'

I remembered something Helen had told me on Thursday about Max's opinion of Lucky. He said that he kept engaging him as a jockey for multiple reasons. Loyalty, a reward for his hard work, but critical at all times was his opinion that Lucky was a capable jockey. He'd been a top-quality trainer for many years so he knew how to evaluate others in the sport. The fact that he didn't train anywhere near the number of winners that the big stables had didn't matter. He was a second-string trainer, but his opinion was as valid as anyone's. While Lucky's ability was ignored by everyone else, the compliments from Max were enough to retain the necessary confidence to keep going.

Mum knocked on our door far earlier than we were prepared for.

'We're going down for breakfast. We mightn't get a chance to eat on the way.'

'Are you kidding?' I said. 'We'll barely stop eating today. The island has so much unbelievable local produce. Even if a lot of it is just taste testing, we won't go hungry. Plus, there's a café at Kettering where we'll have coffee and something to eat while we wait for the ferry.'

'Alright, I'll tell your father we'll wait,' she said.

'Tell him to pick the car up earlier. We want to maximise our time.'

We brought our departure time forward by fifteen minutes and all got ready quickly. I gave up on my plans of doing any more work before we left but packed my laptop into my bag so I could work on things in the car.

'What happened to living in the moment? Seeing those places you only get one chance to see?' Oliver asked.

'Doing too much of that hasn't left me with enough time to get things done. Now I pay the price, but I'm going to make sure I keep that price to a minimum.'

We all went to the hire car outlet together just before 8 am. We had to pick up our hire car from an outlet a few blocks from the hotel, and fortunately, the process was smoother than we'd faced on Friday ahead of our Tasman Peninsula trip.

The drive to Kettering took a bit over half an hour and most of that time I managed to be productive, shaping what I wanted to have prepared for Helen to read through. We did have a couple of delays along the way for roadworks and saw that we were just later than we'd hoped as the ferry left the terminus just as we made the final turn. After initially cursing our timing, I realised it was the one before our planned departure. We now had additional time to take advantage of the bathroom and the shop at the Kettering terminal. We were all in desperate need of a caffeine hit and something to eat, so the time was put to effective use. Our schedule still gave us time for our designated stops on the way down to Helens.

I grabbed a newspaper and had a quick look through it. The news was still dominated by an issue that seemed to be dividing Tasmania, with a stadium being built at enormous expense for a Hobart team to enter the national Australian football competition. From the time we arrived, it seemed to be the only issue being discussed.

The letters to the editor page had been the main reason for getting the paper today. While most of the letters related to the football team and the stadium, it proved worth my while when near the bottom I found one referencing the previous Thursday's article on Lucky.

'Reading about the passing of Lucky O'Shaughnessy reminded me of a day at the Elwick races more than fifty years ago when I had just moved to Tasmania. I knew nothing about Lucky and put $5 on a horse he was riding that looked very good in the yard. Not only did he give me 100/1 on the horse winning, but the bookmaker was so confident that he said he'd give me five times my money back if he just finished the race. I asked why he was so sure the horse wouldn't finish, and he mentioned that Lucky couldn't ride a rocking horse without falling off. At the third jump, the bookie was proven right as Lucky was kissing the turf again. I never made that mistake again.'

There was no offence in the letter, but while I thought any response would be in Lucky's defence, I was proven as wrong as the letter writer in his transaction with the bookie.

That would change once I had finished helping Helen. The next time I perused the paper for Lucky's name I was sure I'd be reading a fairer assessment.

31

11 April 1970

HELEN

As the matron was returning to the nurse's station, she noticed that two of her nurses were perusing the newspaper. Moving closer, she saw it was open at the racing fields.

'Do you think it's appropriate to be reading the racing form guide here and now?' the matron said.

'We were just looking to see if Lucky O'Shaughnessy had a ride today. He does, so we're going to make up his regular room.'

Shirley Murphy told the story with such conviction that everyone accepted it as true. She did live next door to Matron Sue Kelly, so she may have heard this as fact, though it was just as likely that the two of them had created the story for a laugh. Laughter at Lucky's expense didn't concern him, for he often initiated the jokes, but my sense of humour didn't quite work the same way as my husband's.

Shirley's husband Colin had been a moderately successful flat jockey before putting on too much weight and progressing to the ranks of jumps jockeys a year earlier. He'd been reasonably successful over the jumps, sitting comfortably in the top 10 on the premiership table. He was riding a horse named Orwell in Race 2, before his engagement on Mr. Alexander in the third race where he'd be opposed to Lucky aboard Cumberland, the outsider of the field.

I felt guilty thinking about it, but part of me wanted to see Orwell throw Colin off so that I could ask Shirley if he needed to borrow "Lucky's regular room" at the Royal Hobart. It wasn't in my nature to wish anyone the worst and I knew all too well the pain and heartache that jockeys loved ones go through. Sometimes however the attitudes shown towards me tended to rub off more than they should.

Any feelings of guilt didn't last, as Orwell delivered a supreme exhibition of jumping in a comfortable win. I passed Shirley in the grandstand soon after the race and offered my congratulations which were returned with what seemed to be a condescending thanks that made me wish I'd avoided her. Knowing the likely scenarios that would come from the following race, I would be sure to do so.

I stood near the edge of the betting ring and looked at the odds on display for the next race. Cumberland was at 66/1, a comparatively short price for a horse that even Lucky didn't feel confident about. Colin's mount Mr. Alexander wasn't much more fancied at 50/1 so at least I wasn't likely to see more gloating from Shirley. Well, she probably would gloat about Lucky's failure as much as she would from Colin succeeding, so I shouldn't take that thought for granted.

'Why only 66/1?' I asked Jimmy Webb, one of the bookmakers' clerks whose son was one of my students.

'Every time he rides, the legend grows. Every time the legend grows, there's another bunch of people wanting to be here and wanting to say that they backed Lucky O'Shaughnessy the day he won a race. Maybe they just want to keep the ticket as a souvenir, but whatever is causing it, the liability is enough to have us a little scared. We feel almost certain it won't happen, especially not on a horse like this, but even at 66/1 we'd all lose a year's salary paying out on the result. He's probably a 200/1 chance, but if we put up the true odds the entire bookmaking fraternity of Tasmania would be bankrupted if that miracle happened,' he explained.

'I thought you were going to give me a small ray of hope' I said.

'Sorry Mrs. O'Shaughnessy. I hope he stays safe, that's all that matters, right?'

I nodded and gave a slight smile before turning away. Of course, he was right, and I hadn't given any serious contemplation to any success beyond a safe passage before this point of the day. I don't think the honest assessment of his chances concerned me as much as the further explanation of how big Lucky's story had become. He was a joke to the racing community, a novelty to the wider Tasmanian public but rather than it being a shame to him, it was a badge of honour.

'He's got no hope darl,' Lucky said to me last night. He usually overstated the ability of any horse he was riding. Once he referred to a horse as having no chance, it probably meant that he shouldn't be in the race at all.

'Why did you take the ride?' I asked.

'I don't have the option of picking and choosing anymore. Thirty-five rides for zero finishes. When someone offers me ride thirty-six, I have to take it, whatever it is. If I say no to any opportunity I may as well pull the pin on my career altogether.'

'That would make far more sense than riding horses who haven't got a chance of doing anything more than hospitalizing you.'

'There is an upside to falling,' he said. 'You know, I'm becoming a bit of an identity. I reckon more people know me than any jumps jockey in the state.'

'How is that good?' I asked.

'If enough people know you, opportunities follow. I could get a job doing public speaking or advertising don't you think.'

'Advertisers want someone who people aspire to. People aspire to be the winner, not the guy who they know for failing.'

'That's how you see me?' he said with more than a degree of hurt in his voice. We'd been through this so many times, but he always returned to this despite it not being about my view at all.

'No, it's how the community sees you. I see you as a hero because you have the courage to get up every time you fall. Most people have short attention spans. They look at a picture, see the outline and move on. When they look at you, the picture they see is the guy who keeps falling, not the bravery of getting back up and pursuing your dream.'

'You don't understand,' he said.

'Maybe. Though you can never rule out the possibility that it may be *you* who doesn't understand. In the purity, sincerity and innocence that you go about things, you don't realise the full picture that everyone else is seeing.'

He walked out of the room, unwilling or unable to make an argument that was going to further the debate. It was an hour later before we were both in the same room and he spoke again.

'I will continue to ride as long as I am willing and able, which I still am now. I like to think I will win. I like to think I will finish a race. Whatever does happen, I will find a way to make it work as well as it can for us.'

'And I will support you,' I said. 'I want you to fulfill your dreams. I mightn't always agree with the direction that you take to reach them. I'd be happier if you retired which is why I try and influence you that way, but it doesn't mean I won't be standing by you through anything. You will always be my hero.'

As the jockeys made their way out to the mounting yard, I was hopeful that those last six words from last night were at the forefront of his mind. The next minutes would see my anxiety rise to a frightening peak, but as long as he knew he had my love and support, I would have played my role in making things work out as best as I could. As he left the yard on top of Cumberland, I saw him look towards my normal spot in the stand, and I was sure he knew.

It was a two-mile race, the horses starting at the entrance to the back straight and doing approximately one- and three-quarter laps of the course. There's always a level of tension at this point, not just amongst those of us in the stands with loved ones we feared for, but for the competitors themselves. As I later heard, the starter had called out to Lucky as the runners were getting prepared.

'I won't be able to get into the hospital until later in the week Lucky, but I will bring you a fruit basket.'

It would have been the last thing I'd want to hear, yet Lucky would no doubt have laughed, and with that been as relaxed as possible. No doubt the same would have applied to any of his rivals who overheard it.

Cumberland began quite well and was into stride quickly enough to take a forward position. From my perspective, this wasn't as ideal as it may sound. As much as I'd like to watch Lucky's races with confidence, experience doesn't allow me to avoid the thoughts that a fall is never too far away, and a fall was potentially more dangerous the further forward in the field you were. In my target of him finishing safely, the position behind the leader near the rail was nearly as bad as could be.

All the runners made it over the first few hurdles as the field made their way to the winning post with a lap to go. Cumberland was already losing a little ground, but Lucky asked him for a little more approaching the first jump in the back straight. He began to accelerate at the exact point the horse in front of him blundered, throwing the rider. Lucky was a stride away from landing on the fallen jockey but managed to shift out and ease, but with the loss of momentum, Cumberland didn't clear the jump. Not only did the horse come down, but three others behind also lost their riders. One of the fallen jockeys was Colin Murphy. While two of the jockeys were quick to their feet, Lucky and Colin remained almost motionless. I had lived through this trauma enough times, and the fact that there was some small sign of movement gave me some sense of relief.

I rushed downstairs so that I could be as close as possible to any updates, but I was made to regret this very quickly. Shirley Murphy was already there and began yelling at me.

'This is all the fault of your husband. If he wants to kill himself that's all well and good but every time he goes out there his incompetence is risking the lives of every other jockey.'

She was dragged away, still ranting and yelling in my direction, while one of the other attendants, Graham Cash, came to take me to another room in the opposite direction to shield me from the people who were likely to make these difficult moments closer to impossible. Fortunately, the wait was short before some comparatively positive news arrived. Lucky was injured, but conscious. The suspicion was a broken leg, but details like that would only follow his visit to his regular post-race destination of the hospital.

Colin Murphy's injuries were similar in severity to what Lucky faced, but for him and his loved ones, this type of incident was so much more uncommon. In the O'Shaughnessy household, a race that ended with a suspected broken leg would almost be considered a relief, but no doubt it would mean utter devastation to the Murphys. It didn't excuse her behaviour, but it did make sense of it.

I knew what I'd seen during the race, but sometimes it can be difficult to ascertain whether personal bias can lead to false perspective. It was reassuring to have my beliefs confirmed by someone a little less impartial and when Murray Lord came to see me, his take on the fall helped.

'He keeps riding them better and keeps getting worse luck leading to the same result. I don't know if he walked under a ladder or something, but all the hints are there. It is not going to happen for him.' Murray was a moderately successful flat racing jockey whose wife had been at university with me and with time we'd built a good friendship with the couple.

'So the carnage wasn't his fault at all?'

'No, certainly not. He had the horse placed perfectly and the horse in front of him refused at the jump. I hate to think what would have happened to Jimmy Doohan if not for Lucky's brilliant evasive action. Murphy and Clifton only fell because their reflexes were not as good as Lucky's.'

'Shirley Murphy says Lucky's a danger to everyone, and the other guys want him out of the game,' I told him.

'We all believe whatever we need to to stay sane. Her belief couldn't be further from the truth.'

I told him that whatever anyone else wanted, he wouldn't be race-riding for quite some time. I told him if I had my way, that long time would mean forever.

'I'm not surprised,' he said. 'When you're out there, you might not be in control, yet you feel like you are. Like when he avoided that fallen runner. He used his skill and met the challenge. When you're watching from the sidelines, you're equally as invested, but you know that you have zero control. I doubt any wife would ever be disappointed to have their husband retire from this business.'

I doubt any wife would have had as much reason to feel that way as I did. As I left the track and drove to the hospital behind the ambulance, I kept thinking about how I could rephrase my argument to get Lucky to agree with me. Again it was time to sell Bruny Island to him.

32

19 May 2023

ZANIYA

The trip across the channel took just over fifteen minutes. It wasn't hard to separate the tourists from the locals. The locals remained in their cars oblivious to the world outside while most passengers gathered around the edge of the ferry soaking in the sights all around us. It cost us $38 for a return ferry ride, which was purely for the car, and would have been the same whether we had one or four of us. It seemed like a daily commute to Hobart for islanders would be impossible. Given the high cost of hiring the car, it was already an expensive day, so this extra impost seemed just par for the course.

The ferry's arrival point is about halfway down North Bruny Island. While some of the places to the north are said to be stunning, most of the people on day trips head south immediately. As about twenty cars were off the ferry before us, we had plenty of people to follow. A couple of minutes into the drive, we passed the Bruny Island Whiskey Company where Dad wanted to stop.

'You are not drinking whiskey at 10 o'clock,' Mum said. 'Especially with all the driving ahead of you.'

'Don't worry it's not open yet,' I said, uncertain, but reacting to the lack of evident life in the place.

'Ah, but on the way home,' Dad said.

'It will be closed. Everything here is built around tourists and most of them need to be on the ferry back across, like we will be. As a result, everything closes earlier than when we will be back here,' I said, proud of my research.

Within ten minutes we did stop at the Bruny Island Cheese and Beer Company. It would have been easy to spend a lot more time here, but after tasting some of the cheeses and making some purchases it was time to move. It had surprised me that Oliver and Dad didn't insist on doing a beer tasting, but we did find out that their range was available at the hotel, so they were content to wait until lunch to try the local brew. A few minutes down the road we stopped at the Bruny Island Honey Company. We all had different preferences but knew there was only so much honey we'd be able to take once we left Hobart, so just grabbed the one jar, leaving the choice to Mum who tended to come to the fore on such decisions.

The first important stop was about ten minutes later as we arrived at The Neck. Bruny Island almost appears to be two separate islands, but a narrow isthmus connects North and South Bruny. We knew it would be worth it, but when we got out of the car and saw just how many steps there were to the lookout point, we all paused for a moment. I had intended to count the steps, but somewhere along the line, I got distracted. Dad, in his typical exaggerating nature, said it was 8,793, but I have far more faith in Mum's estimate of about 250. Fortunately, none of us were foolish or lazy enough to not proceed as the view at the top was something else. Miles of pristine beach on each side, yet so very different. To our left, the waves crash in as the land is exposed directly to the ocean while on the right, the very gentle waves from the protected straights pass the narrow gap between the bottom of Bruny Island and the main island of Tasmania. Seeing the contrast of the two beaches separated by such a tiny bit of land would have seemed unique if not for our visit to Eaglehawk Neck on Friday. This was however more spectacular, as only one side of the neck at Eaglehawk had a genuine beach, so sheltered was the bay there. Here, the viewing platform and the dual beaches made this absolutely postcard perfect. I didn't need to wait for Dad when it came to cameras. I was already clicking my phone like the stereotypical tourist.

There was a tribute to Truganini, the daughter of the chief of the Bruny Island Aboriginal community when European settlement began here. She was considered the last full-blooded Aboriginal in Tasmania after the horrors inflicted upon their community.

'Remember the Midnight Oil song?' Dad asked.

'Who?'

'A bit before your time. They were a successful Australian rock band. Your Mum and I saw them play once in the UK. Their music was very political, particularly highlighting the plight of indigenous issues. Surely you've heard *Beds Are Burning*?'

'Yeah, I think so,' I said, suspecting that anything less would result in schooling from Dad with hours of their music. I did vaguely recall the song.

'They also had a song called Truganini. The lead singer ended up becoming a government minister. Effectively he had moved from protesting about governments to being part of one. I'm sure he knows better than most that finding and highlighting problems is much easier than fixing them.'

I looked at the beauty all around me and thought about his words. Nature provides us with examples of perfection. The Neck shows us one of these. Around the world there are millions. Amongst these, the existence we experience is filled with imperfection. Even when we work towards one tiny part of our existence, none of us can get things completely right. However hard I strive in my career I will never really achieve my dreams. The more I do achieve, the higher I'll set my goals, and will therefore still fall short.

Lucky dreamed of being a jockey. Once achieved, the dream turned to victory. Had he won a race, the goal would have changed to bigger races, premierships or international success. Whatever point he reached, the goals would have moved, and eventually, he would have fallen short.

We all do. The people most content aren't those who go furthest, it's those who most appreciate each step on the way. If the World Press Prize becomes my goal, it should be just one step, no different to achieving a resolution for Helen.

When the destinations you visit are special enough, dragging yourself away from one amazing sight isn't quite so difficult. You know the next breathtaking view isn't far away, and hanging on to each one will only stop you from reaching others. This is how I felt as I made my way back down the stairs. I wanted to go out onto the beach that looked so magnificent from the top, but I knew we had experiences like that awaiting us further south. We were due at Helens soon and given the rest of the family had set the day aside for my benefit, I had to ensure that I made the most of it. Soaking in all that the island has to offer is certainly part of that, but not at the expense of maximising my time with Helen.

We were only fractionally behind schedule as we saw the signs for Adventure Bay. The problem was we were meant to turn before those signs. I had explained the directions in advance but needed to be paying more attention as we got there. After a bit of ridicule directed both ways, we got on the same wavelength and made it back to the right road. A short way along and here it was, the home of Helen and Lucky for the past 25 years.

'I wasn't worried. I just happened to be outside,' Helen said on our arrival.

'Hard to make up time down here, there is so much to want to stop and look at,' Mum said.

'Not to mention the driver getting lost,' Oliver said.

'Well as much as they blame the driver, they didn't do the greatest job as navigators, I can assure you. They forgot all about the idea of directing me and were far too focused on laughing at me,' Dad said.

'No. Laughing with you, not at you,' I clarified.

33

22 July 1971

HELEN

Early in life, we learn to distinguish between people laughing *at* us and people laughing *with* us. I'm not sure how well Lucky mastered this, but thankfully for his well-being, he interpreted things in the best possible way. At least most times he did.

He had a ride at Elwick in a maiden hurdle one Saturday when several of the top jumps jockeys from the mainland had come to town for a couple of feature races. Given the availability of names like Clark, Lawson, Rafferty and Hunt, it seemed inconceivable that Lucky would get a mount on this day, yet Max's loyalty knew no bounds. When Lucky was fit, he gave him the opportunity. Considering the winners he trained with other jockeys aboard and the continual failures when Lucky rode, this loyalty was either brave or stupid. It all depends on whose opinion you sought.

'He does the work, he earns the opportunity. It's as simple as that.'

'Thirty-eight attempts for thirty-eight failures to finish,' Joe Lyon stated. 'I'd say it is as simple as that.' Lyon had ridden for Max on a couple of occasions and had enquired about the ride on Colossus of Rhodes earlier in the week, only to be told that he'd be engaging Lucky.

'If he rides them badly, he loses the ride. It's a long time since he's ridden a bad race. I can't say that about you, or too many others for that matter. Mostly he's been the victim of circumstances.'

Lucky wouldn't have a job without Max. At times that left me uncertain whether he deserved my ultimate gratitude or my contempt. I wanted something else for him, but I also knew his passion meant any other career would mean regret. It had to be his decision, and at least I knew that until he made that decision, it was best to have the unwavering support of someone who genuinely cared about him and his best interests. Max could never be accused of failing on that score.

In his late seventies, Max was not capable of continuing too much longer. Perhaps he'd transition to retirement by guiding Lucky into a new career as a trainer. Unfortunately, this meant convincing owners to give him their horses to train. Considering his reputation, making headway would be nearly impossible. Max was an incredibly convincing speaker. With several owners, he'd needed these skills to convince them of why Lucky should be given the ride on their horse in a particular race. On more than one occasion he had a horse transferred away from him after he insisted Lucky would ride it, only for the horse to fall in defeat. With his operation shrinking as he entered the twilight of his career, he felt no concern about this.

'There are many elements to training,' Max said at dinner with Lucky and me one night. 'One of those elements is choosing the jockey. Any owner who doesn't let me train their horse in 100 per cent of those elements is someone I am not going to train for. If that means I don't train for anyone else, so be it.'

Colossus of Rhodes was Max's newest hurdler. He'd been bought from New South Wales where he had failed to make a mark in flat racing. His first preparation saw him trained at Randwick by one of Sydney's most prolific trainers. Bred to race over a longer distance, his lack of early success wasn't considered surprising. After stepping up to a mile and a half in his second preparation and still failing to run a place, the horse was transferred to a country trainer at Tamworth. Over the next two years, he raced another eighteen times but never managed to break through for a win. He did prove competitive at this level, with several minor placings, but he seemed like a horse in need of greater staying tests than were available in this region. Hurdles appeared the best option, and this meant a sale to one of the southern states. Max liked the profile of the horse as well as the price tag. He made the purchase.

Both Lucky and Colossus of Rhodes had worked their way into this preparation at a similar rate. Horse and rider had both spent the best part of a year off, until recently beginning a campaign that had them slowly progressing toward peak fitness. Colossus of Rhodes had raced three times on the flat for Max, most recently over a mile and a half where he ran fourth. Max had also given him two trials over the jumps, with Lucky riding him on both occasions. In each trial he had jumped immaculately, finishing third and first respectively. Lucky had been first past the post in trials before, but it was still a thrill to achieve this.

'See,' Lucky told me after the trial win. 'Couldn't ride a horse better than that.'

'Doing it in a race would be better,' I replied.

'Well, he'll be in a maiden hurdle next week. I've got the ride.'

His enthusiasm was generally infectious, but when it came to an-nouncing a race ride, I couldn't share it.

'I'm thrilled,' I said sarcastically. Naturally, I would be there, and I would be hoping more than anything for success. I would also be angst-ridden before and during the race, and if history was any indicator, that feeling would continue long beyond the race as well.

xxx

'Lucky O'Shaughnessy, what a pleasure it is to meet the legend.' South Australian jockey David Clark said walking up to him in the jockey's room. 'I've heard so much about you. Is it true that you don't have children because every time you mount your wife you fall off?' Several of the other jockeys burst into hysterics, but unlike most similar scenarios where he was a willing participant, Lucky glared and walked away.

He never let too much of his personal life out, but after I'd had three miscarriages in the early years of our marriage, we knew children would not be an option. It had devastated both of us, but we'd long since accepted our fate in this regard. For Lucky, this sort of line might have been alright from someone close to him, but as an introduction from a stranger, it smacked of contempt. When the contempt stretched to reminders of painful realities from outside of his career, his sense of humour disappeared.

'These bastards shouldn't be allowed here,' he said to Max when he walked outside.

'Who?' Max asked.

'These arrogant mainlanders coming here and taking our rides. There are few enough opportunities for us,' Lucky said before going on to explain what had happened in the jockeys' room.

'Channel your anger appropriately,' Max said. 'You're never going to stop the best jockeys chasing the biggest prizes. What you have to do, like all the locals for that matter, is perform well enough that you're the chosen riders.'

'You think I ever give anything less than my best? Day in, day out I give everything I have to get the opportunities you give me. There is nothing more I can do in my preparation, my analysis, and my training that can get me better results in any race I ride in. If I got the opportunities that these guys did, I'd get the results that would make me one of the chosen riders.'

He disappeared back to the jockey's room to get his silks on ahead of the race. Max wasn't sure what to think about the frame of mind Lucky was in. Nothing else had worked, so he thought riding angry may be the change he needed, though in theory there had to be a level of potential danger that came with this. An animal that weighs half a tonne is a danger to any person whose focus isn't as it should be. Anger for the right person might not be an issue, but if it led to Lucky losing any small degree of his concentration it could be incredibly dangerous.

Max always felt tense when Lucky rode in a race, but today was now going to have a slightly enhanced level of angst.

Colossus of Rhodes was one of the quickest to begin and settled near the lead as they approached the first of three hurdles on the river side of the track. He jumped cleanly, though shifted out on landing as he had done on occasions during his trials. For this reason, Lucky was ensuring he stayed on the outside. Although this meant covering extra ground, the advantage of the extra space would more than offset this for a horse with his jumping pattern.

At the second jump, he again shifted out slightly, and this time appeared to lose a little ground. The leader, Big Barrel, had moved a couple of lengths clear, and two other horses had now pushed through inside of him to form a line of three behind the leader. At the third, all horses and riders remained safely aboard, leaving the full field of twelve making the tight bend into the straight the first time.

On the first lap, there were four hurdles in a little over two furlongs. The last two of these were the closest to the majority of the crowd, and it was at these two fences that Lucky had most frequently fallen throughout his career. My breathing tended to get a little tighter as they approached this part of the track.

Colossus was so named due to his imposing size as a yearling. He looked bigger than all of his rivals, and the big stride that it gave him made him appear that he was moving in slow motion alongside his rivals. At each hurdle, I held my breath, and when I exhaled on his safe landing, I noticed him lose a bit more ground each time, before reeling them back in the next hundred yards until the pattern repeated at the next hurdle.

It was with extreme relief that I watched him sail over the last obstacle in the straight, just after the winning post. The track staff quickly removed the last two hurdles in the straight so that the next time around, the last fence would be a furlong from home. If only Lucky could still be aboard at that point of the race.

There is a run of nearly two and a half furlongs until they straighten in the back, and in this section of the race, there is only one hurdle to get over. Through this section, Colossus of Rhodes improved from fourth to a clear second, almost at the quarters of the leader. Midas Touch, one of the favourites for the race, had also improved markedly and was coming up on the outside of Lucky. Sean Ryan who was aboard Midas Touch must have noticed the jumping pattern of his rival and gave him sufficient room as they approached the first in the back straight before asking his horse to improve sharply and overtake him soon after. The impact of a horse outside of him, and not a full-length clear, may have impacted him. At the next jump, Colossus of Rhodes gave a half-hearted leap that saw him go through the hurdle and lose all momentum on landing. It was a herculean effort from Lucky to stay aboard, but despite his reputation, this wasn't unusual. He did lose many lengths and was passed by several runners to be in the last three, with all chance of a fairy-tale victory appearing over.

After surviving such a bad jump, part of me thought that it may be a sign that the hoodoo was ready to be broken. Maybe it was more hope than expectation because there were still four hurdles to clear. If the horse repeated the previous jump at any of these, it was unlikely to produce the same result. It didn't take long to find out, as he crashed at the next jump, the impact of the previous one leaving him without sufficient momentum to jump cleanly at this one. The horse fell but was up on his feet immediately and appeared uninjured. The same didn't apply to Lucky.

The medical staff were there immediately, with no other falls having occurred in the race. He was quickly in the ambulance and was on his way immediately to the Royal Hobart. The speed of their actions had my anxiety levels through the roof but thankfully the club doctor was across to me immediately to give me an update.

'He'll be alright Helen' the club doctor said before giving me more details that countered his initial statement. 'He's got broken ribs, most likely a punctured lung as well. He's finding breathing difficult and painful, so we've got him on his way without a wasted moment. I don't think you should drive, so we've got a committee man coming down who will drive you there. He will be in emergency, and you mightn't be able to see him for a while anyway, but I know you'll want to be there.'

'Of course, thank you,' I said. It was hard to describe my mindset. I didn't feel as panicky as the people around me seemed to expect. Perhaps time had made me somewhat numb to these experiences, so frequent had they been. The one racecourse fatality I'd witnessed was Kevin McGregor's, and he never regained consciousness from the moment of the fall. It seemed to me that as soon as Lucky was conscious, I knew that he'd escaped the worst. Beyond that, he'd survived everything there was to survive and I remained comparatively composed knowing he would do so again.

34

19 May 2023

ZANIYA

Helen took us outside to a shed where she kept most of Lucky's memorabilia.

'Other than those couple of photos inside, I don't want most of it on display. As much as it represents a huge part of his life, it is also a reminder of a lot of heartache. To ignore Lucky the jockey is to ignore a big part of who he was, but when it comes to hanging on to memories, we all seek the best moments.'

'Of course,' Mum said. 'Everyone has their wedding photos up. The school photos of their children. We're less likely to retain our own school photos, as we don't usually remember those days as fondly as our parents do, proudly watching us grow and develop as young people.'

For a man who never finished a race, there was far more than I expected. One box was filled with race books and newspapers with the form guide for every race he ever rode in.

'Lucky refused to ever throw a race book out from days he raced. Thankfully he didn't have the same insistence for every race meeting he attended or we'd need a bigger shed.'

I flicked through some, looking at the names that would have meant nothing four days ago, yet now were dominant in my mind. Horses like Roy's Boy, Parvo and Ghost Tour. Jockeys like H. Mortimer, K. McGregor and most notably of all, L. O'Shaughnessy.

Next to the box was a scrapbook featuring every bit of press Lucky ever had.

'When they ran this article the day before his first race, it made sense to keep a record of it. We hoped there would be far more to come. There was, just not the type we had envisaged. For all the doubts I had, I thought he'd either receive ongoing kudos for success, or he would fade into obscurity. With time he started getting more mentions, but less of it was desirable. Lucky insisted that we keep it all so that once things turned around, he'd have ammunition to throw back at the cynics.'

'He maybe should have been given the nickname Optimist rather than Lucky,' Dad said.

'You'd think so when you just scratch the surface,' Helen said, 'but dig deeper and trust me, he was more lucky than optimistic. Have you ever heard the saying, *love what you do, and you'll never work a day in your life*? Well according to that, he never did work a day in his life. That's lucky.

'He often spoke optimistically, but it wasn't a reflection of how he felt. More often than not, it was a feeble attempt to reassure me and stop me from worrying. It was ineffective at achieving that of course.'

'Maybe he was trying to convince himself?' I said, receiving a shrug of the shoulders in response from Helen.

Next, we were shown a collection of photos of Lucky aboard the various horses he used to ride. Some of these were in races, others in trackwork and more still were shots of him sitting aboard posing. A large box next to this had some of his old silks and several helmets, most of which looked much the worse for wear.

'Someone who fell so often naturally had a high turnover of helmets. His got tested more than most others. Why he wanted to keep them was beyond me. Perhaps he sensed the Lucky O'Shaughnessy Museum would one day become one of the state's major attractions. Of course, he probably needed to win every great steeplechase in the world a couple of times for such a place to be instigated, but he wasn't quick to give up hope of that happening.'

'You know, some of this would be worth a fortune,' Dad said. 'There's a huge market for sports memorabilia, and with someone like Lucky, there would be more of an interest in what he wore than in some of his more successful rivals.'

'We struggled financially in our younger years, but by the time I retired from teaching, we were comfortable. Now, what am I going to do with money? It's easier just to hang on to it all, and one day after I'm gone someone can sort through it.'

'You probably don't need anything else, but I found this at Salamanca Markets the other day.' I took out the print that I had bought. 'I don't know if he is in this photo, but it seemed the right era.'

'It is a hurdle race, and that is Elwick. That said, for every hurdle he raced in through the 1960's there were forty more that he missed. I can't be sure, but I think that is Kevin McGregor riding that horse on the right. If Lucky was in the race, he'd be too far behind to have been visible in this picture.'

Despite being unable to see too much clarity of the jockey in question, putting the image alongside what I'd heard of his tragic death, brought an extra sense of reality to the story.

'It wouldn't be the day of his tragic fall?'

'No, that race was at Brighton. This is definitely Elwick.'

She didn't want the print, so it was something to be taking home as a memory of the whole story. Helen added to my memories with a few other items.

'Keep these. It is a way of saying thank you. If your father is right, they can earn you a decent payday. From my perspective, it is more about reminding you. You can tell human stories as a journalist, then walk away. If you want to be making a difference in this world, you never lose sight of the humans that make those stories.'

'Are you sure, I can have these? I will treasure them.' She'd given me race books from Lucky's first and last race, as well as a purple and green jockeys cap, and three photos. The first of these was of Lucky as a teenager sitting aboard Roy's Boy at Max's stables, another posing in his silks before a race and a third of him in action riding Colossus of Rhodes as he clears a hurdle.

'Now, we should get moving,' Helen said. She had booked us in for lunch at the Bruny Hotel before we'd make our way down to the bottom of the island and a tour of the Cape Bruny Lighthouse. We were booked in there for 2 pm, so time was of the essence.

Naturally, the Bruny Hotel supports the myriad of local producers, so lunch started with Bruny Beer and Cider respectively for us all, and a dozen oysters served a variety of different ways to share between the five of us. Helen passed, leaving three each for the rest of us. Although not normally a devotee, I always stick with the *when in Rome* adage. The fact that the local amongst us passed almost had me questioning whether I should to, though I was happy in the end that I took the chance. They were exceptionally good.

I had salmon for my main. Naturally, it was Bruny Island salmon. Even Mum's chicken parmigiana relied on Bruny Island cheese to keep it local, as there was no reference to where the chicken was sourced from. With the boys having lamb and steak, and our Australian friend Helen choosing the British favourite of fish and chips, we got to see the full variety of the menu and it all looked good.

I for one, felt like I'd eaten too much, but rather than sit and let it digest for too long, we were quickly on our way to the lighthouse. We passed through a destination called Lunawanna, which was home to just one thing, a set of public toilets.

'It wouldn't be a huge deal in most places, but there's a lot of people leaving the pub in a hurry to go down to the lighthouse. By this point they realise they need it,' Helen said.

We were a little better prepared and were long past Lunawanna by the end of her explanation. At this point, the drive became significantly less comfortable. We were off the bitumen and on a very rough and rugged dirt road. Helen had made the trek enough times to be rather non-plussed by all the bumps, but Mum, Oliver and I were continually exchanging glances that showed we were struggling.

We were all relieved to see the lighthouse appearing closer and at the last minute a return to bitumen. The road had an impact on bladders as Mum and Dad now needed the restrooms.

While we waited for them, Helen told Oliver and me more about the island and the life that she and Lucky had on it. She remarked that it had changed like everywhere else, but while outsiders may see the changes as less significant in a place like this, to the locals it wasn't like that at all.

'Proportionately, Bruny has probably changed more than anywhere. When we moved down here it was a sleepy little island that few people knew about. The internet age means everyone can be exposed to everything. Now we have tourists flocking here. We have burgeoning businesses to service those tourists. It still might seem slow and laid back to you, but it is incredibly different to what I remember.'

This was true everywhere. People spoke of unspoiled gems, but they were all more spoiled than they used to be. Major tourist hubs like Venice were paying environmental costs from the impact of tourism. The same issues weren't apparent on Bruny Island, but nowhere had been immune to the increasing toll of the exploding visitor numbers before the pandemic. While there had been a period of relief in the past couple of years, that was only ever going to be temporary. Money eventually wins.

'You could spend a week on the island and not see all the best spots, but that's because some of the real highlights we keep secret,' she said. 'Or we have so far. Tourist numbers are continually rising, and with that, more people are seeing more of the beauty, so the secrets are getting out. When we go back, I will show you more of the area around Adventure Bay. It is far from a secret, but it is beautiful. There's a trail there you'd love.'

'If the weather holds out,' Oliver said, noticing the cloud cover getting more ominous.

'We'll plan as though it will stay fine. That was the way Lucky saw life. Don't worry, whatever we plan for, it will all work out when it needs to,' Helen said.

'I thought he wasn't an optimist,' I said.

'Therein lies the difference between belief and hope. He didn't believe things would go his way, but he never lost hope that it would happen. Well, not quite never.'

35

7 August 1973

HELEN

Although Elwick was the premier racecourse of Tasmania, some of the state's feature jumping races were held at Deloraine in the north of the state. Roughly halfway between Devonport and Launceston, jumps racing was the lifeblood of the small town. Lucky had ridden at Deloraine just once, nearly fifteen years earlier. As most of his rides were for Max, there were few opportunities outside of Hobart. Max tended to place his horses in races locally unless they were top-class. In those cases, it was rare that Lucky would get the mount. It wasn't so much that Max wouldn't trust his best horses to Lucky, but he rarely made a change in jockey after a good performance. The horses that made the step up to feature races only did so after victories, and the victories never occurred with Lucky aboard.

Max's best horse, Mile High, had been entered for the feature Deloraine Hurdle. After two straight wins under Colin Murphy, there was no chance of Lucky getting the ride. Max did however offer a consolation. One of the horses he trained and owned, Cashatorio, was to make his hurdling debut in the fourth race. It was an average standard maiden hurdle, and although Cashatorio was limited, Max hoped it was a weak enough race for him to be competitive. Lucky arrived with Max and the horses shortly before the first race. He was keen to watch this to get a feel for the pattern of racing at the smaller track. As always, his preparation was as meticulous as the very best jockeys. A bad fall occurred in the first race, and for one of the rare times in his career, he was on the other end of proceedings, witnessing the misfortune of others rather than experiencing it himself.

Several jockeys were ruled out of action for the rest of the day due to injury and ahead of the third race, there was a shortage of available jockeys. Out of desperation, Darryl Lawson, the trainer of one of the leading chances, Kaa Boy, approached Lucky.

'I've heard enough to say you're not worth putting on my horse, but I haven't got any options. It's you or I scratch him.'

'And you're not going to scratch him?' Lucky said in a joking tone. Seeing the lack of humour in Lawson, he quickly changed tack before Lawson had a chance to rethink. 'I won't let you down,' he said, more in hope than in genuine belief.

It was not as though he doubted his ability, but he was aware enough of his record to be wary of all that could go wrong. He knew he could get horses to settle for him, and he knew he could time the run of his horses, but there was always the fear that something out of the blue would conspire to disunite him from his mount.

He quickly checked on the odds of Kaa Boy which were 6/1 and made him the third favourite for the race. He had never been aboard such a highly fancied starter in a race before. Combined with the last-minute nature of his engagement, he considered it fate that today would be his day.

Twenty minutes before the race an announcement came out across the racecourse of the relevant jockey changes:

'On Number Seven, Kaa Boy, jockey D. McCafferty has been replaced by L. O'Shaughnessy.'

Occasionally announcements like this received some level of interest but on this occasion, the interest rose to several sighs and a far greater volume of laughter. The name Lucky O'Shaughnessy had attracted a few extra people to Deloraine to see the man they'd heard of from down south. Nobody thought his moment would come quite so soon.

Out in the betting ring the impact of the jockey change was quite evident. Some people were trying to get refunds on their bets, though most serious punters were yet to invest and at this stage, they were all dodging Kaa Boy. 6/1 had drifted to 20/1 by the time the horses left the mounting yard. Nobody considered the horse could win with Lucky aboard.

Lawson looked forlorn as he gave Lucky his final instructions. He was already regretting not scratching the horse. He knew he was ready to win and hadn't wanted to waste the day, but he knew all too well the adage that money talks and the betting ring had confirmed that Lucky was far too big a handicap for his steed.

'He's a safe jumper but he hasn't got great pace. Keep it economical early then when you get to the back straight the last time you have four jumps close together. That is when to be on the outside making your move. Hopefully, you can be in front by the bend and then push onward to the finish. Don't use the whip, just hard hands and heels.'

As the race started, Lawson's mood sank further as Kaa Boy was the slowest of the fourteen runners into stride. By the second hurdle, it was down to a field of thirteen. Mercifully it wasn't Lucky that had come off. In keeping with his instructions, he didn't want to take too much out of his horse and allowed him to settle close to last. While the trainer wasn't happy with him being so far back, he was impressed that Lucky had ensured plenty of space for him, by getting the horse to the outside of other runners.

Down the back straight the race began to play out exactly as Lawson had hoped. Into sixth place as he cleared the first jump then fourth by the time he was over the second. Two horses had cleared out to a six-length lead but Lucky was closing ground on them as he moved into third place by the next jump. When one of the leaders, race favourite Clandestine, fell at the last hurdle in the back straight, it took exceptional horsemanship from Lucky to dodge the fallen jockey without impacting his horse's momentum. Turning for home there was only one horse left in his sights.

Mr Vee had been sent out a 10/1 chance for the race. He'd shown great ability throughout his career but while he looked a powerful jumper, he had always shown an inclination to throw in the occasional lazy jump. There had been no sign of that on display at Deloraine as he looked back to his best. Kaa Boy was closing under the hard hands and heels riding of Lucky. As they came to the last it appeared set that the world's worst jockey would be ridding his reputation in the greatest possible way. Less than a length separated the horses as Mr Vee took off for the last hurdle, but he buckled on landing, shifting out onto Kaa Boy. There was not a jockey in the world who could have avoided what happened. He described it in detail to me.

'It was like time moved at the most microscopic speed. It was the blink of an eye, but it felt like a year passed. The horse and rider crashed right in front of me. I yanked at the reigns to move my horse out, but it happened too fast. I'd been as wide of him as I could get, and he'd laid out so far there just wasn't room. Nobody will ever believe it, but I swear this wasn't in any way my fault.'

Mr Vee was destroyed, having broken his pelvis. Kaa Boy hit the ground, but was back up on his feet immediately, albeit without Lucky. For the forty-fourth time, Lucky had started a jumps race and failed to finish. After rolling away to avoid the oncoming horses, he sat motionless and numb. For one of the few times in his career, he had escaped significant injury, yet he was returning to the jockey's room more hurt than after any of his previous catastrophic falls.

There was silence in the jockeys' room. The banter that was always on display was completely non-existent. The presence of Lucky generally ensured a light mood, but for the first time, they saw him not just down, but out. His head remained in his hands. Attempts from others to give him some reassuring words were ignored. He wasn't choosing the response, he was truly incapable of anything else. He didn't come out where I could see him and say anything, so the first opportunity was when he stepped into the mounting yard for the next race.

Throughout Lucky's career, the worse things got, the more he believed he was owed good fortune. Following his worst piece of luck ever, that would have meant payback was due for him in the upcoming ride on Cashatorio. Max, myself, and I suspect even Lucky too, doubted how this would be possible in the mindset he'd now sunk to.

'You should have replaced him,' I yelled across the fence to Max after the horse had gone out onto the track.

He looked over at me and shrugged his shoulders. He knew I was right, yet it came back to the dynamic that Max and Lucky shared. They'd both do anything for each other yet talking honestly about feelings was a step too far. Max would have been too afraid of Lucky's feelings to take him off. Lucky would be too loyal to Max to fail to uphold a commitment. I've never claimed to be a medical expert, but I felt certain that his mental state at that moment was more debilitating than the physical injuries that he previously hadn't been allowed to ride with. I believed he was a danger to himself, the other jockeys and the horses in this current state.

For the forty-fifth time in his career, he started a jumps race. Despite my fears, he had the horse jumping well. He was settled right at the back and out of trouble. At 100/1, the expectations for the horse were low, and not just due to Lucky. Turning into the straight for the first time, the initial field of ten was down to eight, but Lucky was still aboard.

Cashatorio was roughly six lengths behind the second last horse when they passed the post with a lap to go. By the next hurdle, the deficit had moved to eight lengths and by the following jump, it was closer to twelve. There was little to be gained by continuing, however on the occasions he had previously retired a horse from races, he was ridiculed for not taking every opportunity to have his first finish. He wasn't going to make that mistake again, so he continued.

The horse didn't seem to lose any further ground, and with another couple of riders dislodged the field was now down to six. With half a lap to go, there was still the chance of running into the placings, so there was a definite incentive to keep pushing.

With four fallers in the race all getting up and galloping on under their own steam, there was an added level of danger. Jockeys could make errors, but generally under the stewardship of a professional hoop, a horse would not behave too erratically. Riderless horses were another matter. Some continued the course jumping each fence as it came before them. Others tended to run around the hurdles and often scurried well ahead of their mounted rivals.

Then there was Mountain View. He had jumped two fences after falling before running outside of the next two. Continuing his unpredictability, he turned around and decided to race in the reverse direction, and decided he was again ready to jump. He approached the hurdle halfway along the back straight and made a clean jump, landing almost exactly where Cashatorio was about to take off from. The horses made only minimal contact as each reared and sought to stop and change directions, but Lucky had no chance and was flung far and high from the saddle.

For the forty-fifth time, he had failed to finish. The awkwardness of the fall saw him end up with a suspected broken leg. He was taken to the tiny Deloraine District Hospital before being transferred to Launceston General Hospital. They operated, and he was kept in for the first two weeks of his recovery before I could bring him home. Throughout the entirety of his stay in the hospital and his rehabilitation, he never once complained about the injury or how it occurred. He remained inconsolable and depressed in a way I had never seen him about the race before it.

He said it was a good thing he wasn't at the usual Royal Hobart Hospital as the nurses would be upset at his poor mood. The pain from the injury was great, yet no worse than he'd endured previously. He'd worn a smile while coping with similar traumas, but the memory of the incident on Kaa Boy had nothing redeeming about it.

'I don't think I can ride again,' he had said the day after the race. 'I've broken nearly every bone in my body and I always dealt with it, but yesterday broke my heart.'

After all the years I desperately wanted him to give up his career, it looked like the time had now come. Despite all we'd been through, I felt devastated for him. I was finally getting what I'd wished for over so many years. Now that it had arrived, I would have done anything for it not to have happened.

36

19 May 2023

ZANIYA

You don't need to climb to the top of the lighthouse to experience amazing views here, but it is a classic example of making a good thing better. More than a hundred metres above sea level, the spectacular coastal landscapes at the bottom of this island can be appreciated to the fullest. I spent a minute soaking in the vista ahead of me before moving another few metres around, to be exposed to another angle. It was cold, but I couldn't feel that. I was too enamoured by what I could see.

I had left Helen with the rest of the family while I came to the top. The steps are beyond her, so she is staying below. When I come down, Mum, Dad and Oliver will be in the next group to the top. Given the choice, I wouldn't be coming back down, or at least not for a while. I have no say though. The time is strictly monitored. As you can't pass on the narrow spiral staircase, groups come up and spend ten minutes at the top before returning. With one last look to the sea, and then the spectacular landscape of the island, I accept this and join the group heading back to the ground.

'I don't understand. Why is it you love to travel so much?' Helen said as I returned to her.

'New places, new people, new experiences. Every day on the road has something special.'

'I have new experiences every day without needing to leave. I think people are so caught up trying to rush through too many things at once, that they never fully immerse themselves in any one thing.'

'How do you mean?'

'They walk with headphones in their ears or looking at their phones. You cannot be fully immersed in an experience while having one of your senses distracted by something else. People feel this need to have every sense stimulated at once, but if you strip everything back and focus on what is around you in any scene, then you feel its full value. That cloud formation is unique. You will never see exactly that again, yet most people won't even notice it.'

I looked above and couldn't see anything discernibly unusual about the clouds yet didn't want to tell Helen that.

'The people you pass in the street. They are each unique, yet so many go out of their way to avoid eye contact.'

'Yes, people avoid any interaction with strangers,' I said as my mind turned to Toby and I re-evaluated my words. It is true, I don't tend to make eye contact in the street with strangers, yet in the space of such a short time, I was able to completely give myself to one. Of course, as quickly as that happened, it did follow a set of processes that transitioned him from stranger to lover. I wouldn't have made eye contact without a precipitating incident to begin with.

It was as if she was reading my mind as she continued. 'They will all make love to someone who was at some point a stranger. They make lifelong friendships with people who were once strangers. The quality of our life is dependent on those who start out as strangers. Today is what it is for us through interaction that began with us as strangers. Our very existence comes through the uniting of parents who were once strangers.'

'We come across many strangers in life, but all of those situations happen with only the smallest number,' I said.

'True, but we should never ignore someone for the fact they are a stranger. Make eye contact. Interact when, where and how it is appropriate. It is a case of broadening the mind, the very thing that you feel comes from seeing the world, yet I maintain can be done from properly seeing your own part of it.'

'I must admit that complete immersion in the moment comes far more easily to me when I am travelling. My first trip overseas was to Pakistan, nearly a decade ago. I can close my eyes today and see the faces of people I met once. I can smell the spices from the markets in Lahore and hear the pandemonium of the peak hour traffic that was so different to home. I can remember where we ate, what I ate, what we saw and where we went. I can give an hour-by-hour synopsis of events from nine years ago yet couldn't differentiate any day from last month and tell you a single thing I did that was specific to any given date.'

'Is that travel, or a mindset?' she asked.

'Maybe it is the mindset. Maybe my generation is spoiled and takes too much for granted. At the very least, travel reminds us to open our eyes and look up. Maybe the greatest lessons that come from travelling are not the experiences we have while we're away, but the way we need to look at life on an everyday basis.'

'You don't have to win my assent. Everyone has choices to make, I just don't understand why people feel the need to find a different environment before they open their eyes to all the magic around them.'

Helen was one to ensure she got the last word. I let her have it on this topic, partly because I saw the validity of her claim. I always complained that if I travelled for four weeks in a year then there would be forty-eight comparatively uninteresting weeks in that year. I vowed to stop saying no at home to the experiences that I always said yes to abroad. It didn't necessarily mean seeking such experiences but at least being open to them. Places, events, people. Say yes more often and let no be a response that is only given when a reason exists.

We'd wandered down towards the car and stopped at the Lightstation Museum. There was nothing too interesting on display, especially having already had the enrichment of the lighthouse tour guide's discussion of its history.

'Lucky didn't lose out from his career. Matter of fact, he did better than many of the people who were looked up to as successes. Kevin Mc-Gregor died in a race fall. Des Patterson died of a drug overdose, having begun his habit to combat weight issues that threatened his career. Bert Mullins committed suicide or at least that's the official story, though most people down here suggest he was murdered.'

'What?'

'Yes. He won the premiership in his first two years as a senior jockey then chased the bigger dollars in Melbourne. Rumours are that he was deliberately losing on favourites that the bookmakers overlayed. He was getting paid by the bookies to pull them up or fall off, then he was also getting paid by some unsavoury types to pass information on to them. Eventually, he was said to have double-crossed some of these by winning when he was meant to lose. There was so much money involved that they sought the biggest possible retribution.'

It seemed like I had a much bigger story to write after Lucky's. 'Has anyone written about this?' I asked.

'I won't be your source on topics where I can only give you rumour and innuendo. Lucky's story is all I know with certainty. These other people aren't really a part of it, but they do highlight something that lies at the core of Lucky's life. Defining people based on one element of life may be simplistic, but it is futile. Nobody can ever tell me that McGregor, Patterson or Mullins had a more successful life than Lucky. He lived a long life, a happy life, and for all of those falls and failures, he got more out of his natural talent than any of them. Mullins won premierships but died at twenty-three. If it was suicide, he suffered badly before that point. If he was murdered, then he suffered in a very different way. McGregor had a child but died before her birth. Patterson was a shadow of a man for his last 20 years. All of them were gifted and born into the sport following previous generations. Lucky didn't have the talent to ride a horse yet had a longer career than any of them. The wins are all amazing when they happen but are worthless with time. Everything of value that Lucky possessed, never lost value.'

Helen was getting emotional again, and the combination of her tears and her words was impacting me too. I hugged her.

'Often when people talk about someone, they say the person couldn't have wished for more,' I said. 'I don't think it's ever true. Everyone wishes for more in some aspect of life. The better measurement is, would the person have swapped what they had for anything else? I feel sure from all I've heard that Lucky wouldn't have given up what he had in exchange for winning every race in the world.'

Tears still in her eyes, she nodded her head and smiled. She knew I understood.

xxx

On the drive back to Helen's we stopped at Bruny Island Premium Wines and the Bruny Island Chocolate Company. It should have been apparent at our first stops this morning that almost every business here carries the Bruny Island name. It clearly is a selling point, and I can understand why. The quality of the products we tried at all these places was very good, and it was clear that the island was renowned for this. Of course, the prices of most of the products reflected that. I suggested Lucky's beachside horse rides would have been more lucrative if he'd kept his name out of it and just called them Bruny Island Horse Rides.

'I'm not so sure,' Helen said. 'We had a Prime Minister of Australia named Harold Holt. He drowned in the late 1960s and not too many years later he was commemorated with of all things, a swimming pool. We love our ironic names down here, so nothing would sell riding a horse as much as Lucky's name.'

We stopped in the heart of Adventure Bay. There were several small holiday homes and a few bed and breakfasts, but not a huge amount else. There was a bowling and community club, a general store, a playground and an impressive sculpture known as the Bruny Island Arts Globe. Mostly, this area was about the beach.

'Over the years he used a few different spots. He was going up near 'The Neck' at one stage, but mostly around here. There wasn't the volume of people in those days, but most weekends there'd be a few customers. We'd have three or four horses with us including a little pony suitable for young children. We ended up stopping because of the escalating costs of insurance. It began to cost us more than we could make.'

Helen pointed out a few extra spots of interest. She was going to walk back to the house with me to work through a few more things of Lucky's. The rest of the family were going to explore a bit more of the area, including part of the recommended Fluted Cape Walk.

'So, if Lucky retired from racing in 1973 and did the beach horse rides only for a limited time, what else did he do with the rest of his life,' I asked.

'Most people only knew Lucky through his exploits on the track, and from that they all thought it was an ironic name. Look at this island. Imagine living here for half your life without any major responsibilities. What could be luckier?'

'How did he occupy his time?'

'He developed so many interests and he pursued them all vigorously. Even if they weren't working, we always had some rehomed racehorses on our property, and he galloped them, albeit more gently, but as though they were still in training. After the troubles in his childhood, he became a regular cyclist, covering several hundred kilometres a week and covering every inch of the island. He became a fanatical reader, devouring multiple books a week, having dodged books like the plague as a youngster. He did a bit of public speaking too, in the 1980s. He was very well received, speaking to sporting clubs about persistence, speaking to corporations about getting the best out of what you have. He could've done that forever, but he was happier alone, with me, or with the horses, so he lived accordingly.'

'There wasn't a financial strain?'

'Not really. He'd earn good money with the public speaking, but tired of it with time. He then, once again, got very lucky. Max had no family, so when he passed away, he left a significant sum of money to us. It gave us that extra security that we were never going to need a full-time income, let alone two. I taught until twenty years ago, so we were certainly comfortable, particularly with the simplicity of our lifestyle.

It was a life blessed with luck. Even in death, Helen said he didn't suffer greatly, with a massive heart attack taking him quickly, with no forewarning. The only part of life where luck eluded him was the one public part.

'What was the attention like when he announced his retirement?' I asked. 'Was he celebrated at all?'

'Announced his retirement? 'Helen asked. 'He never did.'

37

12 May 1974

HELEN

'I don't want anyone to know I've retired. The moment it's acknowledged it becomes a topic that people will make a big deal about and it's
not going to be a deal that's any good for me.'

'You must be the first person to ever retire from a career without
anyone, including their employer noticing,' I said.

'I haven't retired from my job, just an element of it.'

It was nine months since his last race ride, and he remained certain
of his decision not to ride in races anymore. He had no such inclination
to stop riding trackwork, which he reasoned had been his main source
of income in his time as a jockey.

'I've been back at the track for six months. If I was still available to
ride in races, I probably wouldn't have had a mount in this time anyway.
When you look at it, there isn't any change. I just don't have hope to
cling to anymore.'

Lucky was thirty-seven. He was decades away from the end of his
working life but was incapable of looking into the future as to what
would be possible. He liked to ignore what didn't suit him. Common
sense suggested he couldn't keep riding horses at dawn forever. The
very point of this role was preparation for racing. If you'd lost the
desire or ability to be riding in races, then surely this role wasn't ideal.
The number of hurdlers and steeplechasers in Tasmania was dropping,

which meant the remaining jumps jockeys were becoming more dependent on track riding. While Max would always provide him with what work he could, there weren't too many additional opportunities, and there would be even fewer with time.

'What are you going to do when you can't ride trackwork anymore?

'I don't know. When you've only had one talent, one passion, it's hard to see what follows from there,' he said. George Moore won 2200 races and was probably able to refer to himself as having had a talent. Lucky hadn't finished, let alone won a jumping race so his wording may have been taken to task by most, but I let it go.

'You will need something else, eventually. I will need to get out of suburbia. Bruny Island. The Tasman Peninsula. Some place where the air is fresh, the pace is slow, nature is beautiful, life is peaceful, and stress is a memory.'

'Would be a long drive to Elwick each morning,' he said.

'I was implying that the horses would be a thing of the past.' This had been my mistake all along. It was seemingly impossible to sell him a life without horses.

'Maybe if we had some land, you could rehome some of Max's former racehorses? Keep the connection to the horses and then what is left that you would miss?'

For the first time, I at least had him thinking.

'How would we afford it?'

'We do something with the land. I'm not sure quite what. Ever since they built the casino there's been an increase in tourism to the state and that's only going to keep growing. It isn't going to be the casino that holds them here though, it's going to be the natural magic of the surroundings further south. They all go to Port Arthur and progressively more will go to Bruny Island as well. We could set something up to attract some of those people.'

'How many people go there?'

'More every year. You want to be successful you need to be a step ahead of everyone else, not a step behind.'

'I thought it was all just about staying on top,' he said. 'But what could we do?'

'I don't know,' I said. I was thinking on the run. All of this stemmed from vague thoughts, and I had little idea what we could provide, but Lucky was an identity and if we had something that we could leverage this against, we may have a chance of making it work.

'What about offering horse rides on the beach with you? There'd be so many people who'd be keen to go for that.'

'Wouldn't they be afraid that with every ticket you were guaranteed a broken bone?'

'No. That only happens in hurdle races. Not on beachside walks.'

I'd sewn a seed. It may not have been anything that we'd end up with, but at least it gave him something to think about. It also taught me something important. I had been so focussed on the horses being part of the problem that I had failed to see that they could be part of the solution.

xxx

'What would you do if I quit,' Lucky asked Max after riding work the next morning.

'I'd head down to the church and thank the Lord for finally answering my prayers,' Max said. 'I'm too old to keep doing this. I'd just about had enough a decade ago, but your enthusiasm rubbed off on me. Every year since, I've been thinking, one more, but you keep pushing so I've felt like I should too.'

'You never had to.'

'No, I chose to. Don't get me wrong, I love the horses. I love the sport. But I also love the concept of sleeping in and I think the time is getting close.'

He asked what had prompted the conversation and Lucky explained what he and I had talked about. It was no surprise to Max, having heard me talk about getting him out of racing for many years and he told Lucky that he thought I was right.

'So how can we finish up? Are we going to find a way to get you out on a winner in a jumpers flat? Finish a hurdle?'

Lucky shook his head. 'That day at Deloraine was it for me. Lester Piggott couldn't have ridden that horse better than I did, and I still got the same old result. If it couldn't happen then, I just have to accept it wasn't meant to be.'

He explained that he'd never wanted people to know. 'The public, my peers, they'd all just be making a joke about my career. Kaa Boy didn't just destroy my career, he destroyed my willingness to be the butt of the jokes.'

'You will be if you set up a business built on your reputation,' Max said, though Lucky explained that it would be different once away from the racecourse.

'Once enough time has passed, you can make a joke about a tragedy without it being in poor taste. So long as I am putting myself in the public domain as a professional jockey, the jokes at my expense are an attack. Once I've retired, it's a good-natured ribbing. That's when they can embellish my story and act like I was genuinely useless. It is completely different.'

Max had half a dozen horses in work and said he would keep training them through their current preparations, which would take him through until late in the year. He also had a three-year-old filly who was coming back into the stable who he'd had a high opinion of.

'If she comes up well, I will keep going through to the carnival. Imagine if I could finish off by winning the Oaks. If she isn't measuring up, I might be done in November. Try and sign off with a hurdle winner, even if it isn't with you in the saddle.'

xxx

Max hadn't had a jumping winner all season. His star, Mile High, had been inconsistent, running a couple of placings in good races while failing in easier company. It was only the form of filly Unrepentant and veteran sprinter Losahos that had made his last few months worthwhile. Losahos was named by Max and was meant to be an acronym for Lucky O'Shaughnessy and Helen O'Shaughnessy. He'd given us a small share in the horse when one of the intended partners withdrew. The horse hadn't been a star but had picked up enough prizemoney to pay for the ongoing expenses and had given Lucky an extra sense of purpose away from riding. Losahos had helped Lucky regain his love for the original lure of the sport, the horse.

A late November meeting at Elwick had been set as the last race ever for Losahos, and the last race for Mile High with Max as his trainer. Max thought the horse had earned retirement, but some of the other owners were keen to continue with him for another season. Several of Max's others had already finished their preparation, and those that weren't going to be retired had already been transferred to other trainers. After this day, he'd be left with just one horse in work, Unrepentant, who he considered a race-by-race prospect.

'You never know, she might be good enough to win a Melbourne Cup. That might spur me to continue, but most likely I'll send her to someone else soon.'

We'd reached an agreement on a property on Bruny Island a few weeks earlier, with settlement expected in January. I would be beginning the new school year teaching at Bruny Primary School. Losahos was one of three of Max's horses that would be transferred to our property on the island. Initially, they would be little more than pets, but Lucky and I were working on ideas about how to keep both him and his steeds in productive work.

The crowd at Elwick was comparatively small for Max's virtual finale. It was a rare occasion where both Lucky's mother and my parents were on track, as well as siblings and a couple of our nieces and nephews. Patrick had passed away ten years earlier, and despite the difficulties they'd had for many years, Lucky struggled to get over his loss. From that time, Max's role in his life grew into more of a father figure role than just a boss.

While Lucky's role as a strapper for Max's duo was hardly the glamour of being a jockey, it could well be his last day working in any capacity on a racecourse. However his time in the sport is remembered by others, those who knew him took great pleasure from seeing him do what he loved. When he was riding, we couldn't appreciate the pleasure due to the risks and the results. We never came to watch the simple pleasure he gained from strapping the horses, but now that it was all coming to an end, there was the ability to take joy from this.

The winner's stall was not unfamiliar to Lucky in the role of strapper, but it wasn't to be after the third race as Losahos missed the placings. He had got caught wide in the early stages and after looming up alongside the leaders at the furlong mark, he died on his run to finish fourth. It was a credible result, but not what we'd all hoped for.

Race six was the November Hurdle, the last feature hurdle race in Tasmania for the year. As Lucky helped Colin Murphy to board Mile High, I could tell there was a sense of envy. He may have chosen to step away from race riding, but lifelong dreams never completely disappear, even once reality has been accepted. He'd never ridden Mile High in a race but had ridden him in an official trial and hundreds of times at trackwork. The way he'd dreamed his career, he'd have ridden him in so many wins. Now, all that he could hope for was to wait in the winner's stall when he came back after winning his last race in their team.

Murphy had Mile High placed just behind the leaders through the first lap, and despite being inconvenienced by a riderless horse turning out of the straight the first time, he travelled well throughout. Just inside the half-mile, he pulled him around the heels of the leaders and quickly went alongside them and ahead. On straightening he was nearly two lengths ahead, and with nothing closing ground on him, it was merely a matter of clearing the last two hurdles.

I was suddenly as nervous as if Lucky was riding. The stakes were high. For both Lucky and Max, finishing their time in jumps racing as winners, meant an enormous amount. It was also going to be worth a decent sum of money. I never bet, but I made an exception this time at the insistence of Lucky and Max. They'd focussed three months on getting it right this day, and I'd put a large sum on a victory, as had both my father and Lucky's mother. As Mile High cleared the last now four lengths clear, the noise that we made was sufficient that today's small attendance sounded more like a Hobart Cup Day crowd.

It was unbridled joy. I'd never seen Max happier. The owners of the horse had all won big as well, and it probably stands to reason given the betting fluctuations of 10/1 into 4/1. Although in the role of strapper, Lucky was being treated as a hero. He was deflecting all the attention to the man who had made it all possible and had been doing so since he first spent time here as a child more than twenty years earlier.

All the years we had dreamt of a fairy-tale result on the racecourse, and finally it had happened. We always envisaged Lucky to be in the saddle, but his elation was as great as it would have been riding the winner. He cared for the horse, groomed him and rode all of his preparation work. Whatever anyone else would remember, Lucky was going out a winner.

38

19 May 2023

ZANIYA

'You really must go,' Helen said. 'Once the last ferry leaves that's it. There's no other way back.'

Although I could think of worse places to spend the night, we had to check out of our Hobart hotel in the morning, which would prove quite impossible if we were still stranded here. We said our goodbyes,

'Irrespective of anything else my dear, it has been wonderful to meet you and it has meant more than you can believe, being able to tell Lucky's story to someone who listened to what I said rather than just heard what they chose.'

'Thank you, Helen. I will send you the finished tribute tomorrow. I think the letter is now perfect but send the two items in together.' While we'd waited for the family to return from Fluted Cape, we'd edited the letter Helen would send to the newspaper. I felt certain they would print it, and I was confident there would be some sort of apology forthcoming to Helen as well.

We reached the ferry departure point at Roberts Point with plenty of time to spare. Helen may have done time allocations based on how long Lucky took to get there on horseback. We ended up on the second last ferry but after such a long day we were happy to be getting back early.

'Tonight?' Dad asked.

There was little enthusiastic response from any of us. Dad was trying to gauge what anyone wanted to do for the evening. We had at different stages planned to go across the road to the famous Mures Seafood Restaurant or to Da Angelo's, the place we'd been recommended to visit last night, but those options seemed more than any of us were up to.

I was looking through the photos of Lucky and mentioned that I felt like a quiet night in. I hadn't slept much the past few nights, and while that was the way I liked my travels to be, maximising my waking time eventually caught up with me. Of course, the coming trip to Cradle Mountain was always my planned battery recharge, but so much of the time since arriving in Hobart had been beyond my expectations. I was expecting the mountain, the market, the river and the museum. I couldn't have foreseen the man, the jockey and the widow. Maybe I shouldn't anticipate too much about Cradle Mountain or our following stop, Wynyard. Either of these may turn out to provide something far greater than I've envisaged.

'Last night in the city and you want to go to spend it in your room? Who has run off with my family and replaced them with people I don't know?'

It wasn't out of character at all. It wasn't that I didn't want to be out, I was just preoccupied with the essence of what this trip had become. I was never going to forget my experiences here. I didn't want it to end yet. Bugger it, with one night left I'll fit in with whatever anyone else wants to do. After all, they had fit in with my passion project for the whole time we had been here.

xxx

It is fair to say that Monday nights in Hobart don't offer overwhelming options for a big night out. We skipped the formal dining options and went for a quick bite across the road. Still seafood, still good. Blue Eyed Trevalla was something I'd never heard of, but it was exquisite and a taste of something different from the many oysters, scallops, squid and prawns that had dominated the seafood we'd been eating.

We had a last walk along the wharves, the moon overlooking us above the hills to the east of the city. Buildings from the city's infancy alongside modern constructions, the area was another trendy part of the city, plentiful in bars and restaurants, though most were closed tonight. There was a bar open, so we took the opportunity for a table with views across the water and had a last reflection on the city.

'Never enough time, right,' I said.

'If you feel like you've had enough time in a city, you've had too much,' Dad said. 'You should always be wanting more because there are so many other amazing places that you'll never see at all.'

'It couldn't have been better,' Mum said. 'When I travel, I want togetherness with my loved ones, check. Stunning scenery, check. Great food and wine, check. Meeting new people, check. Unique experiences, check. History, art, and culture, check. Learning, and moving on richer for the experience, check.'

'I still wish we'd found time for Sydney and Melbourne,' Oliver said, 'but at least I know when I do come back to Australia, I have those places to look forward to. I'll also come back here at that point too.'

'It would have been ideal to have three months down here,' Dad said, 'but you make do with what you can. You wouldn't have enjoyed those cities as much anyway because your expectations would have been different. It's the fact that Hobart has surprised you that has made its impact so great.

'I think we should toast Lucky,' Mum said. 'It may have been your project Zan, but he ended up defining the time here for all of us. Going to the races. Bruny Island. It was all about him, and to be fair, I think we all thoroughly enjoyed those experiences.'

'Hear hear,' Dad added.

'To Lucky and to Hobart' I said.

'Courage and persistence personified,' Mum added.

After we clinked our glasses and took a drink, I told them that for all of the stories they'd heard about his racetrack exploits, the main memories I would hold of him stemmed from far after his racing days were over.

'When your significant other is in a profession so demanding, there are times when you're destined to feel secondary to their career. It may not be true, but I'm sure Helen felt that way. Eventually, when the days of being a jockey had passed, he was just a husband. When that time came, the full picture of the man he was, began to make sense.'

39

15 August 2010

HELEN

As we'd been doing regularly for 35 years, we'd come to Hobart today to attend the races at Elwick. We'd left the city behind just a few days after Max and Lucky officially ended their association. While they'd had such a wonderful result with Mile High's win in their last hurdle race, things couldn't have gone worse three weeks later with the talented filly Unrepentant. She finished tailed off in last place. After a vet's inspection, it was found that she had a breathing abnormality caused by a lung issue. She never raced again, and that was the sad ending of Max's training career.

Unrepentant ended up being given to us and lived a happy existence. She was unusually placid for a thoroughbred, and ended up a key part of our business, providing walks along the beach. Lucky led them along, providing anecdotes of his career while highlighting the spectacular coastline of the island. It didn't make our fortune, but it gave Lucky a purpose while making a reasonable enough living. Importantly, it allowed him to maintain a close relationship with horses. Possibly to the disappointment of some of his customers, he never once fell here.

Eventually, the changes in society saw this come to an end. Insurance costs and over-regulation made it impossible to continue, but we've always had horses on our property, and Lucky has always found various ways of using his experiences to entertain new people.

We attended most race meetings at Elwick. Lucky would spend the day chatting with friends old and new. Whether it was fellow retired jockeys or the current breed, other industry members or just the general public, everyone wanted some of his time. For someone who had always struggled to develop friendships, he'd evolved into someone who relished the company of others. There was never any form of condescension in the manner of these people who saw him as a celebrity rather than focussing on what had made him one.

While jumpers had been Lucky's domain, his love for horses and racing in general extended well beyond jumps racing. He was saddened but realistic about the rumours of the end of jumps racing in Tasmania. The number of trainers, riders and horses who were still involved diminished every year, and the reliance kept growing on Victorian competitors to ensure hurdling continued. When the last hurdle race was run in Tasmania in 2007, he was philosophical that it was a sign of the times, but we continued to attend Elwick races with the same enthusiasm.

As time has passed, we've generally spent more of the day sitting on our own in the grandstand. Less of his peers are still around, and those who are seemed to have exhausted the stories that used to entertain them all day. As the last race was run, we watched a dominant win by a horse named End Of An Era, which was one of the very rare times Lucky had tipped a winner. Finally living up to his name, it was also one of the very rare times he'd had a bet.

'How appropriate is that? The last race we ever see here and End of An Era wins. Couldn't have lost, right.'

'What do you mean the last race we ever see?'

'I don't belong here anymore, darling,' he said, a hint of emotion in his voice not sufficient to disguise the certainty he felt. 'This place was the dream of the young boy, the reality of the young man and then the fond memories of the old man. I've recycled the memories too many times now. I keep coming back because it's a routine, but it no longer provides what it did. I don't look forward to coming here anymore.'

The look of puzzlement on my face led him to continue.

'There are fewer people here who know me now,' he said, 'and even fewer who care whether they see me anymore. Maybe that's always been the case, but what is true sometimes matters less than what we believe. When I believed that I belonged, I did belong. Now I no longer believe it, and I've never wanted to be anywhere where I felt that I didn't belong.'

Everyone who knew him said he never belonged on the back of a horse, but he truly believed he did. Just as now, that was all that had mattered.

I must have attended a thousand race meetings at Elwick with Lucky, so the thought of not coming back again was going to be an equally significant change for me too. I wasn't going to miss the races that much, but I didn't like the finality of Lucky's statement. He'd never intimated anything like this, and for it to come in such an out-of-the-blue way made little sense to me.

'You will miss it. The races have always been the great love of your life.'

'No, my greatest love has always been you. The horses may have defined me, but there was no reason for me to be defined at all if it wasn't for you. My dream of being a jockey was never about horse racing. It was to be good at something. To achieve something. To make something of myself which everyone said I'd never do. The reason I wanted to do any of that was to be worthy of you.'

I was in tears. I never doubted the completeness of his love, but hearing it said in this way was something new and truly beautiful.

'Don't get me wrong. I loved the horses. I loved the thrills. I loved pursuing the dream and I loved the fight of proving people wrong. Even in my failures, everyone kept expecting me to be out each time I was down. Every time I got back up, I loved the shock on their faces. But all of those loves were secondary. Now you don't have to share me anymore.'

'After all these years, I don't think an occasional trip to the races means I'm sharing you.'

He may have been wording this as being all about my wishes, but I knew it was more a reflection of his state of mind. All the passing years still had not given him the necessary feeling of security to share all his feelings with me. In good times all the positives were shared, but when he suffered, he was far less forthcoming.

'You've never said anything negative about being here,' I said. 'What has changed?'

'I don't know,' he said.

Earlier in the day, a couple of teenagers approached Lucky and asked him what it was like to be the worst jockey ever. It was the kind of thing he had heard many times and something that he was happy to joke about to this day. It never would have occurred to anyone that it bothered him, for he was so happy to engage with people of all ages. He usually followed these sorts of interactions with the same reflection he'd had with me when the previous similar incident occurred.

'When someone is giving you attention you can't consider it to be completely negative,' he'd said. 'Maybe they're laughing at me, but they don't laugh at you unless you stand out in some way. The truest failures are people who never do anything special enough to stand out.'

'Don't you think some people specifically aim not to stand out? Wouldn't they then only have failed when they do stand out,' I responded, firm in my view that I could never have coped with the sort of recognition that he appreciated.

'Perhaps,' he said. 'But in my career, standing out was the aim. To get opportunities you had be noticed. You needed to stand out. When you won, you stood out more. I never stood out for the right reasons, but standing out kept me in the game far longer than those who blended in. However it has been formed, I have a greater legacy in this sport than 99% of my peers.'

It was true that his career had been more memorable than most, even if the word greater could be questioned. Either way, it summed up his genuine attitude to his career and to life. It contrasted greatly with his attitude to the teenagers who'd mocked him today.

'I only wish that someone would remember me for the right reasons. You can't fall so many times without getting up just as many.'

While I assured him that the people who mattered understood this, the fact I had to do so reflected the state of mind he seemed to be in today and I now assumed that this attitude of not wanting to come back was formed well before End of an Era set foot on the track.

'Those boys earlier today,' I asked. 'They were just like hundreds before yet today they affected you differently than normal. Now this statement of finality.'

'They aren't the cause, they are a symptom,' he said. 'I was always able to take any joke, but only at the right time from the right person. The jockeys all respected me. We all shared the danger every day, not just in races, but in trackwork too. When they joked, they did so in part to lighten the mood and help each other, including me. Even then, they wouldn't laugh on my darkest days. They knew.'

He was remaining composed, but I was tearing up again.

'The boys today, and maybe many others before, had no concept of what I'd achieved. The jokes are only funny when their context is understood. When more people knew me, kids like that heard the whole story. Now it's too convenient to skip the realities and create a simpler version. I don't like it. I've got the horses at home, and I don't want to give them up, but this place is about something else. Egos, dreams, tragedies and triumphs. Our first date. My broken neck. All the things it has been to us, good and bad, are locked in our memory from many years back. Nothing new gets added here to our special memories. It is time to say goodbye.'

40

20 May 2023

ZANIYA

Travel is the quest for new experiences. It seems logical to me that departures should only ever be seen as the essential starting point to the next destination. Logic doesn't matter though, as once again we are leaving a city behind when I'm not quite ready to say goodbye. This seems to happen wherever we go and an extra day or two would make no difference. You maximise the time you have, and while more time allows you to tick more things off your wish list, there will always be something in each city that you reflect on and think '*If only I'd had one more day.*'

Based on everything we'd researched, there is nothing essential that we missed. That only tells part of the truth. We experienced so much here, but far and away the highlight of Hobart was meeting Helen and learning about Lucky. No guidebook or research could have ever prepared us for that. Maybe Lucky's story has a hundred better ones that were worthy of more attention if only they'd been found. No amount of time will ever lead you to these, just circumstances and luck.

I almost felt like I was hijacking my family's trip by devoting so much time to Lucky's story, but each of them became as invested in it as I did. The journalist within me wanted to tell the story, but it was the human within me that had first wanted to know it. The same feeling existed within every member of my family, so they gained almost as much as

I did. Would we have experienced Bruny Island otherwise? Like many of our most special moments when travelling, it was the unplanned experience that ended up being the most memorable.

This morning we drove to Cradle Mountain, where we are spending three days in the most idyllic surroundings imaginable. Tomorrow I will begin to explore these, but today my focus remains on my tribute to Lucky. That was already my plan, but if there was any doubt about that, it was dispelled on the drive this morning.

'Stop the car,' I demanded with a sense of urgency that made Dad panic unnecessarily, thinking something was seriously wrong.

I had seen a horse in a paddock. He was up against the fence, looking in our direction, and I was desperate to stop.

'I have to go over and pat him. All of the talk of horses over the past few days, and this is the first chance to get close and pat one.'

I'd never previously thought twice at the sight of a horse, but the last few days had instilled a passion in me. I didn't expect to have this sort of urge overcome me regularly, but it felt like this horse was calling me.

'Make it worth his while,' Mum said. 'There's a couple of carrots in the shopping bag in the boot. He'll appreciate them even more than your brother would.'

Mum, Dad and Oliver probably thought I had lost my mind, but they all indulged me and wandered across the road with me. The beautiful animal was as placid as could be, not like the racehorses we had seen at Elwick on Sunday. We all took turns patting him and I fed him the carrots which he devoured.

There were many other horses far away on the other side of the paddock, but our presence didn't strike any interest in them. The only figures that did head towards us were an old man and a dog. I thought the man might be concerned about our presence, but as he got closer, I could see the smile on his face.

'Lucky seems to like you,' he called out as he got close enough to be heard.

'Lucky?'

The horse seemed to give a nod of his head to confirm his name.

'That's what we call him. He didn't live up to our hopes on the racecourse, and my co-owners were going to send him to the knackery. I saved him because he was too beautiful to say goodbye to. He was lucky to survive then and once he moved here he had a few other narrow escapes from trouble. The name Lucky stuck.

'Sounds like the Lucky O'Shaughnessy story,' Dad said. 'That's pretty much dominated our time in Tasmania.'

The old man laughed. 'There's a name I haven't heard of in many years. Surprised anyone remembers him.'

'A bit like your beautiful fella here, he may have been a failure in the eyes of many, but to those who knew him better, he was an incomparable legend. There's always more to the story of anyone than what most of us ever see,' I said.

'That's very true,' the old man said as the equine Lucky again nodded and let out a snort.

xxx

It was time to click send. I provided a short tribute that was in keeping with what the newspaper published each Saturday. I used last weekend's paper as a guide. The articles were usually on people with limited public profile and submitted by people who knew them, but not necessarily closely. They were not excessively eulogistic, but I wasn't sure if that said more about the people or those writing the tributes. While trying to stay relatively true to the pattern, I didn't want my tribute to such a great man to be weighed down in dates and events. It defeated the purpose of writing a tribute if not giving the best possible account of what made that person's life special. Nobody is going to be enthused to read about a person without getting an insight into what made that person unique and special. I had to ensure that his soul was captured in my words.

Two months after his passing, there'd been sufficient time for the journalist to do any research necessary. For a professional newspaper to print an article so simplistic as the one they had featured was a blight on Lucky and Helen. He didn't need to be turned into anything that he was not. Portraying Lucky as a star jockey would have been equally inappropriate. My follow-up had countered the flaws of the original, not by saying anything inaccurate or by exaggerating the truth, but by focussing on the parts of his story that best combined general human interest with suitable respect. With this, I hoped Helen would see the article that really should have been featured last week.

A TRUE TASMANIAN LEGEND

Luke (Lucky) O'Shaughnessy. 3/1/1937- 21/2/2023

Former jockey, Lucky O'Shaughnessy passed away after a sudden heart attack at the age of 85. For a man who risked life and limb in his profession, many would have doubted that he'd make such an age, but defying expectations was fundamental to the Lucky O'Shaughnessy story.

The son of a World War II veteran, Lucky grew up just blocks away from Elwick Racecourse. While there was no family connection to the racing industry, Lucky became transfixed by the horses as he watched them train on his walk to school each morning. This fascination fuelled a desire to be more than a spectator, and the dream of joining Hobart's jockey ranks quickly took hold.

To those who knew him, it appeared a dream that would never be fulfilled. While Lucky had a jockey's build, he appeared to lack the natural skillset that was essential to the profession. What nobody had accounted for was his ability to compensate for these shortcomings with an overwhelming set of strengths. He was courageous, hard-working, persistent and resilient. At the age of fifteen, he began working in the stables at Elwick, and by the age of eighteen, to the shock of many, he had achieved his primary ambition with his first race ride.

In the competitive world of horse racing, success seems an easy word to define. Every now and then, a person challenges that definition, such is their ability to transcend our understanding. Lucky was such a man. A jockey whose career resulted in no victories, nor even the completion of a hurdle race, was never considered a success. A deeper look at the man, his life, and his time in the racing industry paints a far more accurate picture.

Lucky maintained a career in the field of his dreams for more than two decades. While he failed to experience the victories he worked so hard to achieve, the ability to make a living fulfilling his passion for such a long period was something few people get to do. For all the injuries he endured, he continued to ride longer than most of his peers. In a sport that is among the most dangerous in the world, he had more than his fair share of knockdowns, but he was never knocked out.

After his last career ride, he continued to work for trainer Max Burton as a stable hand and strapper before he and his wife Helen moved to Bruny Island. Horses continued to play a pivotal role in his life, rehoming several of Burton's former racehorses and giving them a new life by providing beachside walks to tourists on the island. The opportunity to share his love of the horse with new generations brought a whole new enthusiasm to life.

Both during and after his career, Lucky was the source of ridicule for his on-track results. He took this with good humour, as was his nature. He never shied away from his record, even though most good judges agreed that he had ridden many perfect races, only to have misfortune seal his fate. He never sought to lay blame anywhere else, he merely worked harder to give himself the best possible chance next time. Whatever natural talent he lacked, he compensated for with labour.

Never seeking to hide from the humour surrounding his failures, Lucky became sought after on Tasmania's public speaking circuit. Combining the comic elements with the stories of courage and determination that defined his career, he entertained and inspired.

Lucky broke nearly every bone in his body throughout his career. Most people would give up, but nothing could diminish his determination. He persevered, whatever the circumstances. He didn't need the promise of victory to motivate himself. He always gave the best of himself, on and off the track.

Lucky is survived by his beloved wife Helen. They were neighbours as children more than seventy years ago, growing closer through their youth, culminating in a fairy-tale wedding in 1958.

Few people could look at the entirety of his life without feeling admiration. For most, that would also be accompanied by a degree of envy. Lucky achieved everything that most people strive for in life. He made a wife of his childhood love and maintained the happiest of marriages for sixty-four years. He made a career of his childhood dream. Though he endured unspeakable pain from injuries in his younger years, he lived the second half of his life in exceptional health. He had a lifestyle dominated by his passions and the freedom to engage in these without limits.

Each person sets their own definition of success, but under any common criteria, Lucky's life was one of great success. He was an inspirational Tasmanian, and his life provides valuable lessons to us all. Never give up on a dream.

I scanned the photos that Helen had given me the other day and attached them to my article. All of the tributes from Saturday's paper had relatively recent photos with them, but I felt Lucky's story was so defined by his time in the silks, that these older photos would be considered suitable. I wished I had a photo of him with Helen, for her place in his story is even greater. It wouldn't have been used with a tribute like this, but I would have appreciated it amongst my memories.

Time would tell if it appeared in the paper. There were two or three tributes each Saturday, usually within a few weeks of the person's passing. Lucky died two months ago, so it was outside the normal range, but given their article a week earlier, it was still sufficiently newsworthy for consideration. I hoped so.

41

21 May 2023

HELEN

Dear Sir,

I refer to the article "The End of the Biggest Loser" (15/03/23). As the widow of Luke 'Lucky' O'Shaughnessy, I can assure you that he is one of the greatest winners imaginable. Throughout his career, he was the subject of many jokes based on his record. As a man with a great sense of humour, he never hid from these but was willing to play along. Now that he has passed, I feel compelled to ensure that if he is to be remembered, it is based on the full picture.

Losers are those who are afraid to compete when things become too challenging. Losers are those who choose safety when their dreams call on them to take risks. Losers are those who reflect on life with sadness and regret at their unfulfilled dreams.

Those who spend 25 years working in a career that had been their dream since childhood are true winners. Those who have had the passion drive them beyond what a normal person ever experiences, are true winners. Those who spend 64 years married to the love of their life without a single significant argument are true winners. Any person who can look back at the end of life and appreciate the happiness and good fortune that life has brought them, have been the truest winners of all.

My late husband had the worst record of any professional jockey in the world. The article incorrectly stated that he never finished a race, falling in all forty-five career starts. He finished more than a dozen races, but that was conveniently omitted from the article. He indeed failed to finish any of his races over obstacles, but in several of these he did not fall, and there were other factors behind his failure to finish. It appears that the myth is more worthy of newspaper copy than the truth, which saddens me.

There is plenty of good humour to be found within his career record, but it is a small part of a story that is built on the qualities that every champion possesses; courage, determination and passion. Lucky may not have had the talent of the greatest jockeys, but surviving such a brutal career on that basis is part of what made him such an inspiration. Despite his many defeats, Lucky was never a loser.

Any person can achieve when all the cards fall their way, but a hero is someone who fights against all odds and who refuses to accept defeat however tough the battle becomes. 'Tasmania's Biggest Loser' should perhaps have been retitled 'Hobart's Biggest Hero.'

Rest in peace Lucky. Always a winner.

Helen O'Shaughnessy
Bruny Island

I triple-checked everything before clicking send, though it was hardly necessary after the close eye Zaniya gave it on Monday. Whether they print it remains to be seen. It was contrasting with their own journalists' work, but perhaps they may see that lying beneath a simple headline, was a real person with a real story. In such a case, the truth will generally make for a better article than a simplified version. It didn't matter, for I had at least done the right thing by providing the tribute to Lucky. Printed or not, my job was done. I also attached Zaniya's tribute and wondered if that would also get an audience and in doing so, further honour the love of my life.

The wounds won't heal. We were everything to each other and you never recover from losing everything. I'm sure everyone who becomes a widow feels that way when death separates them from their other half. For those without children, the suffering is even more profound, with nobody to share that grief.

Every day the reality sinks in a little more. To say that it gets easier would give the wrong impression. It doesn't feel easier, even if the impact becomes less dominant with time. Every day still throws up memories of him, and the memories rarely end without tears. Finishing the tribute has seen me shed a few more and I doubt it will be the last time today.

Somewhat drained I know it's time to focus some energy outside for a while. I can step out into the fresh air, see the beauty of the land around me, and continue to appreciate life in our little piece of paradise. It may never feel quite the same without him, but I will go on feeding from the courage and perseverance that he inspired me with over all those years. He will always be part of me.

42

24 May 2023

ZANIYA

We have had a few idyllic days at Cradle Mountain, but it is now time to move on. We are just about to make the short trip to Wynyard for the real reason behind our trip, the wedding of our cousin Martin. Oliver is his best man, so we are arriving a week before the wedding to have plenty of time with him, including tonight's comparatively low-key bucks' night. How we will spend an entire week in such a small town is a bit of a question mark, but that was what I had said about Hobart, and time had proven that I had badly misjudged that. We inevitably carry preconceived notions of what to expect when we travel somewhere new, but we should never allow these to close our minds. Places, like people, are full of surprises.

From the door of our cabin at Cradle Mountain to our destination was only going to take a little over an hour. With spectacular scenery most of the way, I didn't want to be wasting my time looking at screens then. I got my laptop out to do some quick journalling and to go through my emails straight after breakfast. Despite having told me she used email, I interpreted that in the same way my grandmother meant it, which was that it got looked at so occasionally that any email was unlikely to be read, and I should never expect communication from her by that means. As I got to my inbox, I was happy to see she had proven me wrong.

Dear Zaniya

My letter was printed in yesterday's paper and what a reaction! Today they printed ten responses all showing solidarity with me, slamming the initial article. I also received an apology from the newspaper. It wasn't a public, printed apology but by being willing to publish the responses they'd effectively acknowledged their wrongdoing. I think they intend to publish your tribute as well, so I expect you will hear from them.

I cannot thank you enough for your assistance in these past few days. I haven't had anyone to talk to about Lucky in such depth. You not only were able to write his story as it should be, but you also helped me beyond belief in coming to terms with my fate. I have lost the love of my life, but how fortunate I was to have had the best part of seven decades of that love. For the first time, I am appreciating rather than mourning. The name Lucky could equally have applied to me as to him.

Of course, the sadness remains, and it always will, but so it should. What it shouldn't do is override the joys that preceded it, but take its place alongside these. This is the step that you have helped me take, and I have the utmost gratitude to you for that.

Please let me know what happens with the story anywhere else. Your account is his true story. Whether the name of Lucky O'Shaughnessy disappears from the memories of all or whether he becomes known to the world does not concern me. So long as his story is told in the manner you have done, where the man beyond the myth is the focus, then I am happy.

I hope your memories of Hobart remain as special as the memories you have left me with.

Kindest regards
Helen

Everyone has a story. The deeper you dig the more you see the uniqueness that makes each person's story something special. His career may have stood out for the wrong reasons, but a lesser man would never have pursued his dream to the extent that he'd have those results.

A lesser man would have settled for an average job for which there were constant opportunities in the booming post-war economy of Australia.

A hero is someone who inspires. It is not the person who wins the most, it is the person who defies the odds the most. It is the person who continues to fight when others quit. The person who battles through the pain for the sake of those he or she loves. The person who never gives up on their dreams, however impossible they appear to be.

Helen needn't worry. I would carry my memories of Hobart with me forever. It is a beautiful city, but it is now so much more than that to me. Through Lucky, I now feel an indelible link to the city which I'm sure will stay with me forever.

Lucky? I couldn't feel luckier.

FROM THE AUTHOR

When I started with the idea of travel novels, I quickly assembled a list of storyline ideas that seemed relevant to different cities. Paris, Berlin, New York, Rome....Hobart. Yes, Australia's southernmost city seemed a little out of step with the rest of the ideas, but travel is not one-dimensional, and I felt this series needed to reflect that. More to the point, I had a character and a story that I felt aligned perfectly with the city. I love Hobart and wanted to tell its story, and through the character of Lucky O'Shaughnessy, I believed I had the perfect vehicle.

Many years ago, my father, sister and I heard a radio interview with former jockey Les Boots. Boots had been known as the world's worst jockey, failing to finish in any of his 39 race starts. It was an amusing story, the comic value of constant failure being exploited as much as possible. We all agreed that someone should write a book about him. As the years passed, I never heard anything more of him, but part of his story always remained imprinted in my mind.

While the comedy of the interview was what gave it such an impact, the more I reflected on the 'world's worst jockey,' the more the story turned to the courage involved in continuing to pursue the career. If nobody was to write a biography of Boots, then the outline for a book on courage against adversity lay in a character based on his career. All well and good, but hardly relevant for the writer of travel fiction.

My honeymoon was in Hobart and its surrounds. It wasn't my first trip to the city, but with time on our hands, we got a more thorough taste of how special the region is. Hobart is an underappreciated gem. Foreign tourists most frequently focus on the East Coast when visiting Australia, and Tasmania, for all of its natural beauty, gets bypassed. The more time I spent in Hobart and its surrounds, the more I began to feel that the region was something far greater than commonly appreciated.

A jockey cannot always be measured by the number of victories he or she has. A city cannot be measured by how many tourists they attract. In both cases, numerous circumstances lead to the results. Often you need to look deeper than numbers, and with this, I saw the link between Hobart and the character that would become Lucky O'Shaughnessy. Although inspired by the statistics of Les Boots, Lucky was Hobart personified. A legendary part of the world. Somewhere to be celebrated, not neglected.

My deepest thanks to my wife Alison. All that I have experienced of Hobart has been with you at my side. As I have written about the city from my experiences of it, you have helped shape every part of it. If that's not enough, then creating the cover for me seals your place in the book! I love you.

My heartfelt thanks to Leonie Page, Ken Rose and Olivia Fergusson for your assistance in the development of the rough story into the polished final product.

Special thanks to my friend Nick Wray who rekindled my love of horse racing when co-owning a couple of racehorses with me. Our success as owners together was similar to Lucky's riding career, but in part that helped build an understanding of the value of following a dream, even when it seems the odds are against you.

To all who have contributed to the book getting seen by as many people as possible, be it through advanced reviews or other promotions, my deepest gratitude. I want as many people as possible to be inspired, both by the city and the characters. Your contribution to this is greatly appreciated.

To Hobart and its people, I hope you feel this book does justice to your amazing home.

To everyone reading the book, thank you for trying travel fiction. I hope you enjoyed it. I hope it has helped you add Hobart to your bucket list. I hope it inspires you to continue reading travel fiction and to explore other books that offer something different to the dominant set of genres. Everyone loves to read, but some people don't know it, as they've never found the right books for them. Hopefully, Hurdles in Hobart has been the right book for you.

See you next time, in Saint Petersburg!

SURVIVAL IN SAINT PETERSBURG

Why does an 87-year-old woman spend hours each day in a doughnut shop?

Saint Petersburg is arguably the world's most beautiful city, but beneath the beauty lies a city that has known trauma and tragedy like nowhere else.

Ekaterina Komarova has experienced it all. Born in the city in the 1930's, she lost her family through Stalin's Purge and the Siege of Leningrad. As an orphan, she was a victim of systematic rape and abuse. She escaped, finding happiness before tragedy again intervened.

When Australian tourists Adam and Louise visit a Soviet era doughnut shop, they are amazed at the crowds and in awe of the authenticity of the step back in time. Before long, their intrigue turns to the mysterious woman hobbling between tables. Neither a customer, nor an employee, they are desperate to gain an understanding of who she is, and what she is doing there.

Through interpreter Yuri, Ekaterina tells her life story. Intermingling with their experiences in the attractions of the city, Adam and Lousie discover what she and her city did to survive against all odds.

ABOUT THE AUTHOR

C.R. Page was born in Adelaide, South Australia. He graduated from the University of South Australia with a degree in business before working for many years in the South Australian public sector.

A love of travel led to him writing articles and short stories, planning to begin a travel blog, but in time the greatest elements he was seeing in places warranted a bigger canvas. The concept of the travel novel began to take shape.

In 2022 he won the Port Adelaide Writers Festival award for his short story, Sanctuary. This was followed by the release of his first novel, The Ride to Work, a story of mental health set on the morning commute to a workplace.

In 2023 he began his travel fiction series with the novel Bedside in Berlin, followed by Paradox in Paris and Hurdles in Hobart.

Follow him on Facebook at CR Page - Travel Fiction.

www.ingramcontent.com/pod-product-compliance
Lightning Source LLC
Chambersburg PA
CBHW020405120726
47904CB00002B/711